FOR THE LOVE OF A GYPSY

MADELYN HILL

SOUL MATE PUBLISHING

New York

FOR THE LOVE OF A GYPSY

Copyright©2015

MADELYN HILL

Cover Design by Anna Lena-Spies

Published in the United States of America by
Soul Mate Publishing
P.O. Box 24
Macedon, New York, 14502

ISBN: 978-1-69291-031-3

ebook ISBN: 978-1-61935-793-8

www.SoulMatePublishing.com

To my entire family.

Acknowledgements

Authors would not be able to exist without a support system. Family, friends, and fellow authors create a supportive group, sounding board, and sometimes an ear to vent when the muse goes missing.

I want to thank my Michigan family who has always supported me, encouraged me, and spread the word far and wide about my novels. Dad, even though you jokingly call this smut, you never stop sharing that I'm a writer and tell people to buy my book. My sisters Shavonne and Janine have also been there for me and encouraged me from the start. The Garner family, especially Aunt Sue, Kim and Dawn, your love has been a huge part of my life. Thank you! And the Martin family—I love your enthusiasm for my writing.

And my mother. You are no longer with us, but I know you were proud of my writing and your strength has been a constant inspiration to me. I miss you terribly.

Prologue

London, England 1811

The magistrate burst into the study. Officers filed in, weapons drawn.

"Declan Forrester, you are under arrest for treason."

Treason?

Declan shot his gaze between the officers and his father as sweat began to bead over his brow. He feinted right, then left, twisting out of their reach.

"Father?" he questioned, begged, as he gauged the distance between him and the only door in the chamber.

His father stared forward unseeing, uncaring, as the magistrate continued to read a list of laws Declan had supposedly broken.

Crimes against the crown? Sedition? Threat on the King's life? He was innocent. How was his father sitting so calmly as his twenty-year-old son was accused of treason?

One officer grabbed his arm. Another gripped his shoulders from behind. They surrounded him. Tried to lock him in chains. He ripped from their grasp, crashed into a table, splinters lodging into his skin. His heart pounded in his ears as he saw the fate before him.

Prison.

"You will receive a trial," the magistrate said as he rolled up the parchment that listed Declan's crimes. "And if God has mercy, you will be put to death and not sent to Newgate."

"Father," Delcan yelled as they dragged him from the

study, his voice screeching, echoing against the walls and falling on deaf ears. "Father!"

No answer to his plea. His father calmly stared ahead as if he hadn't a care in the world. Then he nodded to the magistrate as if saying *Good day*.

Declan's heart crumbled as his world crashed around him. Aye, he was used to his father's apathy. But not when a son was being dragged from the family's English estate. Not when the father was a member of the *ton*.

As they threw him into a locked carriage, Declan gripped the bars in the window and yelled, "Father," as dread seized his heart and cold sweat dripped down his back. He'd no resources, save his father. *I'm as good as dead.*

He spied three black carriages waiting just inside the entrance of the estate as they departed. Two were decorated with a unique familial crest. He committed the crests to memory—one with a rearing steed and white plume, the other with a black knight with a silver shield.

Deep in his gut, he knew the crests would reveal who had accused him of such heinous crimes.

If it took until his dying breath, he'd hunt down the bastards who were sending him to hell.

Chapter 1

Kilkenny, Ireland 1819

He'd been a free man for three years, yet he still felt imprisoned. Instead of steel, the bars around him were made of loosely veiled threats and malcontent conversations.

He couldn't find peace no matter how far he searched. He inhaled and exhaled, yet his lungs never felt as if they were gaining air.

"Saddle my horse," he yelled to the stable hand.

"But, m'lord, Lord Ettenborough demands your attendance."

Declan stopped and pinned the lad with a look that had him squirming. "I don't give a damn what my father-in-law demands. I'm going for a ride."

While he waited for the stable hand to saddle his steed, he slapped his gloves hard against his leg. Did his father-in-law think he could rule him? Dictate his every move? Aye, he'd married Abigail knowing her father would secure his freedom. He didn't know freedom would have so many strings *and* threats attached.

If only the bastard would go back to London.

Declan mounted his stallion, Kindred, damn tired of participating in his ill-fitted life, letting rage suffused his body. As if sensing his rider's urgency, the horse leapt into a smooth gallop.

"That's my lad," Declan urged.

The horse responded further by racing at a full run. Their path was obvious, one trod deeply into the fresh green field. Kindred's thunderous hoof beats nearly drowned out the vicious thoughts coursing through Declan's mind—thoughts that had plagued him for what seemed an eternity. Thoughts he didn't voice, couldn't voice.

One prison exchanged for another.

He thought of his wife. They'd grown to respect each other, created an amicable union, but her father—he made Declan's life miserable.

Now desperation spurred him to nudge Kindred faster and faster as dirt flew and rocks cracked like whips against the saddle and horse's hooves.

He pushed the animal hard, yet at the moment he didn't give a damn as the breeze sifted over his body and the scent of Ireland mingled within it and shrouded him in familiarity. He grinned as he pitched his face toward the wind.

He'd prayed Abigail would accept him, and she did. Even though he knew she pined for another, one her father would never allow her to marry. They each sought an escape—him from prison, her from a domineering father and forbidden love. Yet at every turn the estimable Lord Ettenborough threatened to send him back to hell.

He urged the stallion toward the dense protection of pines. Declan chuckled as the foliage seemed to bow open and consume him as he rode through. A quick camouflage, a cloak from the outside world.

Declan lowered his chest against the horse's neck until he felt as if they were one, breathing and flexing and straining muscles together. The trees shielded him in a cloud of green, tinged with the aroma of pine and loam, and infused him with a peace.

Temporary peace and shade from the sunlight dripping from the sky. The same sunlight that aggravated the megrim pulsing at the base of his neck. As the horse and rider ventured further into the thicket, Declan's mind cleared. He continued to ride mindlessly, eager to be free of problems and worry.

What would it take to be this calm every moment of the day?

The grove of pine thinned as a clearing rose before him. He dismounted and slapped Kindred on his well-muscled hindquarters. The horse trotted toward a stream trickling through the secluded area.

Hands clasped behind his back, Declan searched the glen for something to distract him. The scents of the earth, grass, and air swirled around him in a pleasant aroma. Here, he could breathe. The quiet stretch of field lay empty. Nothing proved worthy as a distraction, unless he counted the winsome croak of a frog and the flutter of a breeze through the tall grass.

His mind continued to think of his predicament. Married to the daughter of the man who'd freed him. The same man who continued to threaten and berate him.

And now Declan was the lord of an estate in Ireland, part of the bounty the English government awarded to English settlers in Ireland during Cromwell's reign. And luckily for him, Ettenborough had an estate that needed a lord, and Ettenborough hated Ireland. 'Twas why he'd sought out Declan who was rotting away in the pits of Newgate prison. He needed a titled suitor for his disgraced daughter.

Titled. He shook his head. The irony of the situation wasn't lost on him. Och, how he hated the term *lord*. It was lords who'd sent him to prison for five years. His father was a lord and upon his death, Declan was now Lord Forrester. An inherited title Declan'd quickly shed if possible.

Not that he'd forsake his responsibility to his tenants and the villagers. Not to mention the numerous staff it took to run Riverton, an estate he'd come to love. The hills of his land offered him an openness he'd savored since arriving in Kilkenny. No longer limited to the rank confines of his cell, Declan moved about the land as much as possible, relishing the feel of loam beneath his feet and the sight of rolling green meadows. Simple tasks such as checking the fields and inspecting the animals gave him solace, even pleasure. He bounced his heels against the earth to see if it was as fertile as his fields. 'Twasn't.

In the distance a dog barked. Another joined in. Declan shook his head to break his reverie and strode in the direction of the barking.

At the edge of the stream, not many lengths from his horse, two handsome Lurchers pranced about, baying, nipping at each other. Their caramel coats glistened in the sun with a brightness that told the dogs were well cared for.

Och, and there was their caretaker. No doubt a caravan was nearby.

He watched the woman as she commanded the dogs. She stood haloed by the light and open glen. Her laughter twinkled along the wind, reaching out to him.

She turned, saw him, and moved to flee, but she hesitated and fully faced him with a curious glint in her eyes, the tilt of her head.

She had large eyes, a full mouth, and high cheekbones. Bright colors comprised her long skirt that failed to hide her bare feet.

A Gypsy.

As he watched her, she narrowed her gaze and gave a signal to her dogs, all without taking her eyes from him.

The woman raced from the area, her dogs giving chase as they melded into the forest and to where ever they'd made camp.

No doubt the villagers had heard. Soon, he'd have an angry crowd to deal with, wanting him to remove the Gypsy clan.

Gypsies were trouble—and he certainly didn't need any more trouble in his life.

Martine ran from the glen until her lungs felt hot and tight and her breathing hitched in her throat. Leaning against a tree, she attempted to slow the rapid beat of her heart as she sucked in heaping gulps of air. She needed to calm herself, gather her composure before returning to the encampment. The dogs circled around her excitedly, then mimicked her relaxed position as they nuzzled close by. She cast a doleful glance at the pair and leaned her head against the rough bark of the tree.

Despair and curiosity battled in her mind. If her brother Rafe knew she'd wandered so far from camp, she'd receive a stern wag of his finger and a lecture on how to behave in relation to her position in the clan.

And if he knew she'd seen a *Gajo*? And a *Gajo* had seen her? Martine shuddered at the thought, remembering he'd threatened to shackle her if she ever spoke to an Irishman. She knew his motives, even agreed with them, but she was sorely tempted to make acquaintances outside of the clan. Something, anything to forge a relationship with the outside world, the world she used to belong to.

Martine chuckled despite the unease rustling in her stomach. The tall Irishman had seen her, had seen her dogs. Gypsies were infamous for training the Lurchers. Perhaps he'd keep it a secret. Aye, and she was the Queen of England. There wasn't hope of silence, that much she knew.

She thought of him again, so different he seemed from the men of her clan. His long hair flowed free of a tether, his shoulders broad, muscular. Her heart skipped a beat as she thought of his purposeful stride. Controlled, regal. Gypsy men were sleek, lanky, not broad and muscle bound. Something about the man had intrigued her even as his presence frightened her. Was it his ardent interest? The slight cock of his brow as he watched her, studied her with too much scrutiny. A tiny flutter filled her abdomen, eased along her limbs, awakening feelings she knew should be held for her betrothed, Magor.

Oh, but the Irishman's eyes—Martine sighed at the mere thought of them—sparkled a rich blue that rivaled any dye her *púridaia* skillfully created. And her grandmother made quite the coin when she bartered her colorful cloth. She'd only crossed the ocean once, but the color, the vibrancy, how shades shifted and merged together created the blue of the Irishman's gaze.

Och, she shouldn't even think upon him. She was betrothed.

To Magor. A man she didn't know but was expected to accept as her husband because the clan deemed it so. Her heart clenched at the prospect of a marriage to a man so foreign to her.

She rose from the damp ground and swept her skirt clean, stalling, she knew. The dogs stood at attention, ears perked for a command.

"Go," she said in a low, even voice. The Lurchers obeyed and trotted toward the caravans.

Martine checked her appearance once more, knowing Rafe would pounce on any dishevelment. His exalted position in the clan as the eldest of the Pentrulengo children caused her undue scrutiny as well.

She followed in the wake of the dogs, their barking antics widened the once hidden path, and her mouth tipped up in a grin at their enthusiasm. The busy activities of the clan proved useful as she slipped into the feminine circle chatting by the fire.

"Martine."

Rafe's tone tangled her nerves. She'd earned the wrath of her brother, and worse, that of their leader. She rose and turned to face him, lifting her gaze from the ground, knowing he was vexed. "The dogs were restless."

"Aye, and mayhap their mistress as well," he said after a shrewd assessment.

Resentment welled up. "I'm not a prisoner, Rafe. I alone know the needs of the dogs."

He nodded. But she didn't miss his scrutiny.

Rafe kept his posture rigid as the wind caught on the full sleeves of his shirt. His dark eyes revealed little, but the clenching of his jaw told her he was aggravated as his scar, shaped like a sliver of the moon, shone white against his tan cheekbone. "You mustn't act so impetuously. The woods are not safe for the likes of us."

Martine clenched her fists in the folds of her full skirt.

"What is it?" her brother demanded. Rafe narrowed his eyes. They seemed like the pits of darkness as they skewered her. "Tell me, *Siskkaar*."

No matter how he was scowling at her, it always touched her when he spoke with endearments, called her sister instead of treating her with the detachment he reserved for other tribesmen. She missed the young man he used to be before he became a leader. The time when the clan had rescued her after a carriage accident had killed her family and she was found lost and injured. But she mustn't allow this slight mellowing to force her to reveal anything of importance.

His scowl told her he didn't believe her. "I am responsible for the safety of the clan."

"Aye," she said as she nodded. Nerves rattled her as sweat began to moisten her palms.

He tipped up her chin. "*Siskkaar*." His tone stiffened and held a warning that he knew she wasn't being truthful. Ire bunched the muscles along his jaw. If she tempted him further she'd be stuck laundering the clan's garments as a punishment.

She sighed as she searched for something to say. "'Twas nothing. Just a man refreshing his horse at the stream."

Rafe grabbed her arms and brought her face close to his. His rough actions contradicted the concern and softness reflected in the lines of his face.

"Next time bring Thomas." His strained voice unnerved her.

"'Twas only a short distance," she stammered.

He lessened his grip, but the imprint of fingers stung her arms. "You are too trusting. These people mean us only harm."

She twisted away and rubbed her arm. "He never saw me," she lied with a simplicity unlike her. What would it be like talking with an Irishman? Was he friendly? Harsh? She knew she'd forsaken her true heritage when she chose to stay with the Rom, but he was one of her own.

"And what if he did? Would you be able to protect yourself?"

She hesitated and he turned with a grunt of disgust.

No, she wouldn't be able to protect herself against the handsome man. And although she was betrothed, Martine wasn't certain she wanted to.

Chapter 2

Declan rode back through his estate, lacking his earlier demons but troubled nonetheless. He squinted at the afternoon sun, and then shielded his eyes. His head still throbbed with a sharp, pounding pain.

As he cleared the dense forest near Riverton, his steward raced toward him.

"M'lord! M'lord!"

Even though the steward rode a most docile horse, he slipped from side to side and his elbows flared out like two flapping wings. Declan hid a chuckle as the lanky Albert Pierce nearly lost his seat in the saddle.

Pulling up beside the anxious man, he waited until Pierce calmed himself.

"Thank the heavens I've found ye, m'lord."

Declan shifted in his saddle. He loathed the title his past afforded, especially since his past represented hell on earth.

"Aye, there's Gypsies about, blast their tanned hides." The man flushed, forcing his freckles to brighten like a bad rash.

"I'm aware." He marveled how swiftly gossip traveled through the village.

"'Tis havoc in the village." Pierce crossed himself twice. "Talk of forcing them to leave."

Heaving a patient sigh, Declan thought for a moment. At least a meeting in the village would keep him from the rattling confines of Riverton. And keep Abigail's father from screeching accusations that lashed at him harder than a prison whip.

While he was responsible for the villagers, he tried to allow them a freedom they'd never experience if Abigail's father were in charge. At least Declan had retained the right to govern as he saw fit. Not that it stopped Ettenborough from challenging each and every decision. The village nestled in the midst of his land. They worked for the estate, were farmers of grain and livestock, sellers of cloth and, thank the Lord, ale.

Regardless, he was reluctant to become involved in the lives of the villagers. It was as if somewhere deep inside him, Declan didn't want to become attached to anyone save his wife and his loyal men. If he did, perhaps his situation would change, shift, and he'd be alone once again, like he'd been so many times in his life. Like when his mother died and his father had allowed him to be dragged away to prison.

"M'lord?"

Declan blinked to clear the vision of his past from his mind. His steward quivered in his boots. Declan surmised his scowl was the cause of the dread on Pierce's thin face.

"I'll speak to the villagers."

Pierce nodded. "Knew ye would. I told meself, Lord Forrester would rid us of their flea-bitten hides."

Declan grimaced. "Where are my men?" he asked as he reined his horse toward the small gathering of shops and thatched-roof homes.

"Aye, they're making their way to the village."

"Thank you, Pierce."

Damn. Not that the news surprised him. The woman in the glen had foretold any trouble.

After Declan had placated the villagers and ensured them he'd handle the matter, he pulled on the reins and turned Kindred toward his estate. In no time, they crossed the lone open field between the village and Riverton. The rhythm of hoof beats pounded through his aching head, each movement pushing the sharp edge further as if a knife twisted within his brain. He'd need an elixir. Considering the circumstances, he loathed to be under its influence.

Which was worse, he wondered? The skull-crushing pain, or asking Ettenborough to have his butler prepare the secret concoction?

Martine ensured the caravan was neat and left the comfort of the small traveling home. The air felt heavy with indefinable energy as the wind whistled like a warning through the treetops. She wrapped her arms around her torso to stem the chills pricking the fine hairs of her arms.

She searched the camp filled with happy children and their mothers completing chores. The men either hunted or enjoyed tobacco not far from the grove. The circle of colorful caravans, twelve of them since a storm had toppled two, made for a protective community, almost like the villages they'd passed through. Her grandmother's stout figure eluded her, however, and Martine felt a wave of rising panic.

A group of young girls just a breath away from womanhood sewed near the fire. She waved and they shouted a greeting, then she continued toward the river that bent its way around the encampment. A sigh of relief escaped her as she walked toward the water.

"*Púridaia*, you shouldn't strain yourself." Martine removed the damp chemise from Anya's gnarled hands and shoved the washing bucket aside.

"Pash, girl. 'Twill be a dire day when I can't be doing my own laundry."

Martine swallowed a chuckle, but concern stayed with her as her gaze swept over the old woman. Her grandmother's once raven hair, now white as a newly born lamb, fell loose from its usual secure bun. Red veins mapped her dark eyes, making them rheumy. The same eyes seemed to bore into her with a knowing intensity.

"You've need of me, then?" Anya dried her hands on a rag and then stared patiently at her.

Martine crossed her arms before her chest. "You were expecting me?" Aye, as the sky expects the sun each day.

Her grandmother shrugged her hunched shoulders and an indulgent smile pulled her lips. "A problem is nagging at your heart. 'Tis written on that fair face o' yers." She gave a chuckle when Martine gasped. "Not to worry, girl. Not many know you as I." The old woman patted the log beside her. "Sit."

Martine complied, but not before she glanced across the creek. Assured no one watched from a distance, she grasped her grandmother's hand in hers. "Has Rafe spoken of the nuptials?"

Anya chuckled, a raspy, humorless laugh as disbelief pinched her features. "Why would he speak to me?"

Bristling, Martine tightened her grip on her grandmother's hand. "You're as close as a mother to me." Pity she didn't have her real mother, the image of the face that had once taken care of her was now a blurry recollection. The image of her father even more vague.

"The council will decide, my dear." Anya tipped Martine's chin with a crooked finger. "Is that yer trouble then? Yer marriage to Magor?"

Martine rose from the log, despair and desperation weighting her shoulders. How could she gain control of her future? Was there another option? "I've never even spoken to him."

Anya shrugged. "'Tis the way."

Of course she was aware of the custom, but it troubled her nonetheless. Most customs she embraced despite her earlier upbringing. Yet how could a council of men determine the best match for her? Her brother must have talked with a honeyed tongue if Magor's clan was willing to accept her despite her true heritage. 'Twas interesting and since she was a woman, she wasn't privy to the conversations between the leaders of the clan. In the end, they had accepted her, Gypsy blood or no.

And no matter how much she begged her brother, he wouldn't relent. And now there would be more than her at stake. Rafe's bartering had brought a steep bridal price.

Like selling cloth to the tailor, she thought with dismay. She had hoped she'd be able to sway her brother by appealing to his heart.

Slowly, Grandmother rose from her seat and Martine witnessed the flash of pain in the old woman's eyes. "Go. Rest."

Anya nodded, seemingly too tired to speak. Martine watched the woman, once graceful and lovely, make slow progress toward her caravan. She couldn't bear to see the lines of pain etched deep into her weathered skin. She'd have to ensure her grandmother rested.

Her fate, sealed and lonely, couldn't be turned by Anya. Regardless, Martine wished there was a different path she could accept. Like the one others accepted for her so many years ago.

"The children are waiting for you, *Siskkaar*."

She turned toward her brother. "Aye, Rafe."

Actually, she looked forward to the distraction of teaching the children to read, an unusual Gypsy trait, but one she'd insisted on. Her own skills were rudimentary, but enough for what she planned for the children.

Martine realized it made the rest of the clan question her presence, but she would share her limited education with them, and Rafe had agreed with her intentions and indulged her. Luckily she remembered how to read when nearly all of her memories had vanished along with the accident.

He watched her, his relentless gaze inspecting her. "Grandmother is well?" he asked.

She nodded, but she never looked away. Deep down, she knew her brother meant well, even loved her in the only way he knew how. But his unwavering insistence that she marry battled with everything she held dear. "I'll have Zoya fix her a draught."

"Ah, the medicine of sleep, keeper of pain." He rubbed the back of his neck. It struck her once again how he differed from the Irishman in the glen. Not only in looks, but demeanor as well. Her brother was serious, mysterious, traditional.

At night before the clan, Rafe became lively as he spoke of their history, sang, and even danced. "Martine . . . the wedding will be in a fortnight."

She gasped and brought her hand up to her mouth. Dread rose within her like a crash of waves ready to bury a wee carrack boat. "Nay," rushed from her despite her clenched teeth. "'Tis too soon." Too soon to be thrust into a loveless marriage. Too soon to be ripped from family and all she held dear.

Rafe's brow arched as if he dared her to say more. "In a one month, twilight will bless your union before both clans, over in the glen. This will unite us, unite two strong, blessed clans." He nodded in the direction of a yellow-roofed wagon. "The children."

She longed to say more but knew it would be futile. Instead, she squared her shoulders and left her brother in exchange for six rambunctious children too impatient to sit and learn. 'Twas a responsibility she normally savored, but today, with thoughts swirling and crowding her mind, she longed to be in the forest training the Lurchers.

A cacophony of little voices reached her at the door. The caravan swayed on its berth as two errant boys wrestled in the corner. Martine ducked into the barrel-shaped structure and silence blanketed the wagon. Solemn bright-eyed faces tilted up toward her, sweet and lovely. A smile tugged at her mouth, sweeping her dour mood away for the moment.

"Martine. Martine."

She looked down and tousled little Katya's raven hair. "Aye, wee one?"

"See," she said pointing to her tester with a pudgy finger, "Me letters are done."

Martine accepted the chipped slate board from the six-year-old and applauded the girl's efforts. She was rewarded with a beaming grin, missing a few upper teeth, and a quick curtsy.

Moments like this she would miss. Once married, Martine would teach no more, see her grandmother only when both clans were in the same area. And her beloved Lurchers—all was to be taken from her. She was powerless. Martine owed the clan for saving her, healing her, and if she were to return to distant relatives, the magistrate would seek the clan and---it was too horrid to think upon. Those who had become so dear to her would be in jeopardy.

Regardless, Rafe and the council's arrangement lay like a heavy cloak blackening her days.

Chapter 3

She stewed for a few days, still vexed about her impending marriage. Just as she was about to share tea with her grandmother, a young man raced by, nearly unsettling her. "'Tis men approaching."

Martine turned around and forced her grandmother back into her caravan. "Please, stay until I come and get you."

Despite her bluster, fear clutched the older woman's face and she trudged back into her berth.

"Remember, Grandmother, wait for me."

After receiving a terse nod, Martine headed toward the center of the clearing. Five riders astride glorious horseflesh trotted through the entrance. The branches of the trees arched over them in twisted brambles. The mist from the river floated around them in a sheen of white clouds. The horses flared their nostrils and pawed at the ground with their hooves. A maelstrom of dirt swirled about the area and formed around the horses and riders, making them look if they sprouted from the earth in one explosive motion.

Her brother stayed in the center of the encampment, feet spread and balled fist secured at his waist. His rigid back a strong wall of energy and power. Martine continued toward him, not allowing his fierce exterior to deter her. One thought came to mind--their leader certainly held the confidence of the clan, but would he be able to dispel the intruders without bloodshed?

With a quick glance, Martine noticed she was the only woman who dared venture into the dilemma. Others gathered in their wagons, heads peeking out due to curiosity, she supposed, most likely a human combination of fear and interest.

She edged closer to Rafe, a silent gesture of support and, she imagined, foolhardiness.

A rider urged his horse forward. He wore a leather doublet of a quality she'd never seen. The black hide was pierced with metal and thick stitching formed elaborate Celtic designs. Regal and rich. His breeches hugged his thighs so closely 'twas indecent, but that didn't stop her gaze from venturing along the hard expanse of his legs. Heat crept up her neck and flushed her face like a flame.

He tipped his head in her brother's direction. Martine gasped.

The stranger from the glen.

"We've business," was all he said.

Rafe nodded, but didn't twitch a muscle. Martine wanted to run from the confrontation, hide in her grandmother's berth safe from the bewitching blue eyes of the intruder. But her feet stayed rooted to the ground.

Och, this man was handsome. Strong jaw, brilliant eyes, and a broad mouth composed a man so striking. His face was a composite of hard planes of granite that matched the intense glare of his eyes.

The man sighed and his comrades inched closer to his side. They dressed as he did, except their clothing lacked the obvious quality she could see stitched in the leather of his.

"The villagers are concerned with your presence, Gypsy."

She could feel the tension in the tight line of her brother's shoulders, taste the anger in the air that hummed about him and the stranger. His jaw clenched and he remained silent.

"I've come to ask you to leave. Gypsies bring foul memories to Riverton." His voice was rough, husky, as he commanded her brother.

Rafe stepped forward. She knew he wished to throttle the tactless man. "We're Tinkers. Men and women with skills and trade."

"And itchy fingers if Lady Bannon's sheep have say

of it," the man behind the stranger spouted. The other men chortled and slapped the man on the back.

The stranger held up his hand and was rewarded with instant silence.

Her brother shrugged, a harmless action unless you were Rafe Petrulengo. "My clan has no need of other people's sheep."

Martine took a step forward.

The stranger's head snapped in her direction.

He leaned forward in his saddle. "You'll leave my land, or pay the consequences." His tone brooked no room for argument.

"We're people of the land, trainers of dogs, and masters of horses."

Her brother's words seemed to befuddle the stranger's friends. They looked to one another, smirks creasing their faces. If only they knew her brother's genius.

"I'm Lord Declan Forrester, Earl of Riverton," the stranger pompously said. "This is my land—and you are to leave."

Rafe bowed deep at the waist, his extended arm almost grazing the dirt before him. "As you wish."

"Be gone by morning. 'Tis all the time I'll give you."

A shiver ran up her spine at the cold gruffness of his voice. He clucked his horse forward, a magnificent animal, well-muscled with a gleaming coat of black.

Martine was so aware of the lord's presence, her skin tingled. And she knew without looking up that trouble was about to ensue. He stopped the horse before her and just sat. When her gaze met his, the lord nodded his head and gave a mocking salute.

She sighed, not knowing why she was reacting so unlike herself, why she was enthralled with the stranger.

With a nudge to his horse's side, he was off without a backward glance at her or her brother.

One look at Rafe and she knew he'd witnessed what had transpired. Rage boiled in his dark eyes and tension pulsed his jaw. He tapped a pointy leather boot against the packed earth. The women of the clan weren't to be appraised by *Gajos*. Especially a *Gajo* who'd ordered the *Kapo* to leave.

No matter, she thought with a smile of satisfaction. Lord Forrester had acknowledged her, and the realization swept through her with unparalleled warmth.

He shook his head as he left the encampment. His words and actions of his men all reeked of Ettenborough and his lordly ways. Yet he had an obligation to keep the villagers and tenants safe. Keep his estate safe.

And the woman—he shouldn't have acknowledged her. But he couldn't help himself. Her leader had mocked them. Declan was privy to some of the ways of the Gypsies. They didn't take kindly to non-Gypsies—*Gajos* looking at their woman. And she had bravely stood by her brother with a shy and curious gaze. No matter, his actions might spur them to leave quicker. He bet they'd be gone before midnight.

Kindred sensed his uncertainty and slowed from a canter to a trot. Declan urged him with a slight squeeze of his legs. The dark-haired woman plagued him much more so than the Gypsies plagued his land. Tinkers, he corrected, as if there were a difference. And as if the leader had spoken the truth. Their dark skin evidenced their lie and all he knew of them.

"We'll form a plan this evening if they do not leave," he said to his men. Then he sent them to the estate as he slowed his horse, trying to delay the return to Riverton so he could contemplate the clan's presence further.

They were industrious, if the camp was any indication. Children had peeked out from wagon windows and their mothers' skirts. Shy, yet daring. He grinned despite the situation.

How he longed for a child, and he knew his wife suffered because she had yet to provide him an heir. No matter how he much he reassured her, she'd often cried herself to sleep.

And her father didn't help matters—the bastard insinuated his wife's youthful transgression had cursed her—that God was punishing her, punishing them, for the sins of their past.

'Twas why they remained in Ireland and hadn't returned to England. Yet Ettenborough had feigned he missed his only child and was now visiting them.

Declan knew better. Ettenborough's visit was to remind him of who controlled his life.

'Twas what drove Declan—the constant threats, innuendos. Drove him to find out more about his past and why he'd been sent to prison without committing a crime. He was determined to discover why he'd rotted away for years. He had to ensure his future was safe—for the sake of his wife and any child with which they were blessed.

Ah, a child. Declan looked forward to the day when he could hold his child in his arms and forge a relationship that had been missing from his life.

A babe would nearly wipe out the harsh realities of his past, his time in Newgate.

Newgate haunted him night and day. The darkness surrounded him, pricking like the stab of a knife pierced his flesh. Haunting cries for freedom echoed off the stone walls and iron bars of the cell. Declan had shifted to ease his weight off his freshly-whipped back. The wounds festered, healed into raised scars crisscrossing the breadth of his shoulders. A man, face hidden in the shadows, his putrid scent giving him away, had reached his filthy hand between the bars that separated them. With obvious intent, he grasped at the bowl of gruel. Crazed with pain, Declan gripped the scrawny arm and jerked the man forward. The prisoner crashed into the iron bars, and the ominous sound of a skull cracking mixed with the howls of other unfortunate imprisoned men.

Unflinchingly, he'd grabbed the bowl and lapped up the meager serving. The poor soul beside him lay, slack-bodied, open-eyed, hopefully in a better place.

He gulped as his heart beat a staccato against his chest. The horrid memories had never abated.

The murder of the prisoner soiled his hands with blood, and he wasn't able to remove it regardless of numerous washings. After he caught his breath, he urged his steed into a gallop, eager to be home, to see Abigail. Hopefully she'd share one of the stories she was forever spinning with him.

As he made his way home, the sun dipped into the horizon, a fiery ball attempting to cling to the day and thwart night's arrival. From his position, he spied villagers finishing their daily routines. Thank God they remained ignorant of his past, despite Ettenborough's threat to tell one and all.

Nay, they saw him as a fair lord. He aided with farming, and when crops had suffered for some reason or another, he'd allowed the tenants leeway with the rents.

No matter. He'd remain at Riverton with his wife.

With that he found solace, a type of peace that would sustain him.

Chapter 4

As Declan neared the manor house, he noticed a flurry of activity near the main entrance. He furrowed his brow as he took long strides to the house.

"There 'e is," screamed Maude.

Declan's gaze snapped to his wife's maid. She'd been crying and her finger pointed to him like a beacon. Dread gripped his stomach as his honed instincts began to hum.

Men from the village gathered closer. Trenmore Grey nudged through the group, rifle in hand. Declan guessed it was primed and ready to shoot if he moved a muscle.

"'E killed me lady."

"Arrest him. He killed my daughter," Ettenborough yelled.

Momentarily perplexed as to why his wife's English maid was speaking with the lilt of an aged Irishwoman, Declan allowed her words to sink into his conscience. Killed Abigail? What the devil was the daft woman speaking of?

He held up his hands, his gaze searching each of the angry faces before him for answers. "Abigail is well." Last he knew she was enjoying the afternoon with her dear friend Sadie.

"Nay, m'lord," Grey countered. Declan wanted to punch the smug look from his face. With a sneer, the man continued. "Your dear wife was found dead less than ten minutes ago."

Shock, anguish, and grief buckled his knees. The moment he went down, the villagers tightened their circle. He couldn't breathe.

His wife was dead.

How the devil did this happen?

He gripped someone's shirt and dragged himself up. Blindly, he shoved through the crowd and raced into his home. Pounding up the stairs, he entered Abigail's chamber.

'Twas true.

Declan stood at the threshold, frozen in place by the grim scene before him as he gasped for breath. Doctor Ramsey sat by Abigail's bedside, shaking his head with a frown tugging his mouth.

"Nothing to be done," he said after he noticed Declan. "The cut across her throat caused her to drown in her own blood."

Declan clutched the door jamb so hard his fingers dug into the wood.

Gone.

She was gone.

Gathering strength, he walked toward the bed as if being dredged through the thickest of moors. His heart broke as he looked over the body of his dead wife and the blood pooled around her neck. Even with its newness, the scent of death permeated the chamber with its acridness and foulness.

How could life prove so cruel?

Doctor Ramsey grabbed his arm. "'Twas quick, lad. Won't you be thankful in that?"

He didn't remember nodding, but the doctor took leave as the crowd of villagers appeared in the hall.

Ettenborough came forward. "We'll put ye in the gaol until the magistrate returns."

Declan swallowed the bile rising in his throat. Prison. The thought was so incredibly horrid he couldn't wrap his mind around it. His chest heaved and his throat tightened close to strangling him.

Never again would he see the inside of a prison.

Never again.

"I didn't kill my wife," he said, his voice raw with grief and burgeoning madness. How could they think he could?

A smirk creased Ettenborough's ugly face. "Ah, well, her maid and Lady Bannon say differently."

Declan raked his fingers through his hair, desperate, perplexed, and furious. The faces in the crowd sneered at him. People he'd helped, given aid, were now turning on him like a pack of wolves. "Let me see to my wife."

Maude pushed through as Sadie attempted to pull her back. "Don't let the man touch me lady."

Grey moved to grab him. "'Tis no secret, *m'lord*, that yer wife had failed you."

Declan twisted away. "Nay. *Never*," he growled.

Little shoved through the crowd and attempted to hold them back. "Let Lord Forrester tend to his wife," the old man yelled as others grabbed him and tossed him aside.

Declan was torn between helping Little to his feet and securing his freedom. The doctor knelt by his valet and helped him stand. Satisfied the old man wasn't injured, Declan had no choice.

"No!" he heard Sadie yell. Desperation ruled his actions. The haunting cries of prisoners, starving and beaten, sounded as though they were in the same room. The scent of rotting flesh rose in the air, voiding the roses on the table before the window. He gagged at the odor of men incarcerated until their death.

Never again would he see the inside of a prison.

Never again.

He shoved Grey aside as he ignored Sadie's plea. Making toward the windows, he reached for the chair by the writing desk. He launched through the window holding the chair before him. Glass shattered everywhere, but he disregarded the shards piercing his flesh as his body ripped through the gaping hole. Declan landed on the balcony and climbed over the railing.

Before making the final plunge, he surveyed the horizon. Villagers peppered the landscape as they made their way to

Riverton. His men sat astride their mounts, with his saddled horse by their side. Even at this distance, he could judge their uncertainty.

Jumping to the ground, he ran to them. Nate looked to him with such confusion and speculation, he stepped back.

"I didn't kill Abigail," he shouted as his breath heaved from his lungs. "She was my wife."

His comrade nodded. "We'll head to London. Randolph sent a missive. He'll arrive soon. He can help you . . . sort out this mess." With a curt nod, he urged his horse forward.

The rest of the men followed suit, each raking Declan with an uncertain glance. Even Pierce, his cowardly butler, was atop a horse. Did he too wish to help Declan, even now? Declan almost went to him to beg him to listen, beg him to believe.

"There 'e is," shouted a villager.

Declan looked toward the manor house. The mob of bystanders had grown two fold. Little led the crowd, confusion in his old eyes and a few ounces of pity as well.

Declan knew he must stay out of prison and its life-choking bars. He had only one option.

Flee.

Wiping blood from his line of vision, Declan grabbed onto Kindred's reins and leapt onto his back. Instinct took over and he urged his horse toward the forest. Declan needed to hide deep within the woods until he could prove his innocence. If he headed to London now, they'd find him. He trusted his men to follow the plan and head to London without him.

Glancing back, he felt panic rise as villagers chased after him. Some were on horseback, others on foot like a pack of hounds trained on a hare.

Declan kicked Kindred's flanks relentlessly, yelling for speed. His hands held fast to the reins as his mount hurdled a creek and raced through the glen.

As he crossed the glen, rain began to fall. *Bollocks*. Now he had the elements to deal with as the terrain turned muddy. One quick look over his shoulder revealed the villagers had not kept up with his neck-breaking speed.

Declan reined in Kindred and sat up. His own heaving breaths matched that of his winded mount. Absently, he patted the horse's neck while he pondered his next course of action.

He must prove his innocence. But how? Who would want his wife dead? And in such a gruesome manner?

They'd planned to grow old together and God willing, raise their children. And now all of those hopes and dreams were futile.

He rubbed his weary eyes and stopped his horse. Blood had dried on his face, yet still oozed from the numerous cuts in his upper and lower body. He regretted running like a guilty man. But survival was his first priority and Abigail didn't need him any longer.

A shout in the distance caught his attention. He tightened his grip on the reins and urged Kindred into a gallop. Once again he ducked branches and kept a tight hold as he guided his horse through the tangled maze of trees. His heart pounded in his chest like an explosive bullet launching from a pistol. Declan shoved his concerns aside as he pushed forward and deeper into the woods.

Kindred jumped over a fallen log, unsettling Declan. The animal skittered to a stop, tossing him onto the wood-strewn ground.

The light of the day faded as darkness enveloped him. His last conscious thought was of his wife, now gone forever.

Lady Sadie Bannon tucked her purchase under her arm and left the millinery. The hat she'd chosen would look fetching with her new gown. 'Twas a gift she had, marrying well, but not for long. She chuckled. Her quick unions had allowed her free reign within the village and its quaint shops. Milliners, the dress makers, bakery, and, ah, the sweet shop, were her favorite haunts. Sure, she spoiled herself rotten, but 'twas no one else at the moment ready and willing to do so.

She strolled down the narrow street, looking forward to tea, offering a genial nod toward the priest and a smile toward Blackstone, the owner of the bank. Why she was so pleased, she didn't know. Abigail was gone. Not a dear friend, but women like herself rarely had women friends. And that tasty morsel Declan Forrester, gone and not a sign in what direction. Nearly five days had passed and the blasted magistrate had no answers.

There were few things in life Sadie was certain of; she loved the power of money and Declan Forrester was a fine example of manhood. How wasted he was with Abigail. The last time she'd seen him, daylight had streamed through the large windows in the main hall, caressing Declan as she herself wished to do. He looked like the statue of a Greek god she'd seen in her husband's books. Except with clothes on, more's the pity. Clothed or no, she wanted to lap him up like a kitten does milk, and she'd not cared a whit about Abigail.

Besides, a lass has to take care of herself, she thought as she brushed her hand over her lovely gown. And being a widow suited her only for the pounds in the bank and the lovely silk that covered her back. She could never go back to living as she did when she married her first husband. He'd plucked her from the serving staff to be his mistress, then she'd moved up the ranks when his wife unfortunately died. Or fortunately, in Sadie's case.

Truthfully, her healthy appetites had been neglected for far too long. And she knew just the man to feed them.

Now that did pose a problem, she thought with a frown. She'd plans for that man and now they were on hold because of one mistake.

"Lady Bannon, 'tis delightful to see ye this fine, fine afternoon."

Sadie stifled a cringe, then thought better of sending the man on his way. "Thank ye, Mister Grey."

He waved his hand at her as one would a persistent fly. "Must we be so formal? 'Twas not too long ago we shared the same school room."

She nodded and grabbed his offered elbow. He was freshly shaven, in a worsted wool suit, and looking quite the man. Hmmm, not a bad picture at all, at all. At least she'd be walking through the village with a handsome gentleman. A gentleman who may have current information on one Lord Declan Forrester.

Sadie smiled and tipped her chin toward her escort. "Tell me, Trenmore, what news can ye be sharing with me?"

He gave a brisk nod of his head. "Lord Ettenborough is not happy with the magistrate."

Nodding her head, she listened as Trenmore relayed the sorrow of Abigail's father and how the estate was now in a precarious position. Lord Ettenborough had no desire to stay in Ireland since the death of his daughter, but he wanted Declan to pay. Aye, he loathed the country and longed for the refinement of his comfortable town home in London.

"M'lady, 'twould be me pleasure if ye had tea with me."

Anticipation of further conversation elated her. "Aye, Trenmore," she replied with a purr. "I'd love to share your tea."

He patted her hand and gave a winning smile. Why, she'd never noticed those golden flecks in his green eyes before. 'Twas a lovely surprise.

They entered the small teahouse and sat before a large bank of windows. Pleased with the advantageous seating, Sadie plumped up her skirts and adjusted the lace fichu around her neck. Now those old birds who gossiped incessantly about her would see she was a force to be reckoned with. She'd been Abigail's friend and confidante and now, aye, now she was having tea with one of the finest catches in the village.

Trenmore ordered from a mousy waitress and set his gaze on Sadie. 'Twas amazing, his interest, and just when she was in need of male attention.

"Declan Forrester will be a sorry man when Ettenborough gets hold of his useless carcass."

Sadie knitted her brow. With all of the attention Trenmore was lavishing on her, she'd forgotten they'd even spoken of Lord Forrester. She tsked silently to herself to keep a rein on her thoughts or at least keep them trained on the conversation at hand.

"We'll not be seeing his hide anytime soon. 'Tis said the magistrate will declare a manhunt for the bastard." He flushed. "Sorry, m'lady. I shouldn't be so bold with ye."

Sadie cast him a glance that told him she forgave him and patted his hand. "Would you care to come to dine, Trenmore?"

"'Twould like nothing better, m'lady."

"Sadie," she corrected him with a promising look. "Sadie."

Chapter 5

Martine paced in her caravan, gripping her quaking stomach as she walked. They had left and found a new safe haven for the clan, one deeper in the wood with a river bending around the wagons like a protective perimeter. Each person had gathered their belongings, secured them in the wide berth of their wagons. Young boys had hitched horses to each wagon, shouting to each other, the excitement of a new journey evident in their young voices. And away they went. Now three days later, they had settled and were back to a normal routine.

"Lass," her grandmother interrupted, "Rafe has need of you."

Martine nodded, a lump forming in her throat as she tried to swallow. One by one, the explanations as to why the lord had recognized her vanished from her mind. How could she defend herself when she was truly in the wrong?

"You best see to him."

Anya placed a gnarled hand on her shoulder and squeezed. Martine patted her hand; the papery smooth surface belied the many years her *púridaia* had toiled. How hard she had worked to support the tribe. They'd all labored endlessly securing enough money, food, and clothing, despite the harsh times that brought the clan sickness, turbulent weather, and battles for their right to exist.

Her grandmother lost her husband in such a way. Fighting for freedom in England had left the clan with a pitiful mix of old men, women, and children. Her grandfather suffered from the shame and never recovered from his injuries. Anya mourned him constantly, Martine knew. Every so often she'd catch such a sad and lonely cast to Anya's gaze. Her grandmother hid it well, but the telltale signs of fresh tears often glimmered in her wise eyes before she masked them.

Now to see her brother.

Martine remembered when he helped lay their grandfather and parents to rest. Such discipline he used to disguise his sorrow. Martine recalled the proud line of his shoulder as he hoisted the coffin to rest upon it and looked forward. He marched as the other men, all many decades older than him, grim and manly despite being just fifteen years old.

That day he entered into the leadership of the tribe. No one disputed his readiness or qualifications. Rafe was a Petrulengo and that proved enough to earn the trust of the elders. Regardless, the tradition of selecting a ruler dictated her brother take the helm no matter his age.

A frown tugged at her mouth. Thinking back, she realized that was when she lost her brother and gained a leader. No more had they fished along a creek, rode recklessly across an open field, her sitting in front of him for safety. No, Rafe held too much responsibility to be gallivanting about with his eight-year-old sister.

Rafe had always accepted her. Held her dear and protected her against the other children who were slow to welcome her presence. 'Twas the Gypsy way—*Gajos* weren't accepted, weren't allowed to be part of the clan. Yet here she was, the *Kapo's siskkaar*. And eventually, the clan came around and thought of her as one of their own, especially when she died her hair and followed their customs.

She removed her grandmother's hand from her shoulder and left the wagon. Rafe was in the center of the encampment training a Vanner. The horse was a gorgeous mix of white and black with a long mane and shaggy hair around its massive hooves. Wind bucked up the dirt, swirling into a little storm in the middle. On the other side of the whorl of dust, her brother stood. He watched her and the horse with those unreadable dark eyes of his. Pricks of uncertainty raced up her spine as she strode toward him. She grasped her hair as it whipped about her face and twisted it into a knot. He still watched her, ignoring the wind, dirt, and his own hair blowing about.

He beckoned a young boy to take the horse to graze. She watched longingly as the horse trotted alongside the boy and away from her brother.

"We've a lot to discuss, *Siskkaar*." He turned and walked toward his caravan. There he lived alone, no wife or children, simply satisfied with leading the clan, yet not providing an heir if he should fall into the trap of ill fate. 'Twas a problem which the clan elders tended to remind him about.

She glanced at the straight line of his back, clothed in a full white shirt. It flapped in the wind like a sail broken loose of its moorings. His strides outpaced hers with his long legs eating up more ground with each step. To keep up, Martine trotted a little, though she loathed appearing too eager.

As they approached his home, men exited and watched as they entered. The elders nodded solemnly at her, their wrinkled faces hiding any indication of what her fate may be. New dread rose at the back of her throat, almost gagging her with fear.

Martine gripped the fabric of her skirt in an attempt to steady her nerves. She tripped on a stone but quickly righted herself before her brother had the opportunity to spy the clumsy action.

"I have spoken with Magor's father," he explained as she sat across from him. "The wedding contract has been agreed and you will hold an exalted position in Magor's clan." He looked pointedly at her. "Until you are wed, you will need to watch all of your actions and the actions of those around you."

She nearly rolled her eyes but stifled the action. "Aye." Her heart raced as she thought of her impending marriage.

How was she to manage without her grandmother? She'd never train dogs again or teach the children to read.

Her brother continued to discuss what the clans had agreed upon in order for her to wed Magor, but she barely heard him.

Life would change with or without her permission.

"*Kapo*," a voice called. "We've found a man!"

"Pash," a pleasant voice said. "You'll tear your bandages."

Declan tried to pull out of the tepid cocoon in which his mind and body rested. Pain free, as if he floated on a mattress softer than clouds in the sky. The voice continued to speak and try as he might, he couldn't force his eyes open.

A hand gently patted his shoulder that he could discern. Then blackness filled him again as he lost his clutch on the easy rhythm of the voice. Humming lulled him back to sleep, a welcome respite regardless of his wish to wake and see who sang to him.

Martine peeked into the wagon in which her grandmother nursed the Irishman. Curiosity drove her, yet her heart held a stake in his safety. How she wanted to replace the gentle woman who now fed him medicinal draughts and slathered ointments on his battered body.

She tipped her head and regarded him as she leaned further into the caravan. If Rafe were here and saw her with her head in the door and her feet sticking out, he'd be furious. She grinned, then steadied herself when she nearly toppled.

Anya moved the sheet further and tsked. Thankfully, the wounds were starting to heal. At first she was shocked at the cuts and bruises over his torso. Some so deep, Anya stitched them with her apt hand. The injury that concerned her the most was the deep gash on his forehead. Stitches jagged across the dark purple bruise and it had swelled horribly.

Once her grandmother's back was turned, Martine snuck into the caravan and sat beside the narrow bed housing Lord Forrester. Awareness of their differences didn't stop her from admiring him. His chest and shoulders bulged with muscles and surpassed the width of the bed. If she touched him, would he be hard? Would he wake? She shook her head to dispel the ridiculous idea. She was a maiden, one who was betrothed.

Still, she thought as she tipped her head to the side. Just a sheet clad him from the waist on down, but it still lent to the firm shape and length of his legs. His feet peeked out and hung over the end of the cot. Tall and strong, the man seemed to draw her with curiosity and, aye, brazen admiration.

"Pash, lass, ye nearly scared me to death," her grandmother said.

Heat rushed over her face as she hastily stood, nearly knocking over the chair. "I wanted to see how he was faring."

Anya chuckled. That wicked all-knowing rumble that amused and annoyed Martine all at once.

"Aye, lass. What do you think happened to him?"

She tapped her lips with her finger and searched the sleeping man's face. He looked less threatening, she thought, less demanding and arrogant. The sharp edge of his jaw still held, but around his eyes, he looked peaceful. Something her mind told her he didn't experience often.

"He's running from something, someone." She touched his warm hand. His fingers curled around hers as if it were the most natural thing in world. Her hand tingled as his heat seeped into her. Glancing at Anya, she reluctantly pulled away. "The cuts look clean, almost as if he were cut by glass."

Her grandmother stood beside her, a rag in one hand and a bottle of ointment in the other. "Aye," she said with an approving nod. Anya patted her arm. "This man has a place in yer life."

She scoffed, looking away. "Aye, he does. He's sleeping in my caravan." She couldn't allow her grandmother to sense her attraction to Lord Forrester. She must keep her thoughts pure and for her betrothed. Lord Forrester wasn't Rom. He was forbidden and must remain forbidden so she did not shame the clan.

A raspy chuckle shook her grandmother's shoulders. "Ye know what I speak of, my dear." She then wagged her finger in Martine's face. "Don't push him away, no matter what Rafe says."

Now confused, Martine kept her gaze on the lord and tried to find the meaning in Anya's words. "Don't you understand? I must do as my brother says."

Anya waved her hand. "No matter, girl. Go see to the children. You know how yer brother likes them to learn their lessons. And make sure to use the dye for yer tresses. The color is fading a bit."

She touched her hair and nodded, torn between watching over the injured man and seeing to the minds of the clan's children. Duty won out, of course, and she left her caravan for the open area of the encampment, far away from the handsome Irishman.

Children raced through the center, playing some game or another. Several little girls circled around a basket of discarded cloth, dolls in their hands as they wrapped them in makeshift clothing. The sun gleamed down on their little heads, shining against their dark Gypsy hair.

She remembered when she was just their age and how she played alone until Maria tucked her under her wing and they'd been thick as thieves ever since.

The young girls noticed her and jumped up to greet her. They hugged her, their tiny faces brushed against her skirt, and she could smell the freshness of their recently bathed bodies. She ruffled their hair and bade them to follow her to the teaching wagon.

They called to their brothers and soon a pack of children crowded the small space. She sat amid them, her legs tucked beneath her as she wrote letters on a slate and had the children repeat the steps.

She tried to concentrate, yet her mind stubbornly returned to Lord Forrester sleeping in her wagon. The image of him clad in a sheet and little else taunted her in a way that perplexed her with curiosity and shame, but och, the way his tan skin pulled over his muscular chest had her blushing at the mere thought. And the way his muscles bunched and strained, then flexed and bulged—'twas outrageous. She didn't mind bunking with Anya, but the intimacy of him sleeping in her bed felt unseemly, forbidden and exciting all at once. Shouldn't the only man to share her home be the man she married?

Marriage. Och, she shivered as a chill raced up her spine.

The word should chime with happiness for her. Instead, she recalled the image of Magor's tall form and stern features. They'd never spoken a word to each other. Her brother negotiated the marriage and somehow Martine felt insulted.

Ridiculous, she thought with a firm shake of her head. 'Twas the custom of the clan and she must support her *Kapo*. He was her leader and the clan would certainly frown if she spoke her mind. Hadn't her awareness of the Irishman caused enough trouble? She'd heard the whispers by the others and their snide remarks about the *Gajo* in their midst. A non-gypsy being nursed in the encampment violated everything the Gypsies held dear and, as for safety, how could they be sure a brigade wouldn't ride in tomorrow seeking the lord?

"Martine, can we go now?" a small voice interrupted her musings and concerns.

She turned to Lucinda. "Aye," she said. "You may all go for the day."

The children bustled out of the wagon with energy she admired. They were so wholesome and without guile.

She bit her lip and hesitated before leaving the protection the caravan provided. Should she venture toward the cooking circle? Not to cook, of course, but Maria was there and it felt like ages since they had a good talk over tea.

Martine stood in the doorway for a few more minutes before she descended the thin wooden steps. As if they had a mind of their own, her feet headed toward her caravan and the bedside of Lord Forrester.

Her home was quiet, her grandmother perhaps mixing her herbs in her own wagon for ointments and salves. The lord lay still on the bed, the covers strew about his body, hugging each oak of a leg like a second skin. She felt a heated blush as her gaze slid along his strong form, embarrassed at her own boldness but not able to help herself.

As she watched him, there was a type of energy tingling along her skin, rushing through her blood as she took in the planes of his face—strong and bold. She was enthralled with the tiny cleft in his chin and she wanted to touch it, if only for a second. His broad mouth tightened as if he were in pain, then relaxed so quickly she thought she'd imagined it. If only she could reach out and soothe his brow without waking him. Martine shook her head. She mustn't think of him. Soon he'd be gone and she'd be on her way to her wedding. All of her wondering about the Irishman would be a memory.

The faint scent of lavender teased his senses. Declan opened his eyes a crack and was rewarded with the vision. The Gypsy stood staring at him with rapt interest. He held back a chuckle at the blatant interest he didn't know a maiden could possess. He kept his gaze hooded. Watching her soothed him, almost helped him forget the injuries troubling his body. Whatever medicine the Gypsy had given him must be wearing off. He felt each cut and bruise and what he thought were stitches as they throbbed. The pounding of a megrim at the base of his neck alerted him that he was unwell, and he didn't have the benefit of Ettenborough's brew. God, Ettenborough must have laid Abigail to rest by now. How he loathed not being with her until the end. His dear friend and wife had died at the hand of a coward and there was naught he could do until he was healed.

Dear God, Abigail. How? Who? He had to find out who killed her. The image of her filled his mind and churned his stomach. How she must have suffered.

A moan escaped as he turned his head before he could squelch it.

"My lord?" the Gypsy asked with her rich voice. 'Twas husky with a hint of an accent he couldn't place, similar to Anya's, yet unique.

At once she was at his side. A damp cloth found its way to his forehead and he heard her mixing something.

"Please do not move so. You'll tear your stitches."

The pleading of her voice stilled his actions. She attempted to help him to sit up, her touch gentle and warm, unnerving. He stopped her, shamed she'd discover injuries not caused by his escape.

Declan stayed silent, just content to allow her to direct the situation. Here he lay in a Gypsy's home, and his mind reeled with the irony. Even when he, a man who'd murdered and spent time in prison, thought the Gypsies represented a baser, lowly type of lifestyle. They'd plagued his land, swindled the villagers and tenants of their meager earnings, and now they sheltered him. He furrowed his brow, frustrated with his anger and confusion. How could they not be what he always thought?

And the Gypsy tended to him. This woman was his enemy and now she was aiding in his recovery.

And Declan didn't know how to react to the guilt and turmoil that raged beneath the surface. He'd been used to remaining aloof, suffering in silence and trying to accept the hand he'd been dealt. His father's neglect, time in prison, Ettenborough's control—they'd all forced his hand and made him cold.

His stomach growled at the smell of soup, ridding his mind of why and who. And if his nose knew what it was doing, he'd be enjoying venison broth with onions and hopefully carrots.

"Take a little at a time," she instructed as she lifted a spoon to his mouth. "'Tis just broth, but if you keep it down, I'll add some meat later."

Instead of disappointment, he leaned up on his elbows and lapped up the soup as quickly as she gave it to him.

"Thank you," Declan croaked, his dry throat not yet soothed fully. "How long have I been here?"

Her gaze avoided his as she busied herself with cleaning up the soup and folding the cloth that cooled his forehead. "Nearly a week."

Bollocks. Declan couldn't wrap his thoughts around the idea that it had been so many days since Abigail had died. His throat nearly closed and he turned his head away from the woman beside him.

He had to discover why his wife was murdered. As a pledge to her, a woman who'd been his friend and partner in marriage when they both had no other option, he would discover who killed her. He knew she mourned the love of her life. Her thoughts of her former lover were never far from her mind. Strange how it didn't bother him, her love for another. Mostly, he felt relief. They weren't a love match and 'twas comforting that they didn't try to woo one another. They married as part of a deal. Declan was free of prison and Abigail's marriage to him would mean her father wouldn't kill the man who'd stolen her virtue.

He moved his head. The movement heightened the megrim and he clenched his eyes shut to void out the light of the day.

"Anya will have something for your aching head."

He scoffed and without opening his eyes, he said, "Who is Anya and how does she know I have a megrim?"

She chuckled, a feminine sound that eased over him like the lap of a gentle wave. Soft and soothing. "She is my *púridaia*. My grandmother is well skilled with medicinal herbs."

The skepticism must have shown on his face.

She folded a rag and allowed an indulgent smile. "Not to worry. 'Tis a miracle you survived that bump on your head. No wonder it pains you."

He gave a slight nod but feared if he opened his eyes or moved more, his head would split open.

Declan heard a shuffle from the direction of the door. "Martine? He's awake?" an aged voice said.

She muttered something beneath her breath, then cleared her throat. "Aye. Just a few moments ago."

"We'll give him this and see if it helps his pain."

Again she chuckled. Were these women witches? Could they just sense his injuries and aid them without further explanation?

The older woman held a cup to his mouth. The smell assailed him with its bitter, woody scent. He looked to the women holding the cup. No doubt she was Anya. Her white hair topped her head in a regal knot and knowledge lined her face in rivers of wrinkles. He accepted the drink, ignoring the acrid taste it left on his tongue.

"That's a lad," she clucked. "It should ease the pain. If ye need more, just tell my granddaughter Martine to fetch me."

"You're not staying to tend him?" The panic in the young woman's voice matched that of her widening eyes.

Anya smiled and patted her hand. "Not to worry, *bitti kom*. You'll do just fine."

"'Tisn't proper, Grandmother." She began wringing her hands and pacing the caravan. "If Rafe were to find out . . ."

"Pah," she said as she waved her hand. "What he doesn't know will not hurt him in the end."

Declan watched as the woman, nay, Martine, turned toward her grandmother, fear and frustration clear on her lovely face. "Rafe always knows what happens within this clan. He's your grandson after all."

She made no sense, and the fear Martine displayed troubled him. Was she in danger if she stayed with him? "I'll do fine on my own," he managed to say, his megrim becoming less and less intense.

Anya threw an angry look in his direction. "And undo all my hard work? Not on yer life, lad."

Martine stepped close to the cot. "Maybe Lord Forrester is right." Hope filled her voice as she appealed to her grandmother. "Declan."

They both looked at him, their brows raised in a question. "Call me Declan."

Martine's doe-eyed look surprised him. Concern ringed her gaze. Why? He attempted to move, yet Anya stilled his hand and scowled openly at him.

"Sit still. Are ye a lad or a man?"

His stitches pulled as he grinned. "You're the one who keeps calling me lad."

When she smiled, he knew her bark was worse than her bite. She wagged a gnarled finger at him and then another smile cracked her wrinkled face. He'd never known his grandparents, but he knew they'd be nothing like the stout Gypsy before him. She was too vibrant, too full of life. She held herself with a beautiful mixture of heritage and grace. His thoughts surprised him, as he'd been known to loathe their existence as much as his villagers and tenants had.

She shrugged and frowned. "Yer built like a warrior?"

He shook his head. "I'm no warrior."

"Pash, lad. Just look at yer chest, 'tis fare too grand for a man who doesn't fight."

"*Púridaia.*" A blush covered Martine's face like the color of the red roses that climbed Riverton's walls.

He started to laugh, but it came out like a weak cough. She patted his shoulder and nodded her head. "You'll tell us when yer ready."

Declan started to protest further, but when she sent him such a reproachful glance, he closed his mouth.

"My lovely Martine will sit by yer side. Don't move an inch," she warned.

Martine sat in the spindly-backed chair beside his cot. He watched her, enjoying her discomfort for the mere reason he wanted her to stay.

There was something calming about her, the softness of her voice, her large questioning eyes.

She looked around the small wagon, obviously attempting not to look at him. He followed her gaze and took in the world in which this woman lived. Colorful weavings bordered the windows and numerous small trunks lined the side opposite his cot. Necklaces hung from nails piercing the wood of the caravan and delicate cloth shoes lay beneath them.

Declan found himself looking at Martine once again. She was dressed in a vibrant hue of blue along with an embroidered white blouse. Her clothing was foreign and exotic, just like the darkness of her hair and the tan of her skin.

She held her hands in her lap, fingers tangled as if she were trying to grip them with too much strength.

"Did you train your dogs this morning?" he asked, nodding toward the leather leashes hanging near the door.

His question startled her and her gaze sought his with a frank innocence that surprised and humbled Declan.

"Your dogs?" he prompted, truly curious about the habits of the Gypsies.

Martine looked at him, her face a study in trying to attempt not to appear excited and failing miserably.

"I train them every day."

He cocked a brow, despite the fact it felt as if his stitch-restrained skin was tearing. "Why is it you do the training?"

She shrugged her shoulders, the gestured belying the excitement in her voice. "I seem to have a way with them."

He regarded her more closely. There was definitely something she wasn't telling him, but he decided not to push the matter. "Tell me about them."

"Oh," she said. Her face flushed scarlet but she began to speak regardless. "I train them for hunting and then they are sold from town to town. Usually, I have two or three at a time."

"And when you sell them? How does that feel?" He sensed sadness in her tone now, and he wished to focus on her, lest she turn the conversation toward him.

A shimmer of tears deepened her dark eyes. They seemed like endless pools, rich and deep. She blinked them away in an instant and her demeanor strengthened before him. "'Tis hard the first couple of days after the sale, but then Rafe brings more puppies for me to begin the process once again."

Before he could ask another question, Anya rushed into the caravan. "Lass, yer needed." The old woman's chest heaved at the extent of her exertion. "The *Kapo* is on his way to speak to Lord Forrester."

Declan watched as Martine paled and swiftly left the caravan. *Kapo* could only mean one thing.

The leader of the Gypsies was on his way.

Chapter 6

A shadow darkened the caravan. A tall man, lean with a hardened glint to his eyes stood at the threshold as if waiting to be welcomed in. Declan recognized him. How could he not? He wore dark pants and a full white shirt cinched at the waist with a broad leather belt. His tanned skin highlighted the white scar that resembled a scythe on the side of his face.

"*Kapo*," Declan said, ready to break the silence and learn more about this man.

The man tipped his head and entered the makeshift sick room. "Rafe Pentrulengo, leader of this clan." His voice, though low, held infinite authority in a calm, menacing way.

"Aye, Tinker." The name hung between them, and Declan remembered the day he ordered the Gypsies to leave and had used his title arrogantly.

"*Lord* Declan Forrester," Rafe corrected. "I remember ye well."

The Gypsy inspected him, his gaze lazy but his intentions clear. He wanted to make Declan squirm. And Declan would be damned if he showed the fatigue that weighted his shoulders.

Rafe waved his hand impatiently in the air. "What are we to do with you, *Lord Declan Forrester*?" He said his name with such a snarl, Declan was ready to leap from the bed and challenge the man to a duel.

"Ah, I know." The grin that curled his lips did little to settle Declan's unease. "Do you think you'd earn yer weight in gold?"

Gold? Did the Gypsy think to auction him off in the village

square? Aye, a hefty price must be wagered for his head by now, and the Gypsies would be all too happy to claim it.

"I've lost a few pounds since I've arrived. Mayhap I'm not worth the money bags I see gleaming in your eyes."

The man's mouth slid into a frown, accentuating the sharp angles of his lean face. "Yer in no condition to bargain for yer worthless life. I know what you've done. 'Tis talk about the village of how your murderous hands killed your wife."

Anger flooded him with indignation. Rage churned his stomach along with grief. A looming question struck bright in his mind. Who would kill Abigail? And so horridly at that?

"I know of you. Yer past isn't as well hidden as you think."

Declan snapped his attention back to the *Kapo*. He watched as delight danced about his dark eyes. Did he really know of Declan's time in prison? Of the fact that although he didn't kill his wife, he was a murderer? Blood stained his hands no matter who had died.

Calling the Gypsy's bluff, Declan said, "What do you know of my past?"

He casually shrugged his shoulders. "I've enough knowledge to know ye don't want the villagers to know you are here. Or the magistrate when he arrives. But enough talk. I grow weary of yer face."

Declan grunted. As if Rafe's face was pleasing to him with its scar and harsh edges. He'd much rather that of Martine or her grandmother, as a matter of fact, a contrast of aged beauty.

The Gypsy turned to leave the wagon. He glanced over his shoulder and stopped. "Hurt my clan, and yer a dead man. Of that be sure."

I've already been dead, Declan thought. The threats lay idle, yet heavy in the air. "As soon as I'm well, I'll be on my way."

The man left the wagon, leaving Declan ample time to think of their conversation. He was once a haunted man. The face of the prisoner, eyes lifeless and pathetic, flashed before him. Now he was hunted. So much plagued him—his wife's death, his time in prison, the identity of the men who sent him there.

Bollocks, he was cursed.

Now the quandary of living with the Gypsies. Their lifestyle was not one he'd bless. Blast his conscience and how it easily molded to the situation. He couldn't judge the clan. God knew he'd met the Devil himself and still paid the price of his actions. No, judging others wouldn't do. He was on his way to hell. Problem was, he hadn't had to leave earth to start the journey.

Five more days. His body lay flaccid on the small cot, limbs lingering over the side like branches from a tree. The only brightness of his days were the visits from Martine. She was shy, but curious. Such a lovely lass with a sweet yet husky voice and a brilliance to her gaze. Her visits were fleeting but gave great insight to her character. She loved her people, adored her grandmother, and relished her time with the children. There was a bit of leeriness when her brother was mentioned, but she obviously respected and loved him as well.

Regardless, he was bored with the lack of activity. Declan sat up, then fell back against the mattress. He gripped the side of the wagon and pulled himself up, thankful no one had seen his struggle. He was nearly upright. His unused muscles ached and his skin stretched as the stitches pulled across his injuries. The dizziness blurred his vision, but he pushed on regardless. When his feet hit the wooden floor, he stayed all motion. Once settled, he pushed up and grabbed onto the wall nearest him. A smile of satisfaction lifted his mouth as he took small steps forward and glanced out the window to view the encampment.

The Gypsies bustled about and many swept the dirt from the steps leading to their meager caravans. Even children took part in the daily work, hauling buckets of water that sloshed over the rims and wetting their path. Grim determination cinched their brows with each laborious step.

Like a voyeur, Declan watched from the cover of the wagon. An outsider, content to stay in the shadows that offered him comfort in the darkness.

Abigail would love this. She was curious about anyone who wasn't English. He'd often chuckle when she'd discover something new in the village and praise the Irish for their industrious endeavors. To her, the Gypsy clan would be exotic, foreign. Something to celebrate, not loathe as many did.

He watched the *Kapo* leading the Gypsy horses to a makeshift pen near the rear of the camp. He had to admit, the Gypsies had a way with Vanners. The animals gleamed beneath their attention and were some of the best-trained animals he'd ever seen. Strong enough to lead the caravans and docile enough to be around the many children racing about the camp.

The *Kapo* then swaggered across the opening to the fire pit surrounded in what appeared to be elder females. They stepped away, making an opening for their leader to advance to the large pot secured over the fire. A hand shot out with a crude bowl. The leader accepted the bowl and ladled his morning meal. He nodded, arrogant, yet a warm smile filled his face. Declan smiled as well as the woman stepped out of the protective circle of ladies. Anya, in her grace and bluster, brought a softness to Declan's heart.

She turned toward the caravan, her eyes narrowed with piercing intensity. Declan felt pinned, and he knew Anya, blast her, had sensed his presence and ardent interest. She strolled through the encampment, her steps measured and slow. The morning sun haloed her white-haired head and a shadow hid her expression.

Declan stepped back to the bed and sat. A thin sheen of sweat covered his torso and trickled down his back. His chest heaved as if he'd just spent an hour training with his men. What a sorry state he was in. Weak as a kitten and alone as the fabled trolls that hid in the hills. He didn't belong here or at Riverton. The thought skewered his heart and it turned as cold as Ettenborough said it to be.

When did longing become one of his emotions?

He thought of his men. Their gazes of uncertainty as they rode out of Riverton still plagued him. He longed to wipe the look of distrust from Nate's face and the frightened grimaces from Matthew's and Lange's faces. Even his butler Pierce didn't seem to welcome his presence and Declan paid him to be loyal and attentive.

The same look he knew creased his face when the mob tried to arrest him, heave the unbearable sentence of prison upon his back once again.

Declan's stomach clenched with dread and the knowledge he'd been duped. And used. And betrayed. Again.

Now to determine by whom.

"Lad," a crackling voice interrupted his taxing thoughts. "I saw ye. Don't be denying it."

Declan swung his gaze toward Anya. Her grin, one of caring despite the fact he was Irish and had ordered them to leave his land, twinkled in her wizened eyes.

"Let me be checking yer stitches." She frowned and inspected him with her shrewd, steely gaze.

Anya silently whipped up one of her medicinal concoctions, all the while watching him, perhaps judging him if life proved as ironic as he thought it to be.

"Stand," she commanded.

He did as she bade, then cringed as she slapped the ointment over each cut, stitch, and bruise on his chest and arms.

"Turn, let me see to yer back." Her voice was terse, its heavy accent mingling with disapproval and a deep furrow between her brows.

"Nay."

"Pash, lad," she said with a swat of her hand. "We couldn't move ye when ye came to us. And Rafe refused to allow the men to help save you. I don't want anything to be festering."

Declan stood still, his muscles rigid and unrelenting as she tried to push between him and the small cot. She sighed, and then with slumped shoulders Anya turned. He relaxed.

She pushed him aside with a strength that startled him. "Ah, lad," she said with a tsking of her tongue. "What did they do to ye?"

Bollocks. She seized an opportunity when he'd released his guard and ran a hand over the scarred welts that crisscrossed the breadth of his back. He clenched his fist and stared out the window of the wagon.

Declan then reached for the linen sheet tangled at the foot of the bed and draped it over his back. It stuck to the lavender-infused ointment.

"'Tis none of your concern." Phantom pain spiked sharp across his skin, now riddled with thick, roped lash marks.

She patted his shoulder with so much affection that he cast his gaze to the ground to block her from his view.

"Ye'll tell me when yer ready. Or," she said with a lilting sweep of her voice, "my granddaughter will bewitch you of yer secrets."

With a raspy hack of laughter, she made her way from the wagon. Her heritage was marked in the stark white blouse and the bright blues, greens, and yellows of her weaved skirt billowing behind her.

Martine may try pull it out of him, but he would not reveal his imprisonment, or what transpired within the cruel stone walls and iron cages. Sometimes he felt as if they still surrounded him, sucking the life from his very soul and the sanity from his mind. Nightmares walking in the light of day, stalking him with their memories, harsh and unrelenting.

Abigail had helped ease the memories. Her smile would pull him back and lulled some sense of sanity into his days and nights. She'd jest and pull a face.

And now she was gone. Was his sanity not far behind?

Martine strode into the caravan, a pile of linen weighting her arms and a smile pulling at her rosebud lips. Her full skirt swept along with her steps, the colorful garment mimicking her grandmother's in pattern and coloring.

Her gaze narrowed at his perusal. He wiped his features clean of any troublesome thoughts. Martine relaxed visibly before him and he knew he must leave.

While he mourned his wife, he knew he never loved her as a man loves a woman. He'd never thought he'd find love that consumed him, drove him to wax poetic, as Abigail had done when she told him of the love of her life.

One look at the Gypsy before him and his mouth went dry and his stomach fluttered.

He'd tried to ignore her loveliness, the curve of her high cheekbones, the sweep of her elegantly drawn brow. There was no way for him to ignore the cadence of her rich voice and the intelligence of her gaze. 'Twas bewitching, her presence. Dangerously welcome to his heart, lethal to his mind and being.

And he was a married man—nay. *Bollocks*. He was not. How strange the truth felt. Abigail was a dear woman and he'd miss her intellect and quick turn of a smile, her acceptance and unwavering friendship.

He blinked, cleared his throat. He'd left her to be buried by her father. A man who'd mocked her, treated her badly. Declan clenched his fist as he envisioned punching his father-in-law squarely in the nose.

"Good morning to you," she said, breaking the laden silence as her gaze slid shyly toward him.

Her voice pulled him from his grief, his guilt. He nodded and tugged the sheet upon his shoulders tighter. He wouldn't expose her to such vileness. 'Twould be exposing her to the bleak underside of the world.

As she moved about the small space, the aroma of a fresh spring breeze tickling the field grass filled the wagon, plunging him deep within her essence, striking a match on his desire. He knew she watched him beneath her long lashes, feathers that wisped becomingly about her dark chestnut-colored eyes and he almost moved forward to touch her dark tresses.

Sanity, however slim, won out. "I'll be leaving as soon as I am able."

"No," she said, then instantly looked chagrinned as she returned to the task of straightening the wagon. "I mean, you mustn't rush."

He hid a smile. "My presence isn't safe for the clan." Hunted men mustn't linger. Hunted men had to seek evidence. And in his case, he not only had to find who killed his wife, he had to find who imprisoned him.

She nodded her head, then inhaled. "We will miss you, Anya and I."

Despite trying to keep strong and focused, he couldn't help but be pleased by her words.

"And I you." He could hear the thickening of his tone. Emotion, somewhat unfamiliar to him, lay heavily between them. "Your kindness . . . I want to repay you."

She waved a hand at him. "Nay, 'tis our pleasure to help those in need."

His eyes widened. The Gypsies weren't known for their kindness to those outside their clan. But he saw the resolve in the line of her jaw and knew she believed what she spoke.

"You don't believe me," she said wryly as she looked pointedly at him. "But my brother has led this tribe in a . . . different fashion than other leaders."

Intrigued, he regarded her a moment before asking, "For example?"

She shrugged. "Other tribes wouldn't allow a woman to train their dogs. Teaching the children to read—"

He cocked his brow. *Damn*, the stitches. "You read?"

"Aye." Pride forced her fist to ball at her waist. "Not quite the itinerants you believed, Lord Forrester?"

Her attitude bemused him. "You must admit, 'tis unusual." Not only unusual, but unheard of. He mulled over what she said and wondered how many of the villagers could read. He glanced at her as she glared down at him, her nose flaring, eyes narrowed and chin set to resolve.

She tipped her head up, her gaze bold and fierce, met his. The shift of her behavior smacked of confidence. "As I said, my *Kapo* leads differently."

He held up his hands in defeat. "I meant no offense."

She snorted and rolled her eyes heavenward.

They chuckled and Martine shook her head.

They spoke of her dogs and her love of training them. He wondered at such a woman who was a contrast to most women he'd known. She was innocent, yet he gathered she'd experienced more than she shared. There was a hesitancy to her, a slight stiffening of her shoulders when she'd change the subject to one not about herself. He allowed the shift, knowing full well he'd be hard pressed to discuss any of his past.

Declan pinched the bridge of his nose. Their conversation taxed him beyond belief. How could he leave the clan if he proved as weak as a hatchling?

"I'm sorry." She patted his shoulder. "You need to rest."

He leaned back onto the cot, still wrapped in the sheet, but too weary to remove it. His mind was heady with her concern and attention. *Bollocks*. Declan cursed his past, father, and life in one breath.

Nay, he must focus on his recovery and then search out the evidence to prove his innocence while finding out who killed Abigail. He owed her as much.

"I'll leave you," Martine whispered. She moved to the doorway, then turned to look at him. She graced him with a swift smile.

"Thank you," he responded when all he wanted to do was reach up and cup her cheek, gently kiss her bowed mouth. Dear God, what had gotten into him?

He was weaker than he thought. Musings such as these proved so. Declan needed his innocence, his men, and peace of mind. It may be meager, but 'twas all he could claim as his own.

He shouldn't dally with a Gypsy.

And he was certain the *Kapo* would agree.

Chapter 7

Martine smoothed her hair beneath a kerchief and straightened her skirt. Giggles and whispers rustled the curtain in her grandmother's caravan. She continued to adjust her appearance, tucking in stray strands of hair. Biting her lip so as not to smile, she placed her hands on her hips and tapped her foot.

"Pah, I know there are no mice in here. Must be kittens, or foxes, and mayhap a rat." She advanced toward the window, looked under the bed, chair, even a pot. More laughter erupted. She whipped back the curtain and three gregarious girls fell to their knees in fits of giggles.

"My, these are the biggest rats I've ever seen." She frowned and knitted her brow. "How must I get rid of them? I know. I'll sweep them out with a broom."

"Nay, Martine. 'Tis just us."

Solemn little faces peaked up at her. Och, they were beauties, the lot of them. She ruffled Emilia's hair and helped Katya up from the floor. Pesha sat cross-legged, dark eyes sparkling and a full grin on her sweet, wee mouth. Martine scooped her up and hugged her tightly. Then she sat Pesha upon the bed. "Are you hungry, then?"

"Aye," they exclaimed. As they chattered, Martine found some biscuits and a few almond cookies. She had some tea left in its cozy, which she poured in tiny cups. She was certain Anya wouldn't mind her using her tea reading cups for the girls.

"Tell us a story," Katya said as she chewed on an almond cookie. "A princess one. Please."

Martine smiled. She pulled back the curtain to check the time. 'Twas mid-afternoon and she'd been banished from her own wagon while Anya bathed Lord Forrester. More's the pity, she thought wickedly, then was instantly aghast at the thought. She wiped her brow. "Aye, I'll tell you a story."

She lifted the other girls onto the bed and grabbed a cookie for herself. After a sip of tea, Martine settled on the floor before them. She hesitated until they begged for her to begin.

"Just a short one. 'Tis nearly time for lessons."

Emilia wrinkled her nose. "Pah, Martine, we know."

She smiled indulgently. "Once there was a brave little girl, lost deep in the woods. She was frightened, but not terribly so. See, her father had taken her through the woods many a time."

"Then why was she lost?" Kayta asked.

Martine tipped her head to the side. "I'm glad you asked. See, her father wasn't with her this time. In fact, it had been many, many years since she'd even seen him."

"Did she cry?" Pesha said with a quiver to her chin.

"Nay." Martine rose and squeezed onto the bed. "She kept walking until she came to a wee pond. Near the edge was a little bird. So little, she'd almost stepped on him."

Emilia snuggled close, so adorable and sweet. Martine smoothed the little girl's hair and continued her story. "The bird had feathers of every imaginable color. Purples, blues and even orange."

"Oh," exclaimed the girls.

"'Twas beautiful. The girl picked up the bird and it began to sing. The song was so touching, the girl began to weep."

"I thought ye said she didn't cry."

"She didn't cry because she was sad, Pesha. It was because of the pure beauty of the bird's song." She smiled at the girls. "Just as the bird ended its song, the grass around the pond blossomed into a rainbow of color. Rabbits and deer came out of the woods and began lapping up the water of the pond. The girl watched, amazed at the sight before her."

"'Tis a lovely story," Katya said with a gapping yawn. "Did the bird grant her a wish?"

"Nay. But the bird did lay an egg. One large egg with the most amazing shade of purple on its shell." As she glanced at each of the expectant faces of the children, she felt her heart lurch. To have a babe of her own would almost be worth the sacrifice of marriage to Magor. Och, she loathed the thought, but knew it was necessary in order to have children.

Emilia jumped off the bed and began parading in the small area. "See, I'm the bird." She tweeted as she flapped her arms. The other girls followed suit, and soon the cacophony of tweeting filled the air.

Martine chuckled and mimicked the girl's actions.

A shadow darkened the doorway. All eyes sought the intruder in silence.

"So *Siskaar*, ye've time to play?"

She crossed her arms before her chest and tapped her foot. The girls stared solemnly at Rafe. They scurried past her brother as quickly as their little feet could take them. "You needn't scare them to death."

He chuckled. She hadn't heard the sound in so long, she nearly smiled. "'Tis good to see ye enjoying yerself."

She watched him, uncertain of what he wanted.

Rafe came further into the caravan and inspected the area. "You'll soon have your wagon back. That must please ye."

"Aye, 'tis my home."

He touched her sleeve. "Martine . . . ye must understand."

Ignoring his touch and gentle tone, she busied herself by cleaning up cookie crumbs and teacups.

Rafe rested his hands on her shoulders and looked into her eyes. "'Tis well past time you wed."

Martine nodded mutely. She could never trust her brother with her fears. He wouldn't understand how she wanted to ignore tradition and the honor of the clan, even though she'd followed their traditions ever since they found her. There was a part of her willing to rebel; the other part was too beholden to the clan. But mostly, her heart was theirs and she loved them as if they were truly her family.

Regardless, his scrutiny unsettled her. "Leave," she said. "I've lessons to do."

After a probing glance, he nodded and left. And all she could think of was that she'd be married to Magor too soon. Her life would be over too soon.

He'd stayed abed long enough. For the past four days he'd moved about the length of the caravan, trying to strengthen his muscles, remove the hitch caused by his injuries. He left the wagon, wearing the clothing of the Gypsies, since his seemed to have vanished. They were comfortable, loose, and freeing. Slowly, he walked into the wooded area surrounding the caravan. He'd garnered stares from the clan, but he shook them off, longing to move his legs and breathe some fresh air.

His strides were slow and a little unsure, but he relished stretching his legs a bit.

An evenly pitched whistle drew his attention. He inspected the picturesque scenery of the glen in an attempt to find its source.

Ah, Martine. She was lovely in contrast to the greenery surrounding her with her bright blue skirt, crisp white shirt, and colorful kerchief. Luxuriant hair spilled down her back in an endless wave of black silk. Her curves, her femininity, sent fire through his loins.

He stopped, dragged his fingers through his hair. Did he move forward—or scurry back to the caravan? His attraction was pleasurable and troubling at once.

His gaze sought her once again. She held herself regally, her chin tipped up as if she were attempting to soak up the heat of the sun. Moreover, he suddenly longed to do the same, feel the heated, soft caresses of the sun and mimic her carefree actions. The dogs danced around her, jumping and yapping at her heels.

Declan stepped out of the shadows as he paced toward her. She swished her colorful skirt at the dogs in a graceful movement; they seemed to enjoy the teasing and became more excited. She pursed her lips and whistled low, a sound that skipped through the wind and calmed the errant canines. Amazed, Declan wondered how she'd won such easy compliance from the two robust creatures.

Her eyes narrowed, then they widened. Eyes that tipped up at the corners, framed by long, dark lashes. He peered closer and marveled as her eyes shifted from dark brown to a softer hue flecked with gold. Her mouth resembled a plump bow tied on a Christmas present.

This beauty captured his attention as the hum of awareness tightened his muscles and befuddled his mind. She was lovely against the rugged landscape, her beauty unique and exotic.

Guilt filled him with shame. He wiped the back of his neck as he stopped walking.

You're a good man, he heard Abigail remind him in her clipped English tone. She'd often told him how *good* he was. She thanked him more times than he could count. Thanked him for marrying her when no one else with a title would and putting up with her attachment to the love of her life. He'd pick up her hand and kiss her soft skin. *'Twas my pleasure*, was his constant reply. And he meant it, because it was true. If he had any choice, he'd have picked Abigail. She was smart, lively, and could tell a ribald joke better than a sailor.

Friends? she'd asked just a few days before her death.

Aye, he'd returned. *Forever*.

She waved a hand at him and laughed before a somber look stole over her face. *When you find her, I want you to forget about me. You've suffered too much. You deserve the love I cannot give you.*

Tears smarted his eyes. He tipped his head up and grinned. *Thank you,* he said in silent prayer. *Thank you for your kindness and understanding.*

She'd approve of Martine, Declan was certain of it. The Gypsy had captivated him from the moment he woke in her caravan, no matter how he tried not to be enticed. His body now thrummed with energy and desire.

He strode with purpose and a need to be near her.

"Good morn," he greeted. His voice sounded rusty, rough from the memories and his determination.

Her gaze darkened and she quickly glanced toward the camp. After a moment, she said, "You're exploring."

He relaxed and grinned at her. "Aye, as lovely as your wagon is, I was going mad."

Declan's gaze roamed over her hungrily. Every soft curve beckoned exploration.

She nodded toward him, her watchful gaze distrusting, obviously unnerved by his regard. He immediately masked his desire, not wanting her to flee when he finally had the strength to walk about the land—and, *bollocks,* the strength to admit his attraction to the beautiful woman before him.

He nodded toward the dogs, obediently flanking her as if waiting for a command. "Grand animals, your dogs."

"Aye," she said so softly that he almost couldn't hear her.

He grinned. "You're right, you do have a way with them."

A grin softened her mouth. "Aye."

He watched her pace the dogs a bit longer, his body pleased he was moving about, but fatigue was setting in.

Martine touched his arm, concern furrowing her brow. "We'll head back."

Och, his legs trembled, he was such a weak man. This wee woman was going to help him return to the wagon. "Only if you are done training." He drew up, straightened his shoulders. He wasn't going to allow her to see how weak he truly was.

"Pah, the dogs would train all day if I allowed it." With a quick grin, she whistled to the animals and they flanked her side in an instant.

She tipped her chin up at him, the line of her jaw softening as she held out her hand to him. "I know you're trying to be strong, but I can see the pain in your eyes."

He reached up and touched the side of her cheek. 'Twas silky and warmed by the sun and her exercise with the dogs. Her eyes widened to those of a doe beneath the accurate bow of a hunter. Fear, uncertainty. She stepped back. He stepped forward.

"You are lovely."

A flush rushed up her neck and reddened her cheeks. And all he wanted to do was touch her again.

An unbearable moment passed before he lifted her chin with his forefinger. Declan leaned down, kissed her bowed mouth softly. Lovely. He pulled back, looked into her ardent gaze and descended into heaven once again. She shifted into him, fit her body against his as if she were made for him. Curve for curve, dip for dip. Her lips—soft, succulent. He continued to enjoy her as a soft moan eased from her.

He tangled his fingers through the rich strands of her hair, cradled her head as he slipped his tongue into her mouth. His blood rushed. He couldn't get enough of her.

Hot, spicy. God, heaven.

He left her mouth and kissed along her jaw, the silky skin along her neck. Her pulse ratcheted against his lips as a sigh escaped her mouth.

Her dogs barked. She ripped from him, and her hand flew to her mouth. Panic widened her eyes. "What have I done?" she cried.

Martine looked to him, then she fled and the dogs trailed behind her.

He shook his head and dragged his finger through his hair to give her a moment to arrive at the camp before him. He was an *eejit*.

No matter. As he headed toward the camp, his strides slow, he recalled the pleasure of holding Martine. Soft, warm—she truly brought him to a place of peace.

He knew he shouldn't have kissed her, but he made no apologies. She was worth it. The kiss was worth it.

The kiss was imprinted in his mind forever, for there would never be another so perfect.

Chapter 8

Trenmore Grey left Sadie's home whistling a jaunty tune and possessing a certain kick to his step. Sadie watched from her bedchamber quite pleased with the interest the man had taken in her. She rang for her maid. After an afternoon of love making, she was in need of a soothing bath for her sore muscles.

"M'lady?"

She turned, too lazy to hold the pretense of her station and smiled at her faithful maid, Hannah. "Draw a bath for me, please."

Shock registered on the maid's face, but Sadie paid no mind. Nay, she'd plans. Lord Forrester still weighed heavily in them. Blast the man for hiding for so long. It had been too many days since Abigail's death and Sadie lacked the patience to wait for him to come to her.

He would, she thought as she removed her robe. A man such as him needed the comfort of a woman. Her bed, her loving embrace, the haven between her thighs. Trenmore had certainly been more compliant since their . . . arrangement. Temporary, but a pleasing arrangement to say the least.

Hannah brought in one more bucket of steaming water and Sadie plunged into the rose-scented tub. Dear Lord, was there anything more glorious than a hot bath filled with rose petals?

Never did she think her aspirations would be fulfilled. But her first husband, God rest his soul, had plucked her from his staff, rescuing her from lye-blistered hands and a cragged worn face.

She had appreciated him, well and truly, Sadie mused as she ran a cloth down her arm and over her shoulder. Leaning back, she closed her eyes and enjoyed the moment. A sigh slipped past her lips as tension and overuse eased out of her limbs.

When her first husband had passed, the second had come along quickly enough. Now he was a fine lover, that one. Frisky at all times of the day, and creative. Their appetites matched for a while, until he met with death while hunting.

"Hmmm," she moaned as she relaxed further and further into the copper tub. "Number three didn't last but a year."

"Pardon m'lady?"

Chuckling, Sadie said, "'Tis nothing, Hannah. Just some memories."

"Aye, m'lady."

She heard the maid busying herself by straightening the room. Sadie ignored her, as she envisioned Declan in the bath with her, saturated with bubbles and longing for her. Her abdomen clenched with desire she knew would need to be fulfilled sooner rather than later.

Lord Declan Forrester would be hers, to be sure. She'd planned it since she first laid eyes on the handsome lad, *and* when she cleared the way for him to be with her.

Now, she just needed him to be here, with her, sharing her bed and heart.

Declan was the only man she'd ever loved.

Chapter 9

A breezed tugged at her hair, sweeping its length across her face and catching on her lips. Martine stared over the creek, in the direction of Lord Forrester's manor house. It had taken her a while to find it and she truly shouldn't be here, but she was allowing her curiosity to get the better of her. The man intrigued her, befuddled her. She touched her lips and sighed.

And the man had kissed her.

She'd never been kissed before and the heady rush of blood had raced through her when he'd pulled her to him and . . . and leaned down to capture her mouth. She smiled at the memory of his commanding mouth. How she allowed him such liberties without stopping him was beyond her.

And now she was looking at his estate located just a half hour walk from their new camp. She nearly laughed at the fact that Rafe had moved them as requested, but just past Lord Forrester's property.

No matter, a Gypsy camp and a grand estate—the difference was glaringly obvious.

She dug her bare toe into the soft earth near the creek. *What was it like living in such luxury and security?* Staying in the same home and town, having servants and abundant food. To her it seemed so foreign, yet somewhat like paradise.

"Martine?"

She looked over her shoulder. Rafe stood behind her, his ire alive in his rigid stance. Returning her gaze to the creek, she heard his step crunch across the dry grass. Tension eased up her spine, slowly, as he sat beside her and looked out in the distance.

They stayed that way, the silence as brutal as the bite of her brother's usual acerbic wit.

"You followed me," she accused, frustrated with the silence.

After a few moments, he spoke, his low voice commanding, ensuring no room for argument no matter how dearly she longed too. "We'll be leaving soon."

"But what of Lord . . ."

Rafe scowled, his brow creating a furrow deep enough to plant a row of oats. The same scowl she remembered from the moment he became *Kapo*. "Forget the lord," he practically growled. "He's been here for more than a fortnight. If Magor learns ye've been looking after him, he'll withdrawal his offer. An offer that merges strong families. Families of honor and tradition."

She turned to her brother, her heart hammering against her chest as frustration filled her. She stepped closer, close enough to see the slight clenching of his jaw. She tilted her head and looked at him and took a step back. Not that she was afraid of him—his bark was worse than his bite—but the unchecked anger in his dark eyes made her cautious. "And Magor will accept me? Even though I am not Rom?"

Rafe shifted uncomfortably, then met her gaze with a firm resolve. "Aye, his father wants the clans joined. We've raised ye since ye were a young lass. You've embraced our traditions. They know this as true."

Regardless, deep within her, though she knew it was wrong, Martine hoped her betrothed would refuse her. Not because of her actions. They were loathsome, and so against the Rom way. To be alone with a man who wasn't her father, brother, or husband was unheard of. To have him recovering in her caravan, lying in her bed with his glorious body pressed against her sheets—

Not to mention the kiss. She'd replayed the embrace over and over, and she didn't regret it. Nay, she wanted it to happen again and again. But that was the problem. It couldn't happen again.

"Tell the Irishman we'll celebrate in two days and he's to join us."

She looked to him, startled at the request. How unlike her brother to be making it. To have an outsider view their evening ritual was more than unusual. 'Twas never done. Just outside the encampment, they built a fire and would partake in entertainment. The entire clan would join in for dancing and storytelling. Her brother would regale them with tales from the past, ones passed down from his father and his father before him. It would be a magical time when all seemed right with the world, at least the world of a Gypsy clan. And she loved it.

"'Tis strange, I know," her brother said as if reading her thoughts, "but I want him to see the difference between us. As broad as the difference between the sun and the earth, the grass of his meadows and the dry grass beneath you—of a lord and an itinerant."

She scowled at him and fisted her hands at her waist. "I'm not itinerant."

He scoffed and shook his head. "Aye, but the Brits believe we are."

Martine held her anger in check but couldn't help saying, "You're imagining his desires. He told me that he is leaving as soon as he is able. Your judgment is as harsh as always, *Kapo*."

A gust of wind whipped his hair across his face and he angrily pushed it away. "He can't be leaving at his own whim. And how are we to know he won't search out the magistrate to come after us?"

She brought her hand up to her mouth, the damp air nearly sucking the wind from her. The pleasure of the creek was now voided by her brother's nonsense. "He'd *never* do that."

The smirk that curled his lips churned her stomach. "Tell him to join us and then stay away from him. You've mocked our traditions. Have Anya tend him until he can truly leave."

Traditions, her mind screamed. How they smothered her with unbearable weight. How they tore at her, piece by piece, as she fought to keep them separate from her memories of her life before the Rom.

And just as she sometimes hated the traditions, she knew she'd never forsake the clan that saved her, took her in as one of their own. Nurtured her.

She was one of them.

Again her brother read her mind. "By staying with us, you've accepted our ways."

Close to tears, she merely nodded, fearful the sadness and rage pulsing through her veins would be relayed in her words and irritate Rafe further.

"Make sure he's ready."

Martine swept her skirt clean. The ordinary action forced her hands into action, lest they find themselves around her brother's neck.

"I'll tell him," she said, not at all certain he'd comply, and secretly hoping he wouldn't. Yet, she thought about him, about Lord Forrester sitting next to her as members of the clan danced, circling around the fire pit as darkness seeped in and an almost wantonness urged the music into a frenzy. Sometimes, if they were lucky, the stars and moon would light the sky and grace them with enough glow to continue the dancing and rivalry until the wee hours of the morning.

She left her brother, clutching her chest, a little breathless and anxious. Definitely excited and curiously in control of her anger.

"Martine."

She bit her lip to hold onto the retort she wished to brandish against him. "Aye, Rafe."

He rose and stood looming in front of her. "Send Anya. You've spent too much time with the lord."

She headed back to the encampment. When she entered, she quickly looked for her grandmother.

With a weary sigh, she headed toward the cooking fire. No doubt she'd find Anya there.

As she rounded the corner of a caravan, the sight before her made her smile. Anya sat like a mighty queen in a circle of women who either stirred what Martine knew was dye in the kettles or were wringing cotton dry of its coloring.

Maria bound forward. "Come and see," she said with a chuckle. She pulled Martine over to the pots of dye.

"Lass, ye've come just in time."

Martine smiled down at her grandmother, her hands dipped in a steamy mixture of deep red dye.

Realization struck her.

They were making her wedding dress.

It took a moment for her to gather her senses before she could speak. Her voice seemed locked within her throat, afraid to appear lest it cracked and croaked her request.

Maria talked to her, her hands gesturing excitedly as she spoke of the special stitching and color of the gown.

She could only think of the idea she'd be married soon. Married to a man she did not know, had never spoken to. Dread filled her as tears pooled in her eyes.

"Rafe would like you to speak to the Irishman." The hollow cadence of her words sounded queer to her, and it garnered the attention of the women, their piercing gazes pointing at her like sharp darts.

Anya raised her brow. "And ye can't be doing that for me?"

Martine pulled herself straight, prideful and stubborn. And not willing to admit the truth of it. "I've the children to teach."

The falsehood must have rang true enough in Anya's mind, for she rose, wiped her hands on her apron, now stained a muddle of reds. Her curt nod cut off further conversation and Martine watched as the hunched woman crossed the center of the camp and made her way into the caravan. How she longed to join her, speak with Declan.

How the Irishman consumed her thoughts, even though it was wrong.

She remained near the other women, listened to their chatter about the upcoming wedding. Maria laughed and began laying the material in the high grass so it would dry. Martine just watched as if the reality was happening to someone else. If only that were true.

Despite their kiss, she found comfort speaking with Declan. His interest in the dog training and her part in it made her feel important. Rare it was that any paid attention to her actions, since they were so used to her working with the dogs. And he was curious about their way of life. When he'd first arrived she knew his disdain, but now he asked question after question about their traditions and lifestyle. He had mellowed and began accepting their ways.

The dark shadows that tainted his azure eyes remained with her as she recalled their conversation. His dulcet tones still teased her with their deep, rumbling quality. To connect with another outsider and be allowed into their life was lovely.

"Didn't you have to see to the children?"

Martine turned toward Linka.

"Get girl," she said with a hostile scowl. "You have to teach them to *read*, don't you know it."

Her sarcasm wasn't lost on Martine. But, as usual, Martine brushed her comment aside with a casual shrug. The older generations of the Rom didn't understand her teaching the children to read, but along with keeping their trading fair and legal, Rafe and Martine had brought a sense of respectability to the group.

"High and mighty, you are, girl. And without an ounce of trueness to you, *poshrat*."

Martine felt a snap of anger curl her tongue at the insult. "If you've a problem with our *Kapo's* practices, you should speak with him." Satisfaction flowed through her as the woman blanched at the idea of going to the *Kapo*.

Maria stood close and gripped her hand in a show of solidarity. Linka backed away, yet anger sparkled in her dark gaze.

Armed with more courage, Martine left Linka, disregarding her brother's instruction, and headed toward her caravan.

Before she entered, she straightened her skirt and wished for a pair of shoes to cover her dirty feet. Yet, her slippers were saved for special occasions, and they didn't quite suit the rough wool of her skirt or the oft-washed linen of her chemise.

With a quick twist of her dark hair, Martine steadied herself with a sigh and entered her home.

Her grandmother sat beside the cot.

She gasped.

Declan lay on his stomach exposing his broad back, tan and scarred.

Anya heard her and turned with a finger before her lips. Martine quietly strode forward.

The closer she came, the more disturbing Declan's back became. Och! How could someone prove so cruel to inflict such punishment?

Her stomach clenched at the pain he must have felt, how it was obvious they'd festered in their gnarled raised lines. She wanted to run her hands across his back, bring the warmth of her palms to the scars and siphon away the anguish they represented.

He stirred but did not wake. She felt relief. For she could imagine he wouldn't be pleased she'd seen beyond the injuries that had brought him to the Rom.

"Will ye be watching him then?" Anya whispered.

Martine nodded and sat in the chair her grandmother had occupied, her mind still reeling over the scars. Her heart clenched over the pain and suffering Declan had endured. Tears filled her eyes as she looked at the angry scars crisscrossing the breadth of his back.

"I'll keep Rafe from coming this way as much as I can manage." The elderly woman stretched and rubbed her back with her aged hands. "Yer doing the right thing, lass. 'Tis a fine man here."

"I feel something," she admitted as she avoided her grandmother's gaze. "But I also don't know if it is good or will bring shame to our clan."

Anya wagged a finger in Martine's face. Her white brows met at the furrow above her nose as she spoke in their native tongue. "Ye've given yer life up for this clan. Are ye certain it is worth it? Snatch a bit of happiness for yerself, despite the loyalty ye feel for Rafe."

Her heart pounded against her chest as she fiercely whispered, "I can't forsake the clan. Surely you can see that."

Anya patted her arm. "Aye, you can, my *bitti chovexani*."

Martine cringed. She wasn't a little witch, but her grandmother insisted on calling her such.

If only she were, she'd be able to find a way out of her impending, loveless marriage.

He felt rested, almost peaceful. No doubt Anya had tainted the medicinal draught with an ingredient to induce sleep. Yet, Declan wasn't angered. No. It had been years since he'd slept without the haunting reminder of his father's treachery and the years spent in prison.

He rolled onto his back, much relieved after the salve Anya had slapped upon it. Startled, he pulled the sheet over his bare chest.

There sat his Gypsy.

Calm, even amused, if her raised brow was any indication. For a moment, he enjoyed the twinkle in her eyes, not the black pits like her brother's, but lighter—brighter, reflected the light with golden flecks.

She tipped her chin at him with a haughtiness that now satisfied him instead of vexing him. God, she was lovely. Her skin a mix of honey and gold, soft and satiny. He wanted to kiss his way from the arch of her winged brow to the hollow of her elegant neck now peeking from her white blouse.

Such thoughts rocked him. He must dismiss her beauty, turn his head toward proving his innocence, not taking hers. Nay, his focus couldn't be turned by a comely lass.

"Good afternoon," she said, her smile flowing into her tone. "You slept well?"

"Aye." Declan stilled the grin tilting his lips.

Martine's brows knitted, then they smoothed as she rose from her chair. "My grandmother prepared a broth for you."

"Please allow it to have meat in it," he grumbled.

"Pah, 'tis filled with venison and wild onion." She placed the bowl on the small table beside the cot. "Eat up. You'll need your strength. And then this evening you can eat *bolkoli*."

"*Bolkoli?*" he asked, butchering the pronunciation of the unfamiliar word.

"'Tis a tasty pancake filled with meat."

Declan nodded and raised up on his elbows, conscious of his bare chest and how unseemly it must be for her to even be in his presence. He noticed how her gaze lit on everything but him, and how roses blossomed on her cheeks. The sight was captivating and endearing all at once.

"Here's your shirt," she said with her arm extended toward him.

His shirt dangled from the end of her long fingers, mended and laundered, smelling fresh as the outdoors, not the blood that had saturated the linen.

He grasped the material, purposely allowing his fingers to graze hers, relishing the slight shiver that trembled her hand.

No matter how she tried to hide it, his Gypsy had fire within her just waiting to ignite and flame her passion. Desire like he'd never known flared in him just from the touch of her hand.

"You're to join the clan in two days for our entertainment."

Her statement doused all desire. He lifted his brow. "Entertainment?"

She nodded. "My brother leads the clan in music and dancing."

He frowned. "Dancing?"

She chuckled and he couldn't help but grin at the lovely sound. When she laughed, her eyes lit up with such joy.

"Music, dancing, storytelling, food." A furrow appeared between her brows. "'Tis tradition."

Join them around the fire? Eat with his enemy, the very man who mocked his authority and challenged his innocence. Her *Kapo*, her brother, and the man ready to send her away to a stranger? Aye, Declan had heard her grandmother gossiping with her cohorts. Rafe Petrulengo would see his sister wed to a man whom Anya claimed treated women like dogs and she could do naught to stop it. All to strengthen the powerful clans with a merger—marriage between them. Surely there was another way?

Declan should steal Martine away from the awful fate of marrying a man who wouldn't appreciate her. The fineness of her voice, the intellect of her eyes, the sheer beauty of her. Her betrothed didn't deserve Martine, a doe amongst goats.

Bollocks, who was he to judge? A murderer, prisoner. What could he offer her that proved better than what awaited her? Nothing.

Martine handed him a spoon, pulling his attention away from his thoughts and back to the small caravan and the woman beside him.

"Eat," she prodded. "You'll feel better."

"Only if you sit and talk with me." Declan wondered at the quick shift in her gaze. How she glanced at the doorway and then back to him. Nodding, she sat and folded her hands in her lap.

"Tell me more about the clan."

Martine smiled and began talking about the tribe. When she regaled him with stories during her teaching sessions, light danced in her eyes and excitement laced her voice. Her hands became animated, gesturing, emphasizing the antics of her pupils.

He chuckled when she told him how the boys had hidden all of the slates so they could fish instead of study. "'Tis unusual, teaching in a Gypsy clan."

She narrowed her eyes and her hands stopped midair. "Ah, you do believe we are the dregs of society."

"Nay," he said, his hand raised, palm up. Truly he didn't. In the past he wouldn't have been so generous. But now, after spending time with the clan, his mind had changed and mayhap his heart as well.

She shrugged and stayed silent. After a few moments, she spoke again. "I had the good fortune to learn to read, and I convinced my brother to allow me to teach others."

"How did you learn?" he asked, interest piqued. He knew many Irish children who did not have the fortune to learn to read, let alone Gypsy children.

She remained silent as she lifted from the chair.

Declan feared she'd flee the caravan. "No matter, let's talk about something else." His words appeared to soothe her and she sat back in the chair after a moment and her shoulders relaxed.

"What of you?" Martine said with challenging tone. "Tell me of your life at Riverton."

Declan grunted. Martine cocked her brow and looked down her nose, haughty, impossibly regal. He believed her in the role of Gypsy princess. It suited her, whether her feet were bare or if she were dressed in gilded finery.

He shrugged. "I enjoyed training my men."

She smiled, apparently amused with something he said, although he wasn't sure what. He sat up and leaned against the caravan wall. "Ah, and what did you train them for?"

"I . . . needed to have men ready to protect my . . . estate." *Damn*, answering questions wasn't his forte.

"And your wife, what was she like?"

Declan hesitated as his heart nearly stopped. She obviously knew he'd been married. Did her brother share how his wife died? If he did, surely she wouldn't be at his bedside. He grappled with sharing the story, the accusations, then quickly decided not to. It wasn't as if making her privy to some of his demons would rid him of them. Nay, it would only make her look at him as if he were a monster.

Sympathy filled her gaze and she reached out to touch his arm. "I'm sorry. Anya always says I don't know when to leave good enough alone."

"Nay," Declan replied. How was it possible her brother hadn't shared his wife's murder with Martine? "My wife died just before I arrived here."

He didn't want to talk about his wife. She was—she was one of the saving graces of his life and now she was gone. And it was certainly awkward to speak of her with Martine. He rubbed the back of his neck as he grappled with what to say. Abigail's advice came to him, what she always said to him prior to her father's visit.

You are worthy of love, Declan. And you should find her, find the love that is worthy of you.

He always wondered what would have happened if a woman, a woman like Martine, had arrived on the estate when Abigail was alive. Did she truly think he'd leave her and run away like she urged him to do?

Remember Declan, she'd say in the efficient manner of hers, *love, true love, comes once in a lifetime.*

He mulled over Abigail's words and how she'd often push him to leave her. He couldn't—not that she believed him—but he'd made a promise and said vows. But now, Abigail was gone. He held her memory close to his heart and he'd fondly remember her. But he couldn't help but wonder if the memories were trying to tell him something, push him to move forward. As if Abigail, God rest her soul, were there with a gentle hand on his shoulder, giving a squeeze, then a slight push.

Martine bit at her lip, an action that appeared innocent, but it made Declan want to slowly feast on her ripe mouth.

He thought about their kiss in the glen and how every time he'd seen her since all he wanted to do was gather her in his arms and kiss her again. Not just kiss her, but embrace her until they could kiss no more. Rather unfaithful thoughts for a newly widowed man, but true nonetheless.

"I'm sorry. Rafe mentioned she had died. Please excuse my thoughtlessness," she said as she reached for his hand. Her touch was gentle, caring, and enticing.

"Thank you," he said with a thick voice.

"Declan, I am sorry." Tears filled her eyes as she moved the chair closer.

"Aye."

Martine rubbed his arm to console him. Did she realize that her touch inflamed him? "Abigail, my wife, was English." God, he felt guilty talking about her—just as he felt guilty not revealing the true nature of her death.

She nodded but continued to gently rub his arm, her attention fully on him as if what he said was the most important thing in the world.

He watched her, the gentleness of her actions, the pure loveliness of *her*. Never had he met a woman who had so much compassion for others. Would she still feel compassion toward him if he revealed the accusations against him?

"I miss her." He gripped her hand. "Abigail—she and I—it was never a love match."

A flash of anger flared in her eyes. Darkening them, making them as murky as a lough.

Martine seethed inside. Marriage without love. Why would a man choose to marry if not for love? Power, money— what else could prompt him to make a woman miserable as Martine would surely be once she wed Magor?

"Pah, not a love match. You men certainly hold the world's arrogance. Forcing women to marry you regardless of their feelings." Rage gripped her tongue before she could stop it as she ripped her hand from his grasp and stood to pace the caravan. "Bully your way into her bed. And then expect her to endure your presence."

Declan stared at her, a perplexed expression marring his perfect features. *Nay*, she thought, *ignore his handsomeness before it draws you once again.*

He blinked then narrowed his gaze as the lines around his mouth tightened. "My wife's father arranged the marriage. 'Twas not I."

She didn't ignore the low growl of his voice, or the snap of fury stiffening his shoulders and pulsing at his jaw. But she didn't allow it to deter her train of thought.

"You could have refused. Her father most likely forced the matter on her to begin with."

Ah, how his face now resembled a brutal storm, harsh with thunder and fierce with lightening, his blue eyes a tempest of dark midnight. "I wasn't in the position to refuse. Marrying Abigail ensured my freedom—and hers. Without the marriage we'd both be living in hell."

Martine flushed. Heat raced up her neck and lodged itself on her face. Duly chastised, she held her tongue. Not an expert on the way of aristocracy, she didn't know what to presume. The more she thought about it, she knew a man of Declan's obvious resourcefulness must have been in a dire situation if he wed a woman not of his choosing.

She sighed, trying to temper her tone and demeanor. "Tell me why."

A knock rattled the wagon's door. "Martine," a voice whispered, "The *Kapo* is headed in this direction."

Martine quickly stood as she gripped the chair about to topple. "I'll see you before the fire?"

He nodded. Oh, how she wanted to reach down and touch his face, perhaps kiss his cheek.

Yet, if her brother found them—it would be disastrous.

And he'd be murderous.

Chapter 10

Tired of wasting away in the little caravan or *vurdon* as Martine called it, Declan breached the berth and walked, albeit slowly, toward the center of the encampment. 'Twas odd how he was learning the Gypsy language when before he loathed their existence. Each day, he absorbed more and more. The dynamics of the clan were much different than that of his society but just as noble. The elders advised the *Kapo* and he assumed the many women of the clan advised their elder husbands. Children worked hard, obeyed their parents, and played with abandon. Much like Irish children, impish enough to gain a smile from their parents and mayhap a treat or two.

He passed by the fire blazing beneath a cast iron pot. The scent emanating from its boiling center was the venison broth he'd enjoyed earlier. And while he'd enjoyed a hearty serving, his stomach grumbled from the savory aroma.

Martine's kinsmen continued to notice his appearance, yet kept their distance as if he carried a lethal disease. A group of men, strong and armed, raced into the camp. Declan watched as they went to the largest caravan. The richly appointed home on wheels was obviously the *Kapo's*. A deep burgundy covered the wooden boards that formed the walls and gilded trim accented the edge of the windows. A tin roof capped the home. Rafe emerged at the commotion, his face stern and intense.

"'Tis riders near," one of the men said as he caught his breath. "They've been following us."

Declan's stomach clenched with the hollow resonance of regret. He'd brought the wrath on these people. In their effort to assist him, they'd put themselves in danger. Walking closer to hear what the leader said, Declan found he was limping. The realization annoyed him, reaffirmed his inability to make a safe exit.

"Come this way," a voice whispered from behind.

He turned and saw Martine partially hidden by the brush. She crooked her finger at him and he found himself drawn to the lighthearted action. She skipped far into the woods swinging her deep blue skirt, her dogs dutifully following without so much as a whimper. He paced himself as his legs stubbornly refused to navigate the brambles and fallen logs. His height allowed him a visual connection with her and the Lurchers, despite his slow stride.

They continued to walk until he heard a brook tinkle in the distance, with a steady rush of water and the sweet sounds of the woodland animals that flourished near it. The clearing offered the dogs the ideal area for a quick romp as Martine quietly laughed at their antics and tossed a small branch into their midst.

"Come," she called, "your turn to play."

He glanced over his shoulder. Surely they were far enough away from the encampment. The riders hadn't followed and he shrugged away any uncertainty that had settled into knots between his shoulders. He smiled, reached for a small twig, and tossed it. The dogs lunged and then went sprawling about as they frolicked with one another.

Declan inspected the area once again, doubtful they were truly alone, but hopeful regardless. He ran his fingers through his hair, anxious yet wanting to enjoy the carefree moment. He sat near Martine on a fallen log. She tipped her head back and closed her eyes. A soft murmur eased past her full lips as she smiled at the sky. The sun filtered through the clouds and the leaves above, freckling the ground around them. They stayed in comfortable silence as the dogs barked and yapped as they chased each other into the brook.

"They'll scare all the fish."

He shrugged. "Aye, but why ruin their fun."

She chuckled and opened her eyes. "They do enjoy life, do they not?"

Declan reached for her hand. Long, graceful fingers gripped his own. "How do you calm them?"

"They know the signals. I've taught them since they were wee pups and weaned from their dame." As if to accentuate her point, she thinned her lips and whistled. It was low, barely perceptible to his ears, and he sat just beside her. The dogs' response was immediate. They now stood before her, their golden ears perked for more commands. This time she whistled through her fingers and then gave a hand command.

He watched, transfixed by the astute intelligence of Martine. 'Twasn't a womanly thing to do, training dogs, yet it suited her in its uniqueness.

"Try," she said. A challenge sparkled in her dark eyes, one he wasn't going to forsake.

Declan attempted a low whistle, yet barely managed a pitiful copy of Martine's well-practiced one.

"Here," she said as she pinched in his cheeks. "Blow over your tongue and keep your cheeks in."

He tried again. No luck.

She laughed a joyous peal of music that distracted him and the dogs. He wanted to pull her into his arms, feast upon her lips, feel her heart beat against his chest just to know they were both alive. "You're trying too hard." She leaned closer and grabbed his hands. "Feel my face." He rested his palms on her cheeks. Her smooth skin beckoned a caress. She ducked her gaze, then placed her hand over his. The intimate gesture nearly undid him.

A Lurcher came between them, as if the animal sensed to interfere with the moment. She grinned and tousled the dog's caramel coat.

Captivated, he said, "Show me again."

She complied. He smiled and grabbed her hand. He slipped her fingers into his mouth. Declan barely focused on the whistle as he suckled on her fingers. The brush of air in the form of a low whistle eased past his lips. Sensual, erotic. Him suckling her fingers, the sun heating the clearing, and the swift thickening of his loins.

She pulled back, as if suddenly conscious of what she'd just done. Declan cupped the back of her neck and brought her in for a kiss. *Damn*, 'twas worth it. If this were his last moment of freedom and the magistrate was back with the clan waiting to shackle him forever, the taste of her lips was worth it.

He delved into her, matching the eagerness of her lips. Her ripe body leaned into him, the curves of her breasts and hips melded into his body, urging him to pull her even closer. His heart surged as if claiming Martine as its own.

What a tangle of limbs and emotions. The deeper the kiss, the more his mind reeled at the thought of Martine in his arms. He nipped at her full lower lip. She moaned, sweet and soft, dragging his mind out of the embrace and back to the situation at hand.

"Declan?" she asked breathlessly as he pulled away.

He shook his head and whispered a curse. *Bollocks*, he'd forsaken all common sense and it compelled him to act beyond reason. "We can't. Your brother would be as mad as the Devil himself if he found out."

A grin creased the corner of her eyes. "Pah. Are you afraid of my brother?"

'Twas his turn to grin. "Not afraid, just respectful." Not to mentioned she was betrothed. Reluctantly, but betrothed regardless.

Martine nodded and rose from the log. After brushing

her skirt free of dirt, she called to the dogs. "Come, Lord Declan Forrester, we need to return to the camp."

He accepted her hand and they walked toward the caravans. Regret filled him as he glanced at her profile. Strong and lovely, he knew he'd never forget her and his time spent with the clan. But she'd do better to forget him, especially in light of her upcoming nuptials. What he wouldn't do to trade places with Magor. To be the husband of such a passionate woman would probably send him to an early grave, yet with a full smile plastered on his face, to be sure.

They hovered near the camp to see if the riders were still there. She eased him through the thicket surrounding the camp and he was satisfied there wasn't a threat. Whatever the *Kapo* had said must have worked, for there wasn't a magistrate, not even Trenmore to whisk him back to prison.

Declan needed to leave, and quick. His mind had been too long from the important matters at Riverton and his past. Without discovering the reason for his imprisonment and Abigail's death, he'd never have peace.

Not even peace brought by the lovely Gypsy woman walking beside him.

Chapter 11

Mist lay heavy in the air as a boisterous wind blew across the encampment opening, trying to push it aside. Martine straightened her skirt and retucked her yellow blouse. The necklaces around her neck jingled along with her movements, mixing with the sounds of the night. A fire blazed in its pit, lapping into the darkness, warming some of the mist and the members of the clan surrounding it. She sat near her grandmother and a few children joined her. She wiggled her toes, unaccustomed to the tightness of her slippers, the golden silk damp from the dewy night.

Martine placed a hand over her heart. It battered against her chest as fast as a hummingbird beats its wings. In and out, her breaths came in rapid succession, until she nearly swooned.

The shadow of a man stirred across the fire. Tall and broad of shoulder, Declan broke through the darkness like an avenging angel. Firelight danced about his strong features as it kissed his skin with an amber hue. Martine sucked in her breath at his handsomeness, then expelled it at the glowering set of his jaw. Firelight failed to reach his eyes; they stayed dark and impenetrable.

Rafe approached him and pointed to the nearest seat, a mere patch of grass with a woolen blanket thrown upon it. Declan complied, yet she sensed his displeasure, saw the stiffness of his movements.

He found her with his gaze, intense, probing. She fingered her necklaces, attempting to ignore his attention. Failing miserably, she turned toward him and gave a weak smile. He tipped his head in her direction, then focused on her brother.

"Tell me, Irishman, have you ever seen the light of the moon as stars sprinkled around it? Lit from above with sparks of gold and silver? Tell me, can ye see how we are the sun and you—you are the earth? Dark as loam sucking our rays from us." Rafe's voice lifted over the roar of the fire, commanding and filled with sarcasm. He threw his arm up and opened his hand. Sparks glowed against the night sky. The glimmers flitted down around him, making her brother appear magical.

Declan appeared confused, or was it anger in the firm set of his mouth over her brother's taunting?

The clan's musicians began picking away at a song. Ronal, the clan's *boshomèngro*, played his violin. Dulcet tones eased around them, visibly relaxing many who witnessed the scene. Linka's husband Wilhelm strummed a *bouzouki,* joining in Ronal's song.

Anya hummed beside her, slowly rocking back and forth to the rhythm.

Her brother strode before the group, his hands fisted at his waist. Fury shook her as she watched his arrogant posture as he paced in Declan's direction.

"Do you wish to see my sister dance?" he prodded with a broad sweep of his arm.

The crowd ignored her brother's uncivil tone and applauded. Rafe cut them a nasty glare, then turned to Declan once again.

"What say you, Irish?"

Martine cringed. She knew the tone, the daring, accusation coating the words that displayed her brother's rage.

Declan stood, towering over Rafe in both height and brawn. If it weren't for the animosity sizzling around them, Martine could appreciate the virile masculinity of Lord Forrester.

She went to stand, yet Anya pulled her back. "Let them figure it out, the mule-headed goats."

Her grandmother chuckled, then rasped with coughing.

She quickly wrapped her arm around her. "You should go to bed. 'Tis too damp."

Anya shook her head. "And miss the excitement? Ye know me better than that, my *bitti kom*."

"Martine," her brother called. "Our Irishman would like to see ye dance."

Mortified, she stood, heady consciousness looming over her. How could she dance before him as a spectacle to her brother's animosity?

She began stiffly, the dance so familiar she could perform the steps in her sleep. The tempo quickened as did the glide of her movements, the swirl of the stars above her as she turned and turned graceful pirouettes around the fire. Lost in the music, she ignored those watching, couldn't care if they enjoyed the spectacle or not. The strum of the *bouzouki* fueled her desire to perform as if it vibrated within the beat of her heart and urged her soul to continue with energy and happiness.

Declan gripped his hands as he watched the seductive rhythm of Martine's dance. Sweat tricked down his back and wet his forehead as his breathing nearly halted. Never had he seen such a sensuous display, yet innocent as the smile now curving her lips. Her sheer enjoyment of the dance was obvious, as was the fact that every man surrounding him lusted after her.

Her curvaceous figure moved tantalizingly in front of the clan. Some clapped, others just watched, amazement obvious on their faces.

Declan controlled the urge to jump up and join her, carry her over his shoulder and back to her caravan. There, he'd ravish her in the small bed.

His loins tightened, nearly exploding from months of unspent desire. Declan clenched his jaw tight as the song slowed and her movements did the same. He envisioned her doing the same with him. Their skin exposed, slipping against each other as they explored, enticed, and made love. With each second, he grew more uncomfortable. Physically, emotionally. How he wanted Martine to be his.

How desperately, uncontrollably.

A few men stood and circled around her. They clapped over their shoulders in rhythm to the drum and then snapped their fingers as they moved their legs in tandem.

He rose and left the circle, aware of the stares and the sudden halt of the music. Though it pained him, he paced to the caravan in need of a cold dip in the river and a sound thrashing for his thoughts. He couldn't, nay wouldn't, ruin her.

He was a haunted man. A hunted man. With many more secrets than emotional tangles. She'd soon wilt under his attentions because he wasn't free.

Declan threw open the door to the wagon, nearly unhinging it as he did so. He grabbed a change of clothing and headed toward the river he knew ran along the camp. He stayed in the shadows, behind the protection of the wagons.

The gurgle of the river greeted him as he stripped down to nothing and waded into the icy coldness of the water. Desire was immediately doused and his heart beat rapidly because of the coldness, not the lust surging through his veins.

The music in the distance tapered off and he could hear voices. Some shouting, laughter, and camaraderie. Then the music started once again.

Bitterness tainted his tongue. What he wouldn't give to be back at Riverton—all like it was before Abigail was murdered. He wouldn't have decisions to make, temptations to forsake. But mostly, he missed the friendship of Nate and his men. Regret twisted in his gut, tumbling him into a melancholy mood.

A dog bayed in the distance, pulling his attention to his impromptu bath. The wind still tousled the leaves and the crunch of footsteps sounded nearby. Declan stilled and pulled beneath the protection of an overhanging tree.

He crouched in the shallow depths of the frigid water.

"Lord Forrester," a melodious voice called. A voice that had entered his dreams and now tormented his sanity.

He raked his fingers through his wet hair. "Go away, lass."

"Are you well, then?"

"That and more. If you stay, you're likely to see more than permitted." He remained beneath the branches.

"Oh."

Declan chuckled. Then sobered. She'd be ruined, he argued. Yet the Devil tempted him beyond his sense of control.

"Step away," he warned once again. "I've to get my clothing."

The rustle of leaves indicated her retreat. Declan lifted from the river and shook his head free of water. The invigorating temperature had cooled his ardor, yet the thought of Martine seeing him naked fueled the fire once again and his blood raged with a lusty fervor.

He glanced up. There she stood. Her gaze brave and watchful. Blood rushed through his veins as if it were on fire.

"I warned you," rasped from his throat.

"Aye," she whispered as she stepped closer, her gaze never veering from his. "I'm tired of warnings and apprehension."

Declan reached past her for his shirt and pants. Her breath, warm and sweet, tickled his neck. One swift movement and she'd be in his arms, then another and he'd be deep within her. God, how he wanted to quench his desire in the goodness of her.

The very thought had him searching for her lips, giving nips and kisses down her jaw. Along her elegant neck, pulsing and soft. She eased into his arms, pressed against him, and ground her hips against his arousal. Ah, God, he was home.

"*Martine*," he said with reverence. "Please, I've only so much strength."

She turned her head as their mouths met in a gentle war of lips and biting. Heat and passion. Longing and need. Martine moaned as he tangled his fingers into her thick mane of hair, slid his tongue into her hot, moist mouth. She parried with him as she raked her fingers along the back of his neck onto his bare shoulders. Lightly, then kneading, they pressed into his skin, alighting the fire within him so intensely he nearly howled with pleasure.

He splayed his hands along her back, then lower over her slim waist and down the swell of her hips.

"Please," Martine whispered, "please don't stop."

They tumbled onto the ground, onto the clothing he'd never put on. Declan eased her chemise over the round of her shoulder, down past her glorious breasts, peaked and begging for his touch. "Beautiful," he said in wonder as he suckled.

Martine writhed beneath him, moaning with pleasure. Her hands gripped his head and pressed him deeper. Her enthusiasm surprised and delighted him. Never had he dreamed she'd react with such abandon.

Declan's pulse surged through him, setting his body on the undeniable edge of losing all control. Such desire and longing fueled him, pushing him to continue the gentle onslaught.

An owl hooted in the distance. Declan stopped, his gaze soaking in the beauty before him, the creaminess of her moonlit skin. The passion shining in her eyes. His body begged for release, her touch. His mind saw clearly. He couldn't go any further. She'd be ruined.

"Damn," he swore as he rested his forehead against hers.

"Declan?" Martine dragged a finger down his face and tipped up his chin.

He sighed, torn between delving into heaven and being honorable. Even as his body trembled with desire for her.

She cupped his face in her hand, her gaze searching his, her voice pleading. "Do not stop. I want this, am asking for this." She traced a finger along his shoulder, down his arm. She moved to his back and cupped his buttocks. He closed his eyes and groaned.

"Do you like that?" she asked as she gazed at him.

"Aye," was all he could muster.

She slipped her hand between them, tentatively tracing his aching cock. When she grasped the hard length of him, he lost all control. Declan grit his teeth. "Martine, you know not what you do."

She laughed, husky, sensual. "I want this, Declan. How else can I convince you?" She continued to grip him, sending him close to oblivion.

He shook his head, panting with need. "I can't. You're to be wed." In his short time with the Rom, he'd learned of their code of honor, something totally unexpected and enlightening. "You'd be marked. I can't do that to you, lass."

"My sweet, sweet man," she crooned as tears shimmered in her eyes. "How can I face a marriage lacking of love without first experiencing what love is with you."

The rope on his reserve began to unravel. Temptation lay in his arms. How right her body felt—soft, giving. So seductive in pureness.

"Make it your gift to me." She spoke so sincerely he'd grant her anything. "A gift I will treasure always."

"How can I take such a precious gift from you and then leave you?" Could he stay? The thought fettered about in his mind, tangling with his present state and the mess he'd left at Riverton.

Could he offer for her?

Declan pulled up at the very thought of marrying Martine. Keeping her for himself, taking from another of her kind.

"Marry me."

Martine gasped. "I'm betrothed. You don't understand our ways. How it would be impossible for me to marry a *Gajo*?" She looked away, severing the passionate moment.

He stiffened. "But you wish to make love with a *Gajo*."

She looked at him, serious, determined. "Aye. 'Tis shameful. Shameful in the eyes of my clan. Not to me. But I . . . I have to experience our love. Can you understand?"

He tried to, but the thought of her marrying Magor made him furious. "We do not need to remain in Ireland."

She shook her head. "Nay, my clan would be shamed. My brother has signed an agreement. We would never be accepted. Our children would never be accepted in either of our worlds."

He watched her, read the pain in her gaze, the confusion creasing her brow.

God, how he wanted her—forever. The thought of loving her snuck up on him like an attack from an enemy. Yet this enemy would save his soul.

They lay together, silent save for the babbling creek and hoots and chirps of the animals of the night. The night came alive around them, blanketing them with a cloak of darkness.

"Marry me," he repeated as he trailed kisses along her brow.

"Please, Declan." She turned, her body snug against him, fitting as if God created her especially for him. "I cannot marry one who isn't my kind. I would be shunned. The clan would suffer."

He cupped her cheek. "I love you."

She sniffled. Her tears glistened in the moonlight against the high curve of her cheek. "Then show me," she said softly.

He needed no more invitation as he eased her skirt down her hips and into a pile on the ground. The moonlight cast a golden hue over her long legs, the dark apex between her thighs. Unable to bear any more temptation, Declan devoured her lips as he nudged his manhood between her thighs and slowly entered into her wet silkiness. He hesitated as she gasped. "'Twill ease, my love."

He laved her neck, her jaw. She shifted and together they moved, synchronized in their pleasure and thrust. A hot, demanding need drove them each to moan, gasp out each other's name. Loving each other, groping, kissing, and flesh against flesh. Needing each other as if they had no salvation.

He slowly eased in and out of her, so tight and soft, slick. Ah, so drenched in her desire.

Never had she thought it would be like this. She moved her hand over his back. The hard plane of muscles shifted beneath her attention as she tickled, gripped, as Declan nuzzled the tender spot at the base of her neck. Ah, oh, tingling pleasure heated her deep within her womb.

"Declan," whispered past her lips. He lifted, a cocksure grin tipped up his mouth and heady desire burned intensely in his eyes. The moonlight filtered around them, almost as if they were in a protective cocoon.

She cradled his face between her hands, shifted, then kissed him. There was so much pleasure and emotion surging through her. She lifted her hips to draw him deeper. The need to be closer, one and part of each other, drove her into a frenzy. Her heart pounded against her chest, pumping her heated blood to every limb.

Declan kissed along the round of her shoulder, feathered tiny kisses down her arm while he continued to slide in and out. Slow, long thrusts shifted into quick short thrusts. She arched, pushing her breasts against his chest. The soft covering of hair tickled her, thrilled her. He lapped the soft flesh of the crook of her arm, continuing up her toward her breasts. He nibbled and then cupped her breasts, dividing his attention between both of them. He lavished them with kisses until he pulled on her nipple, suckling. Heat and moisture flooded the apex of her thighs. Surely her body could only take so much pleasure?

He gripped her buttocks, holding her tight as tremors of pleasure cascaded over them.

"I never thought . . ." Martine said as she tangled her fingers in his hair and lifted her hips to continue to grind hard against his.

Martine climaxed, her lips parted and eyes widened. Awe whispered from her. Declan filled her until he reared back and growled his shout of release. He panted as he cradled her in his arms, both sated, both exhausted.

"I will love you until I die, Declan Forrester."

He smiled into her hair and inhaled. "And I you."

Declan awoke to the splash of water and the burgeoning ripples of daylight. His muscles protested as he lifted from the ground. Disappointment pierced him when he realized Martine was gone.

He picked up his wrinkled clothing and began to put it on.

"Aren't you going to join me?"

Declan gazed to the river. She stood in a deep pool, water caressing up to her shoulders. He threw down his breeches and tread into the water. Ignoring the coldness, he grasped her in his arms and captured her lips with his. His body immediately sprang to life, prompting him to push her legs around his waist.

"What a perfect way to take a bath," she whispered into his mouth.

"Are you sore? Do you want me to stop?" Not that he could. He could feel the heat of her apex even in the cold water.

She shook her head and pressed against him. He entered her in one swift movement.

They groaned in unison as each brought pleasure to the other. Martine feasted on his neck, lapping the water, sucking his skin. Their actions were frenzied, manic, and totally insatiable. She gave as well as he did, amazing him once again with her passion. No matter, she was his, no matter.

He stifled her cry of pleasure with his mouth and succumbed to his own. Depleted, he lifted her out of the water and laid her on his clothing.

The sun had crested the horizon and began awakening the earth and its inhabitants. Birds sang and insects buzzed in rhythm to Declan's heart and breathing. He watched her dry off with his shirt. Martine smiled. His gut twisted at the thought of losing her.

"Run away with me," he demanded.

Her smile vanished and she stayed silent.

Declan knelt in front of her and swept her hands into his own. They were graceful, fine, yet showed the signs of hard work. He wanted to take her away from the nomadic life of the Rom, clothe her in luxuries, and bath her in jewels. It was his dream, one dreamt in the arms of a siren on the bank of a river.

"We'll go to England. I have holdings there."

Her gaze changed to one of sadness. "I cannot."

"Your brother is smart. He will find a way not to lose face." He needed her, it was right. His mind and body told him so. Most importantly, his heart was begging for her.

"These are my people. England won't accept me. Ireland won't accept me. How could we live like that?"

"We'll go to Italy, France."

She ripped her hands from his, rose and turned away. Still in naked glory, Martine turned her back to him. "I cannot."

Declan starred at her back. Black rivulets of water trickled down.

He came forward and touched her hair.

"No," she yelled as she twisted out of his grasp.

He frowned and looked at the color staining his fingers as his heart pounded in his throat. "What's this? Is your hair dyed?"

Martine looked to the ground, avoided his gaze. He wrapped his hands around her shoulders. "Look at me," he demanded. "Why do you dye your hair? Why?"

Tears overflowed her lashes as panic filled her gaze. "I never meant to deceive you."

He gritted his teeth as he tangled his fingers in her decidedly auburn hair. Black dye continued to run down the length of his hand and over his wrist. "Tell me? Are you Rom?"

Her eyes widened, fear and pain mixing within her gaze. She tried to pull away from him, but he held steady.

"Are you Rom?" he demanded.

"I am Rom," she said as she pounded her chest.

If that were true, why did she not look him in the eyes? "Martine, are you Rom?"

She looked toward the ground. After what seemed like an eternity, she whispered, "No."

Although softly spoken, the words roared through his mind. No? If she wasn't Rom, why was she so intent on this marriage? Why would she insist that she wouldn't be accepted outside the Rom? "You played me. I'm such a fool," he ground out.

Declan released her and grabbed his clothing.

"You don't understand," she pleaded as she tried to grab his hand as he turned from her. "They are my family, my clan. I have nowhere else to go."

"You could've come with me, to be sure. Didn't I offer such to you?" Anger, sharp and bright, blurred his vision. He'd given her a chance. If she truly loved him, 'twould have been simple, instinctive. Her heart would have made the decision easily.

She waved her hands. "Pah, I will never be accepted in your society again. I've lived with the Rom for too many years."

Declan shook his head. "You'd rather marry a stranger instead of the one you love?" The thought seemed incredulous to him. "You'd rather sacrifice yourself for a brother who'd barter you like cloth."

She rubbed her brow in frustration. "You don't understand!" Again she tried to grab him, pull him closer to her. "I do love you. But with the Rom, I am the *Kapo's* sister. I am respectable. I can have children and not be ashamed. I will be accepted!"

He narrowed his gaze, tipping his head to the side as he contemplated what he wanted to say. "Are you certain?" he countered. "Do you really think deep down they grant you the same respectability as your *brother*?" His tone held the blunt edge of sarcasm. He didn't care about his harshness. She must realize that life with him would be better than marrying a man she didn't love. "We can be together. In England they don't know you as a Rom. The dye is already washed from your hair."

She reached for him and rested her hand on his arm. "How? The way I talk, the way I dress—it is Rom. The way I think, what I eat, is Rom. Even my name, Declan—'tis the only name I remember—is Rom. I've been with them for more than half my life. I cannot remember the ways of the Irish, and the English loathe us." She tipped her chin at him, challenging him with her darkened gaze. "The magistrate is looking for you and I do not even know why." She moved away and began dressing before she stilled and said, "We both have secrets, Declan. Secrets we are willing to protect, no matter the cost."

She rubbed her brow before she looked at him, deeply gazing into his eyes. "What we have shared will never be far from my thoughts. If I die tomorrow, 'twill be worth it."

Declan cringed as he realized life with him was worth naught to her. He couldn't force her or obviously change her mind. It was set. Now all they had to do was live with the consequences. Whatever they might be. He knew he'd continue to live in purgatory. Deep in hell on earth.

Bollocks. He had to hope, keep the hope Abigail had insisted love was his for the taking. She knew there was another woman for him and here she was, slipping away from him.

"Please," he attempted once more, "come with me. We'll find the answers together."

She shook her head. "We both have secrets, Declan, as I said. You've yet to share yours with me. How do I know what awaits us if you don't trust me, share your secrets?"

He dragged his fingers through his hair. To tell her would mean he'd have to leave no details out, and the details were harsh, grisly. "I . . . I must prove my innocence and then I'll share all."

"Innocence for what?" she cried. "See, you can't even tell me. You do not trust me." She pounded a finger into his chest.

He gripped her shoulders and looked directly into her sad eyes. "I want to protect you."

She wrenched away, disgust filling her gaze as she forced her mouth into a straight line. "I do not need your protection, Declan. I need you to trust and love me."

He pinched the bridge of his nose. Without his innocence, he was nothing to her. They'd never be safe. "I will, I promise, but first I have to leave you."

She turned to the water. Her spine rigid and unyielding. "Go," Martine said with tears in her voice. "Go and find your happiness elsewhere."

"Wait for me, Martine." He stood behind her, reached out to touch her shoulder, then let his arm fall to his side. "Wait to marry until I have proven my innocence—trust me. If I have your trust, I know you'll wait for me."

She remained silent. The pain in his gut intensified as if someone had taken a knife and twisted it. How could he leave her behind?

She was wrong. He did trust her, far more than he'd trusted anyone else. Once he had his innocence, he'd move heaven and earth to make others accept her. Once he went to England and cleared his name, they could each begin anew. Together. Didn't she see this?

Declan left, determined more than ever to prove he didn't

kill his wife and solve the mystery of his imprisonment so he could claim the woman he loved.

Martine crumpled onto the bank of the river. Tears racked her body as grief consumed her.

She stayed there, attempting to find solace in the last place she'd ever find happiness.

As the sun crested and heated the earth, she wept. Clouds invaded the sky and her mind, bringing torrents of harsh thoughts. She was a fool, she kept saying to herself. She'd never find the love Declan offered her again. She couldn't help but think it was the price she'd pay for her sins.

Near midday, she finished dressing, yet stayed along the bank of the river. She hated the thought of returning to the camp, fearful others may guess her sinful actions. But also, she didn't want to leave the place in which she'd given herself to Declan.

"Martine?"

She cringed and braced herself. "Aye, Grandmother."

Her grandmother paced near, her aged movements hindering her steps. Martine rose to help her and guide her to sit on a stump.

Deep lines etched her face in an expression Martine knew as concern.

Anya peered up at the sky, brooding or thinking, she wasn't sure.

"I didn't think ye'd still be here, my *bitti kom*."

Martine shrugged. The action careless, so contradictory to how she was truly feeling. "Declan has left."

"That I know. I can feel yer despair." She lifted a gnarled hand and gripped her arm with surprising strength. "You should have left. 'Twas yer destiny."

She reined in the words she wanted to spew. God, how she hated the duty she felt, the gratitude. Aye, the clan had rescued and saved her. But the pain of the obligation weighted her shoulders with unrelenting force as her heart broke, shattered.

"I can't sacrifice the clan for my destiny alone." She shuddered, a warning tremor skittering up her spine. "Does the *Kapo* know I am here?" She glanced around, trying to find what prompted her sudden unease. A breeze crossed the river and chilled her further with a bracing wind.

"Nay, *bitti kom*. He's in his *vurdon* talking with Lord Forrester."

She gripped her grandmother's hand. "What?" She stood and straightened her clothing. "I must go to them." She helped Anya stand.

"Go," she said with a wave. "See if you can make your brother see reason."

She narrowed her gaze as she glanced in the direction of the camp.

Aye, see reason. But first she'd have to tell him—tell him she'd lost her innocence with his foe, the Irishman.

Chapter 12

Declan paced toward the *Kapo's* caravan. He banged his fist against the heavy wooden door, then shoved it open as a voice bid entry.

Rafe Petrulengo sat at a large table strewn with papers. He scowled at Declan, then nodded toward a chair. Declan refused the offer and remained standing before the Gypsy leader.

"Why is she here?" he raged as he clenched his fist. "Why?"

The *Kapo* leapt from the chair, scattering papers onto the floor. "What has she told ye?" A suspicious gleam entered his dark eyes. He was a formidable man, to be sure. Declan didn't give a damn. He wanted Martine as his wife.

He glared at the tinker. "She *is not* Rom."

Rafe cocked his brow. "That is all she told ye, Irish?"

Declan raked his fingers through his hair and he expelled a grunt. "'Twas enough."

Rafe began picking up the scattered maps. Declan was surprised once again at the intellect of the Gypsies. How the man had been measuring, marking the maps. Perhaps planning their next move.

As he adjusted the maps, the man stayed infuriatingly silent.

"Ye have no sense of what she's been through," he finally said. "An orphan—no, an angel, she was to us in our time of need."

Confused, Declan just listened and prayed the man would reveal something useful. While he listened, he paced back and forth in the small home.

"So many had died. Pah, murdered." Rafe rubbed the

back of his neck, his dark eyes unreadable. "Tell me, Irish. What is yer interest in my *siskaar*?"

Declan pulled up to his full height and fisted his hands at his waist. "I want to wed her."

His eyes widened, then suspicion narrowed them. "Nay. Never. She belongs to another of her kind."

Declan scoffed. "*Your* kind?"

"Aye," he replied with a quick swipe of his hand. "She is one of us."

"Nay. She is not Rom." He raked his fingers through his hair. Why the deception?

"She has little memory of her old life." Rafe sat in the chair by a table littered with maps. "Her family is dead. She is as Rom as I."

Dear God.

He narrowed his gaze at the Gypsy leader. "How is she with you?"

Rafe indicated the chair across from him with a sweep of his arm. "Sit, Irish, and I will tell ye."

He sat and waited. He had to know why she would refuse him for a marriage without the hope of love. He'd lived that and wouldn't subject her to such an ambiguous union, even though his had been filled with admiration and a comfortable sense of friendship.

"A carriage accident took her mother, father, and brother." He shrugged. "We do not know why she was saved from death, but my father deemed her an angel."

Declan shook his head. He still didn't understand why she stayed all these years.

"We'd lost my grandfather, the *Kapo,* my mother, and the clan were mourning such a great loss. It was a terrible fight between the English and my clan. They tried to banish us, wanted to kill us all." He waved his hand dismissively. "No matter. She was injured and we healed her. *Anya* healed her and she wouldn't leave my grandmother's side unless it was to be with me."

Declan absorbed the information. Too many details were missing and the shock of it all brought out sympathy for Martine. *God, how she'd suffered.* "And what of her family? Did you search for others who'd claim her?"

A wry smile creased his face as he poured a tumbler of whiskey. He tipped his head to Declan and poured another. "Pah, she has plenty of family that would claim her. She's an Earl's daughter."

He stood, knocking the tumbler from the table. "What?"

Rafe had the audacity to laugh. "Aye, Irish. Her land and estates have moved on to others, since they thought all were dead, but," he said with a shrug, "one can assume her family would not welcome her appearance. And if we'd approached the magistrate after the accident, certainly we'd be blamed for causing it."

Bollocks. He never thought this was her story. Even when she was standing in the creek and 'twas obvious she wasn't Rom, his mind never ventured to the idea she was an earl's daughter. "I'm sure the magistrate would be interested in her."

Rafe drew back, his eyes narrowed, and the muscles ticked along his jaw. "Ye'd ruin her? How would her family accept her after she has spent so many years with us?"

He cringed and let out a breath. "Nay. I'd never hurt her."

The *Kapo* crossed his arms before his chest and eased his long legs out. "As I thought, Irish."

He took a long look at the leader. Weighed his next words, actions. Did he confess to what had transpired the night before? Or did he wait and see if Martine would change her mind and come with him?

"*Kapo!*" a young lad yelled as he barreled into the wagon. "*Kapo*, the magistrate is here."

They both swore beneath their breath and stood. "I will distract them. Leave us before ye bring more wrath onto my clan."

Declan looked out the small window of the wagon in search of Martine. He must say goodbye. Aye, she'd refused him, but he couldn't leave her without a goodbye.

The leader grabbed him by his shoulders and growled, "Leave, Irish. Leave now or I tell the magistrate all."

He glanced at the door, then to the window. He could not risk going to prison. She'd understand. Aye, she'd understand.

He had to leave before the magistrate found him and locked him back in hell.

She took her time returning to camp. She had to gather her thoughts before she spoke to her brother. Mayhap Declan had already confessed and Rafe was ready to void the marriage contract with Magor.

Aye and she was truly Rom. She was fooling herself if she thought her brother would shame the clan all because of her indiscretion.

She continued to linger as a way to deny what she'd refused, thrown away. She'd seen the anger on Declan's face when she'd pushed him away, made it seem as if his love meant nothing when quite the opposite was true. Martine's heart clenched within her chest. She surely couldn't survive and it pained her so. She stopped and held onto a tree to catch her breath, then proceeded further toward the life she'd chosen and farther from the one given to her as a gift.

Her arrival at camp went unnoticed. Fellow Rom gathered near her brother's caravan. Urgency and fear overwhelmed her, washed over her as the rain washed over Ireland.

They know, a little voice said. They know you are soiled. She pushed toward her own wagon to shut out the voice and any speculation from the clan. She collapsed on her bed, ready for rest and the cleansing abyss of dreams. She tossed and turned until a fitful sleep overtook her.

Her faithful Lurchers chased her about the clearing, yapping with enthusiasm only dogs could manage. A form loomed at the gap in the tree line. Tall, dark, formidable. A scar glowed in the darkness. Rafe. Fury pinched his brow and narrowed his intense eyes. She tried to run in the other direction, follow her dogs and their playful antics. Each turn she took, her brother appeared, growing larger and larger. Martine fell to her knees, her head cast in shame. He spoke to her—harsh condemning words. Tradition, he repeated, tradition of the Rom. The words crashed over her in waves of pain and regret. Never would she forget the look of disappointment that filled his dark gaze. He left her, a crumpled mess on the field grass, her dogs howling in the distance out of her reach.

Martine attempted to catch her breath as she bolted awake. She threw back the blanket and wiped the sweat from her brow. Her dream appeared so vivid and true. Her mind raced as she tried to glean the meaning of her brother's appearance. Then her thoughts stopped when all was clear. She'd mocked the traditions of the Rom, slapped the very face that had saved her so many years before.

God help her, she must tell her brother what she'd done. Then, if she were banished, 'twould be her own doing and with that shame she'd live for the rest of her days.

Chapter 13

Declan raced through the forest, oblivious to the branches ripping through his flesh and the drenching rain. He arrived at Riverton tired, sodden, and hungry. Watching from a copse of trees, he waited to see if there was any life about. He slipped into the barn, empty save Kindred. Thank God his steed had made his way back home.

He raked his fingers through his hair, then grabbed a saddle pad and made his bed in an empty stall.

When sleep finally came, Declan rid his mind of Martine and the Gypsies and allowed darkness to consume him.

"There you are, you wee bastard."

Declan wrenched awake as he jolted to his feet. Before him stood the most glorious sight of all.

Finn Randolph.

He grinned and reached to shake his friend's hand. Randolph tugged him into a tight hug and patted his back.

"'Tis time you returned. I've been watching for you."

Declan rubbed weariness from his eyes and sat back upon the blanket and straw. His body fatigued beyond reason, his muscles protested the slightest movement. "Welcome to my palace," he said with a sweep of his arm. "Sit."

His childhood friend sat and reached into a leather saddle bag. His pants were filthy, shirt untucked, and jacket rumpled. Aye, 'twas Finn all right. And with that roguish gleam in his eye and that long hair, he'd sent many a lass into a swoon with one look. "I was sure you'd be hungry." He tossed a loaf of bread at him and then reached for more. An apple and chunk of cheese followed. Declan devoured them as if it were his last meal. When Randolph produced a tankard of ale, Declan nearly kissed him square on the mouth.

"What took you so long to come, you *eejit*?"

Declan smiled at their familiar insult. "A certain Gypsy beauty."

"Aye, she's a beaut to be sure, but what of yer innocence. Doesn't that matter to you?"

Declan frowned, his anger now curdling his breakfast. "What do you know of Martine?"

Finn cocked an arrogant brow and anyone but Declan would be intimidated. "I've been trying to locate you for the past fortnight. I spied the Gypsies, even visited the camp looking for you and only one could garner yer sniveling attention."

Ah, the men who'd visited and sent him and Martine to the clearing. He decided to steer the subject away from the love he lost to something more attainable. "What have you learned in London?"

A smile some would call sinister spread across Finn's handsome face. "Aye, we've some enemies there, to be sure. Ettenborough has weaved a fine tale, but some truth came out regardless. Yer name is wagging on many a tongue."

Declan clenched his fist at the mention of Abigail's father. The man had made both he and Abigail suffer.

"'Tis that English bastard Broderick who worries me. He runs deep in yer past. Yer father and him were friends at one point. He wouldn't mention anyone else but yer father. Ranted about him—and you. Not altogether, that one."

"Why?" Declan asked. "Why do they hound me?"

Finn hunched his shoulders. "Aye, he wants to hound you to hell, that one. 'Tis about politics. Yer fathers and Brodericks, Ettenboroughs, and some other man who has yet to reveal himself."

He gripped his friend by the shoulders. "Why, damn it?"

Finn patted him on the shoulder. "I was close, but then he clammed up on me, the bastard. Even when I broke into his townhome, I found nothing." Finn rose and swept his black clothing clean of straw. "I was ready to return to London when I met up with yer men."

Declan stood as well. "Where are they?"

"Just outside of town."

He leaned against the stall door. "'Tis too dangerous for them."

Finn chuckled. "Och, Declan, they're not bairns in need of a nursemaid. Grown men, they are. Ready to prove yer innocence."

He doubted that. When Nate had left, 'twas distrust in his all-seeing eyes. They proceeded out of the protection of the stables. The estate was silent, save for the chickens clucking a few feet away.

"The estate is empty. Ettenborough cleaned the place out except for yer chambers. I," he said with a gleam to his eye, "have been using them."

Declan punched at his friend, then eased into pacing beside him and thought of the next plan of action. "Did the villagers question your presence?"

"I was careful, you ken. No candlelight at night and I stayed in the shadows during the day."

Declan shook his head. Of course his friend knew how to remain undetected. It had saved his life many a time. "We must go to London."

Finn stopped and looked at him. "And yer beauty? What of her?"

He tried to speak, yet the torture of admitting her refusal lodged in his throat. He glanced away and shrugged his shoulders. "I have to prove my innocence."

Finn nodded and walked up the front steps to Riverton. No candlelight burned welcome, nary a servant was available to ensure comfort. Nay, only solitude, damn solitude.

"I'll leave at dawn."

Declan watched his friend, uncertain whether he should ask him to stay. The haunting cries from prison rose to a crescendo in his mind along with the cries for justice from the villagers. "I'll go with you."

Finn turned to him, his dark eyes searching his face. "Aye, 'twould do me good to have company. I just don't want you blathering on about yer lass, bonny or no."

Chuckling, Declan entered his chamber, opened the armoire and grabbed clean clothing. The full linen shirt of the Rom and straight black trousers had long ago replaced the waistcoat and breeches he was wearing when he'd left Riverton. Their comfort had surprised him. Now, they only reminded him of what he'd lost. Stripping down, he accepted the washbowl of water from Finn and began administering to his numerous cuts and bruises.

His friend cocked an arrogant brow. "You've a fair share more than when I left you."

He nodded and hissed when he washed a particularly deep gash. He folded the Rom clothing and set them inside the armoire. He couldn't part with them just yet.

Back in his own clothing, Declan lay upon his bed and crossed his arms behind his head. He'd strode past Abigail's chamber when they'd entered the estate, not able to look in. Mayhap later he'd venture into her room and say a quick prayer. Try to think of the happier memories of their union.

Finn sat in the wing chair before the fireplace. His friend kicked his feet onto the small stool and leaned back into the damask upholstery.

"Nate sends his concern. They seem to be waiting. For what I'm not sure. But they'll be glad to see you."

He grunted. "The last time I saw them, Nate wanted to skin me alive."

Finn sighed. "Been a time or two I've been wanting to do the same."

Declan chuckled. "You're a bastard, you are." The camaraderie felt good. Damn good. "Rest," he said, "then we'll have ourselves a wee feast before we head to London."

"'Twill take a while, lad. And yer not in the best of shape, you ken?"

Inwardly, he wanted to scoff at Finn's words, but he knew it was the truth of it. While he knew his friend spoke of his physical state, his hear hurt more than anything else. The image of Martine with the tears streaking down her face came to him. If only he'd remained in control. She'd still have her innocence and he'd still have his sanity. After one taste of her, he knew he was spoiled for life and none would ever compare. "I'll manage."

"Aye, I'm sure you will."

With that said Finn closed his eyes and rested his hand on the hilt of his knife. It reassured Declan that all would be well. 'Twas the knife that had staved off many a fight when they visited pubs.

Aye, 'twas good to see Finn Randolph. He just hoped the rest of his men were truly as glad to see him.

Sadie crouched behind a yew. The window was partially blocked by curtains, yet she'd know that tall masculine form anywhere.

Lord Declan Forrester was at Riverton.

She moistened her lips with the tip of her tongue. Despite Trenmore's devoted attention, she felt a lack of excitement. But it appeared as if that were about to change.

Sadie shivered as gooseflesh skittered over her arms. Aye, 'twas more than excitement. 'Twas near bliss she felt.

Another man moved into her view. "Hmmm," she cooed. Bollocks, this one was almost as grand as Declan. Tall, dark. Dangerous.

"Forgive me, Abigail, but Declan will be mine," she whispered. "I can't help myself." She inched away from the window and strolled back toward the kitchen entrance. As luck would have it, the dark one had left. She grinned. She'd welcome Declan home in the proper manner. And if the other one returned, why she'd take care of him like she'd taken care of her husbands.

For one moment, sympathy for Trenmore seeped into her mind. He'd been such a dear. Accommodating, a fine cut of a man, but without the viral masculinity Lord Forrester exuded. Such was life, she surmised with a lift of her shoulders. Sadie rummaged through a drawer to find a knife and sliced some bread. Abigail's father hadn't removed everything, it appeared. A few thick cuts of ham, apricot crumb cake, and a pickled egg. 'Twasn't fine fair, but 'twould do. She laid out the food on an ornate tray and found a not so wrinkled cloth napkin.

Now she just had to wait.

Chapter 14

"I'm ready to marry."

Rafe whipped around. "Pah, as if you had a choice."

Martine shrugged as if her brother's words didn't emphasize how little control she had over her own life.

Her brother advanced and stood too close. The scar across his cheek whitened. She braced herself for his words, although she wished they would remain unspoken.

"I make the decisions, *Siskaar*." He retreated a step, yet fury still reigned over his face and in his posture. "What makes you certain your Magor would welcome you now?"

Martine twisted her hands together. "He must. 'Twas arranged."

Rafe sliced his hand through the air. "The clan is in a precarious position. I fear word of the Irishman may have reached Magor's clan."

She cast her gaze to the floor. She rubbed her brow, her head now aching at the worry and heartbreak. 'Twas obvious Declan didn't reveal what had happened the night before. He'd left as he said he would, and now she knew what was expected of her. Martine inhaled deeply before she spoke. "I know I must wed."

Rafe tipped up her chin. "'Tis time for you to have a husband and a family of your own."

She looked into his eyes, now filled with concern and compassion. Aye, she'd miss him dearly, her moody brother. Rafe and Anya were the only family she'd known. She so wanted to stay, remain with them forever.

Just as she thought of it, the idea of family and babes of her own sent her heart careening.

He let go of her and tugged at his chin. He placed his free hand on his waist as he tapped a booted foot. "Go, we must prepare. You must wed. You know it, and Anya knows."

"Anya knows what?"

They both turned toward the doorway. Anya stood watching them, obviously disgruntled. She bustled forward and wrapped a protective arm around Martine. "'Tisn't her fate. Didn't I tell you, *bitti chovexani?*"

Martine nodded, not trusting her voice to speak. Rafe shook his head as he filled a cup with whiskey.

"*Púridaia*, you know as well as I, 'tis done. The bride price has been paid and Magor awaits our lovely Martine."

"Pash," Anya said as she strode to his side. She helped herself to some spirits and glared at her grandson.

"Our clan will lose the respect we have earned over the generations."

"Nay," Anya said with a growl as she set her cup down with a thud. The whiskey splashed over the side and spread over the maps on the table. Rafe whisked them up and set them on his cot.

"Please, don't argue." Martine took a rag from a shelf and began blotting the maps. The action helped her ignore the tension, thick and palpable, humming through the wagon. "I'll marry Magor."

"What of Lord Forrester?"

She looked at her grandmother, drew from her strength. "He has left." And she gave him no encouragement to return.

"Are you certain?" Anya asked as she came closer.

Martine took comfort in her presence, but struggled with voicing the words once again. He'd asked her to wait, but that wasn't possible. He'd never return before her wedding.

"Aye," Rafe said harshly. "When the magistrate arrived,

he fled." He looked pointedly at her as if trying to convey a message. "He will not return."

Anya took the rag from her hand and enveloped her in a hug. "'Tis right," she whispered with heavy resignation and the tremble of tears in her voice. "The Irishman is gone. Remember him in yer heart, but in yer mind, replace him with Magor. Yer fate changed when Declan left and you did not follow."

Realization flashed in her brother's eyes. They swirled into a thunderstorm of fury. "All I can see is dishonor," her brother said. He paced to the door and looked out over the encampment. "Gossip is swift and tart. Never will Magor truly trust you or me again."

She shook her head, tears threatening. "Nay. I'll make sure he does."

Rafe's pointed gaze found her, intense and sad. "No, my *siskaar*, 'tisn't the way of the Rom."

Tears flooded her vision. How could something as beautiful and pure as her love for Declan have resulted in such gut wrenching pain and despair?

Her grandmother tugged on her arm. "Come, *bitti kom*."

Martine gripped her stomach as it churned over the tension.

Rafe spat. "'Tis glad I am the Forrester is out of our midst. He brought dishonor."

She glared at her brother, her mind well past the point of anger and treading fast into fury. "He was a good man in need of help."

"Ha," Rafe said with a humorless chuckle. "He killed his wife. Why not try to steal you away as well?"

Her knees buckled. Anya tried to stop her from falling onto the floor. The old woman lacked strength and Martine landed with a resounding thud. Her leader, her brother, came forward and offered a hand. She looked at his hand and then at his face. She accepted, no longer certain of her attachment to him and his to her. He seemed to have no loyalty to anything but the clan as a whole. Not even his brotherly love had softened his words.

"Why do you think he ran? A wealthy lord, living among the Gypsies. He was hunted."

"No," she said softly. "Declan would never kill. He is too kind. Too gentle."

Rafe cocked a brow. She braced herself for more, as she could feel his anticipation.

"Grandson, ye've said enough. Leave the poor lass alone."

He held up his hand. "Nay, *Púridaia*. She must know so she can forget him. Let us hope Magor will still have her."

Anya pushed between them, her face awash in concern. "'Tis enough, *Kapo*. See to the clan. They have questions for you. Make certain you have the right answers."

He opened his mouth to speak, and then closed it. With a brisk nod, he left his caravan to address the clan and elders. 'Twould be a night of heated discussion, she knew, but necessarily so.

Martine sat on the edge of the cot. Her shoulders drooped with fatigue and the burdensome weight of remorse. "Declan, a murderer? I do not believe it."

"Nor do I," her grandmother said with conviction. "Why did he leave?"

"He said he had to prove his innocence." She cringed when she realized her ignorance. Declan's innocence had to be tied to his wife's death.

Anya nodded. "Aye, he is innocent. I know it deep in my bones."

Did she agree? Aye, her Declan would never kill another.

Her grandmother tipped her chin up with a crooked finger. "Can you be wearing red for yer wedding?"

She ducked her gaze, her body trembling at the thought of her confession. "Nay," she whispered.

"Martine. You need to wed quickly before any sign of a babe is apparent."

She moved her hand to her stomach. Dare she hope that they'd created a child together? 'Twould be enough, she thought, to live out her days with Declan's child as a reminder of their love. Would Magor know? Declan had dark hair. Would that fool her future husband? Och, what a mess she'd made of her life. What a liar she'd become.

She furrowed her brow at the deception. She'd be banned from the tribe. No home, no love—how could she survive?

The thought of a baby was dulled by her brother's announcement. Declan wasn't a murderer. She knew it deep within her heart—soul. He couldn't have done what her brother had said. She'd never believe.

Martine left the caravan after a few moments to gather her thoughts and dry her tears. The night air lay heavy over the area, cool and oppressive. The elders gathered in the middle by the fire, her brother standing before them in his usual rigid stance. Many shouted out as each attempted to have their say. She stayed to the back, not wanting to gain their attention and perhaps the brunt of their anger.

"We must get the Irishman."

"He brought the magistrate to our camp. We should hang 'im."

Rafe held up his hands for silence. "Nay, we'd just bring more of the wrath of the magistrate on us. Forrester is gone. He will pay for his crimes once the people of Riverton see him."

"Nay, *Kapo*," Linka's husband yelled. "If Magor refuses her, we must have justice. The union would bring great honor and now we may have great shame."

Her brother rubbed the back of his neck. Martine felt for him, his position one of great importance, yet little yield. Before she could think better of it, she walked to his side. He was her brother and she'd support him, even if that meant bringing their wrath upon her.

When she put her hand on his shoulder, he flinched.

"'Tis Martine's fault. She kept the man here."

Once again Rafe held up his hands to still the verbal lashing by the crowd. "My sister has been nothing but loyal to the Rom. Even," he said with warning and a pointed glare at Linka's husband, "when she has been treated with hostility. Do not forget, I allowed her to watch over the Irishman."

Linka's husband glowered at her. How she wanted to appear strong, but she quivered beneath his scrutiny.

"Go," her brother said. "You're needed elsewhere."

She nodded, relieved to leave the boiling pot of Rom emotions and escape to her caravan where she could regain her composure.

Racing along the dewy grass, she reached her caravan quickly. A light flickered through the window, and Martine knew the privacy she sought was not to be had.

She inhaled, then released her breath as she opened the door. Her grandmother sat in a chair with a cup of tea poised in her hand.

"Sit," Anya said without a trace of the usual softness.

Martine complied, then glumly stared at her hands. "I…I don't know what to do."

"That much I know," Anya scoffed.

Tears threaded down her cheeks. She wiped them with the back of her hand and continued. "I love him." She began to hiccup along with crying.

Anya rose, stiff, appearing older than Martine thought possible. "There, there, *bitti chovexani*." She patted her head and smoothed her gnarled hands over her hair. "'Tisn't yer fault."

"I should have told Rafe," she wailed.

"Yer brother wouldn't have listened," her grandmother insisted. "Each of us has our own destiny, Martine. Yers was forever changed when we rescued you."

She nodded with little conviction, the guilt too strong to ignore, much less disregard. "What if Magor refuses me?" She touched her stomach as it churned with guilt and doubt.

"'Tis done," Anya simply said. "The contracts signed. He will not refuse you."

The crushing weight of the day nearly overrode any sense she had left. She gripped the wall, her body tired and weak.

"To bed with you. All will still be in shambles tomorrow." Anya guided her to her bed.

Martine mustered a small chuckle before she shucked her clothing and climbed into bed.

So many questions swirled about her mind, plaguing her with uncertainty and fear. Sleep eluded her for a torturous amount of time. She rose from her bed and sat by the small window. Silence rang through the camp, the men and women long left for their beds. The moon crested in the sky beneath a blanket of clouds.

Where was Declan? Was he thinking of her? Or still running, if her brother's words held any truth?

Her heart pattered against her chest with longing to see him once more. Again her hand found its way to her stomach.

Please, she prayed, let his child be within me.

Chapter 15

Declan rose slowly, stretching against the soft cushion of his bed and the warm weight of the counterpane. For a moment he smiled, then the reality of his life appeared to vex him. *Right*, he thought, *I'm still a hunted man.*

The cock had crowed its last warning that daybreak was upon Kilkenny. Declan rolled out of bed and planted his feet on the cool flooring of his chamber. Heavy drapes barred the sun like a shield protecting a warrior. Shadows clogged the corners and emerged from under his bed, grasping for his feet. Cold sweat moistened his palms and raced down his back as he tried to overcome the gut-wrenching panic threatening to consume him.

For a moment, his time in prison flashed before his eyes. The beatings, starvation, humiliation—all spiked his anxiety.

Declan ran a hand over his bed covering. The thick damask brought him back to where he was. In his manor home—not a prison cell. In a warm, huge bed—not a dirt floor with threadbare clothing to stave off the unbearable cold. Ready to break his fast with more food than imaginable— not wiping up gruel with filthy fingers, even stooping to lick the dirt clean of any drippings.

"I'm going insane," he said aloud.

Although he knew the contrary, saying the words helped him realize it more clearly. Who wouldn't have nightmares after what he'd gone through? He raked his fingers through his hair and stood to glance about the chamber in an attempt to slow the rapid beat of his heart. Neat, luxurious, yet barren of any identity. No mementos, not even a shirt tossed hastily aside. It looked as if he'd never lived here, and that made him lonelier than he could bear.

Declan sat again, the wind taken from him. There was Little, his men, and Finn Randolph. Besides Randolph, only Nate held a close relationship that would endure.

Bollocks. He needed to stop feeling sorry for himself. He hated the weakness, the cowardly thoughts. If one of his men were to act in such a manner, he'd triple his training to drive the whining from him.

On that dour note, he began to dress. With a longing look, he glanced at the armoire, thinking of the Rom clothing and his desire to wear them. Aye, wouldn't that startle the English when he and Finn rode across London Bridge?

Forgoing the urge to wear the uniform of the Gypsies, Declan slipped on a pair of dark wool pants, a shirt, and leather doublet. 'Twould be comfortable for the long ride and dark enough to hide them as they rode through the night.

He trotted down the stairs two at a time, eager to find Finn and head toward proving his innocence.

The clatter of dishes sounded from the direction of the kitchen. He grinned, more than ready to sate his hunger with a fine meal.

Declan pushed open the door and stilled.

Sadie Bannon was laying out food on the servant's table as if she did so every day. She obviously sensed his appearance and flashed him an all too knowing smile. "Glad to see you again, Lord Forrester."

He crossed his arms before his chest. "And what are you doing here, Sadie?"

She flashed him a grin. "'Tisn't the welcome I expected, but 'twill do."

"*Sadie.*"

She waved a hand at him and continued to fill cups with steaming tea. "Sit and eat. You've the look of a ghost about you."

He cocked a brow at her. "I'll not play these games with you. Where is Randolph?"

She wrinkled her brow and pouted. "I've worked hard to prepare a lovely meal for you. The least you can do is sit and enjoy it."

He took a step forward. "Where is Randolph?" he growled.

She sighed. "He rode out at sunset. Just barreled out of the barn and headed to the village."

Bollocks. Declan wiped his brow of sweat. Where the hell did Finn go?

"You have a choice, m'lord. Either you can sit yourself down and eat, or I can be making my way to the magistrate now ensconced in Trenmore's parlor for a morning respite. Now, won't you be choosing to stay?"

He observed the haughty tip of her chin and the flash of challenge in her gaze. Aye, she'd do it, blast her. For the moment he had no choice. At the first possible moment he'd be following Finn's path.

She hid her grin of satisfaction. Och, her plan was well on its way to fruition. Sadie watched Declan devour his meal as he glowered at her. Such a hot-blooded man. And so handsome. A shiver ran up her spine in anticipation of the evening she had sketched in her mind. Her, Declan, a fire and brandy. Then it would all fall into place.

"I'm leaving now," Declan said as he interrupted her pleasant musings. "You are to stay here as long as you wish. Don't follow me."

Sadie reached and patted his hand. "Now, now. Won't you be staying until I say otherwise?"

He scoffed and moved to leave the kitchen. "A wee lass such as yourself? How will you keep me here?"

She winked at him. "I've me ways, m'lord."

She watched as realization flashed harshly across his face. With one fell swoop, the food and plates on the table landed on the floor with a resonating crash at the sweep of his hand.

"Damn you, Sadie." He wobbled as he stood, just as she had planned.

"Tsk, tsk, Declan. Now just lean on me and we'll find a place for you to rest." She bore his weight as she lugged him toward the stairs. His body pitched forward, and she caught him before he landed on his handsome face. Declan stumbled and he was obviously barely conscious of his actions as a few guttural curses erupted from his mouth.

"Aye, m'lord, we'll be resting together soon."

Her words did not sooth him. Quite the opposite. He swaggered away from her, nearly pulling them down the unforgiving wood stairs.

Finally, Sadie thought with a sigh of relief, as they entered Declan's chamber. She nudged him onto the bed and swung his feet up. Removing his boots, she regarded his sleeping form. 'Twas good fortune she'd wrestled a sleep draught from the village doctor despite his reluctance. Her theatrics had served her well in the wake of Abigail's death. "Maybe I'm ready for the stage in Dublin," she said with a chuckle.

Removing as much clothing as she could manage, she covered Declan with the counterpane and then stripped down to her chemise and linen petticoat.

Feeling peckish, she made her way back to the kitchen for a light snack. She made certain she did not stand before windows, lest someone from the village detect her appearance. Not that many wandered near the house since Abigail's death and her father's quick retreat after he laid her to rest.

'Twas a shame to leave such a grand house unoccupied. Sadie strolled through the main hall and elegant dining room. Even her home couldn't compare to Riverton's size and carved woodwork. Aye, she'd look well as hostess of this estate. She deserved it, truly earned it.

Sadie finished a crumpet and took a last sip of tea before heading back up to Declan's chamber. Once there, she slipped into his bed and snuggled up to his muscular body. The heat of him warmed her instantly. She moved closer, roaming her hands over his hard muscles. Aye, he was a finely built man. In the morn, she'd present him with their deeds of the night, the passion they shared, and sweet love they made.

The honor she knew was deeply imbedded in him would warrant he marry her. Of that, she was certain.

Declan woke groggy, his head throbbing. He hadn't a megrim such as this since he arrived at the Gypsy camp. He rubbed his temples and wished for Anya's concoction to ease the pain. Reaching for a pillow to cover his face from the strong morning sun, his hand collided with a decidedly human body.

"Och, m'lord, 'tis a fine way to start the day."

He bolted upright, his head swimming at the effort. "*Bollocks.*"

"No need for that, Declan."

He glared at Sadie Bannon, freshly risen and wearing only a chemise.

Nay. He couldn't have.

She wagged a finger at him and in a light-hearted tone said, "Since we worked up such an appetite last night, I'll fix us breakfast."

Declan groaned. The last thing he remembered was eating with Sadie the day before. He couldn't remember anything after that. *Damn*, he wished Finn was here. Where the hell had his friend gone?

Knowing the mess wouldn't be sorted out with him still abed, Declan dressed and went to the kitchen. His rubbed his aching head and looked for a water picture to quench his thirst.

Sadie grinned as she moved away from the stove. "Ah, I see you've decided to join me."

As if he had any choice. "Tell me everything."

She flashed a feline smile as she set down a platter of biscuits. "'Twas pure bliss, to be sure. You were the most attentive lover."

He scoffed as a foreboding chill raised the hairs on his neck. He remembered nothing of the night—nothing. "You are a liar."

She frowned. "Nay, Declan. I speak the truth of it."

He pushed open the door that led to the estate's kitchen garden. Fresh air slapped him like a wave of cold water. He inhaled, trying to rid himself of the putrid feeling deep inside. He was certain he was rotting from the inside out, his gut clenched as beads of sweat dripped down his forehead and back.

"M'lord, your food grows cold," Sadie purred from behind him.

He ignored her and paced toward the stables. How, he questioned himself, could he have forsaken Martine by coupling with Sadie?

The image of Martine appeared before him, her face softly lit by candlelight. Her luxurious hair cascaded over her bare shoulders, teasing across her breast. He rubbed the back of his neck as Declan remembered his love and her wish he leave. He should have stayed, pleaded with her to see the sense of plan.

Sadie curled her hand over his shoulder and attempted to pull him toward her.

He remembered.

It flooded his mind with murky illusions. Sadie grinning across the table. Her proclamation they'd be together, him stumbling up the stairs, his vision blurred, his throat parched.

Declan turned to Sadie, his anger traveling as fast as an errant ember catches dry timber on fire. He clenched his fist at his side, wanting to pummel her for her deceit. "What did you do to me?"

The feigned innocence of her gaze incensed him further. He couldn't quell his fury. "Tell me," he demanded.

"Declan," she began as she stepped backward. "Don't ye see? We should be together."

"Me and *you*?" He sneered at her, his mouth a frown as tension ran its course through his body.

Her lip trembled. "Aye. I wanted you to see how we should be together."

"You drugged me?" he growled.

She paled a bit and tears filled her eyes. "Aye," whispered past her lips. "We did not . . . we . . . you were too drugged."

He slammed his fist against the side of the barn. "Damn you, Sadie."

She threw herself at him, wrapped him in an embrace so tight he was forced to struggle out of it.

He ripped Sadie's arms from their strangle hold around his neck.

"Go," he said as he pointed to the house. "Gather your things and go."

With steely determination, she straightened and made her way to the house. "The magistrate will hear about this, mark my word," she threatened as she paced away from him.

"I'm headed to the magistrate myself. I'll save you the trip." He entered the barn and began to ready Kindred for the ride to the village.

"That's my lad," he said to his steed as he brushed his coat to gleaming. The horse stomped in response, obviously eager to go for a ride.

As he hefted the saddle onto the stallion's back, an acrid smell drifted into the barn. He sniffed again and tossed the saddle aside.

He raced from the barn. Black smoke billowed from the estate. *Riverton.*

He picked up his pace, then broke into a run.

Riverton was ablaze.

'Twas a lost cause. Never could he stomp out the fire licking up the roof and lapping angrily out the windows.

A movement near the main entrance attracted his attention. He moved closer, then ran to the bottom of the steps.

Sadie Bannon stood just inside the door. A look of madness widened her eyes as she shook her fist at him. "'Tis mine, Declan. All mine."

He bound up the stairs and clutched the edge of her gown. She wrestled from him, delving into the pit of hell burning within the estate.

"Sadie," he yelled. She disappeared near his study. He ducked as a beam fell behind him. Smoke clogged his lungs and singed his eyes. Still, he searched for her. "Sadie!"

A flash of white near the kitchen lured him further into the inferno.

He wiped sweat from his brow and crouched close to the floor and continued. Coughing fiercely, he leapt over a hole burned into the floor. He entered the kitchen, yet there was no Sadie. *Bollocks*, where had the blasted woman gone? Beams crashed behind him, blocking his retreat to the front of the house. Declan skirted a flash of flames near the stove and broke through the garden door.

He rolled on the grass and vegetables, cooling his body and extinguishing sparks on his clothing. Sadie wasn't there.

He lifted from his knees and moved away from the burning building.

"What a lovely sight, to be sure."

He turned toward the voice. Sadie stood behind him, pistol drawn. Her dress was scorched along the hem and ashes smudged against her fair skin.

"Come, Declan."

"Put the gun down."

She shrugged, but wildness filled her eyes. "Now why would I be doing that?"

"You want me, so you have me." He kept his voice low, placating, as he slowly walked toward her.

"Aye, I have you, love. Not like Abigail, she couldn't handle a man such as you."

Her manic gaze darted between him and the direction of the village.

He held up his hand and spoke in a soft tone. "Abigail was your friend."

"Ha," she snorted. "She loved another and her father was poisoning you."

Declan furrowed his brow. Sadie had supported his wife while she lived. What had changed her mind? What? *Poisoned*? "Calm down and we'll talk."

"No," she said with an eerie, high pitch to her voice. She waved the gun toward him. "Don't move, Declan."

He had to defuse the situation. "Sadie, what did Abigail do to you?"

Her face lit up, and the waving gun stopped. "Why she stole you from me. Can't you see? We are made for each other."

The woman was daft. "I married Abigail in London. I didn't meet you until we arrived at Riverton."

As if sensing its name spoken, the west wall of the estate groaned and crumbled. The shattering clamor of broken glass mixed with the collapse of wood beneath the flames echoed across the yard.

Sadie didn't so much as blink. "Nay. Weren't ye always mine, now? She tried to take you away."

He rubbed the back of his neck. He had to move her toward the village and hopefully toward the magistrate. "You speak madness."

The manic gleam appeared once again in her eyes. "The villagers are coming. Quick, we must go."

He glanced over his shoulder. Aye, 'twas the truth of it. Anger and frustration snapped through him. "Only if you tell me everything."

She sighed and attempted to sweep her skirt clean of soot and ashes. "He planned to kill you."

Ettenborough? Declan scoffed. "Not possible."

Sadie laughed, a hollow, ear-piercing howl. "The elixir for your megrims was poison."

He was speechless. Nay. Even Ettenborough couldn't have been so mercenary.

"I see you don't believe me, you fool. But his blasted servant gave him the mixture. When you had megrims, he gave you more and more," her agitated voice skittered up his spine. "You see, don't you? The megrims were when the poison was wearing off. You were an addict."

Declan raked his fingers through his hair while trying to keep an eye on the crazed Sadie and the approaching villagers.

"Don't you believe me, my love?"

"Aye," he answered under his breath, still trying to absorb all that had happened. Could circumstances be any stranger?

Sadie cackled. "Ettenborough was trying to kill you and *his daughter* ended up dead." She shuffled a little jig with glee.

Declan took the opportunity and lunged at Sadie. She toppled to the ground. The gun landed several feet away from them.

"Nay," Sadie bellowed. "You're mine. Didn't I make sure she was out of the way?"

He grasped her shoulders and shook her. "You killed Abigail?"

She nodded and reached up and caressed his cheek. "We can wed. And we can have beautiful children."

Thunderous hoof beats echoed across the clearing, matching the rising chaos in his mind. Villagers now crowded behind them, their curiosity forcing them to close in, nearly sealing off any air. Declan tried to catch his breath, not sure of what to say as grief washed over him anew.

"Let her go," Trenmore Grey ordered as he pushed through the crowd.

"Nay," he said with a rasping voice. This woman had killed his wife. He was truly innocent.

"We heard what she said," one of the villagers yelled. "You can let her go."

He rose, emotions swimming in his mind and forming tears in his eyes. His wife had been murdered all for the obsession of one woman.

The waste devastated him.

He stumbled away from her. Trenmore leaned down and assisted Sadie to her feet. "That's it, my love. Just lean on me." His gentle tones soothed the crazed woman, who now resembled a child more than a murderer.

The magistrate, Martin Connelly, rode up on a huge gelding. "Grey, what the devil is going on?" The man dismounted from his horse and straightened his suit coat. He swaggered closer, a scowl on his face. "Is that you, Forrester?"

Declan nodded yet remained silent.

"Won't I be needing to talk with you?"

Again he nodded.

"'Twas Lady Bannon," someone in the crowd yelled. "She killed Lady Abigail."

Connelly cocked a bushy brow and looked pointedly at Trenmore Grey. "Is that the truth of it?"

Sadie leaned her head on Grey's shoulder and began to weep. "Aye, 'tis the truth," he replied.

The magistrate nodded to the men standing behind him. "To the gaol with her."

Grey held up his hand. "I'll take her if ye don't mind."

Connelly hesitated, then acquiesced with a shrugged of his broad shoulders.

The crowd followed Trenmore and a cowed Sadie as they slowly walked toward the village. Inquiring whispers reached Declan as he watched with a mix of anger and pity.

All he could think of was finding Martine. He turned and looked in the direction of the camp. Were they still there? Or had they moved once again in preparation for the marriage ceremony?

He was torn. Should he go to her now that he had been proven innocent of killing his wife? Or should he ferret out the truth of his incarceration first?

Glancing quickly at the villagers still making their way to the gaol, he turned back to the woods—to Martine.

He was going after her.

Chapter 16

He grabbed Kindred, threw on a bridle, and leapt onto his bare back.

They raced toward the clan's camp. Declan heart swelled with eagerness to find her. Find the love of his life.

A steady rain began. A slight tug on the reins and his steed slowed to a walk. He lifted his head toward the sky and allowed the water to wash over him. Aye, he felt alive.

"Declan."

He opened his eyes and couldn't believe the sight before him. There she stood—his love—his angel.

Within a moment he'd slipped from Kindred's back and was running toward her. All he could think was to have her in his arms.

"Martine," he said as he kissed all over her face.

She laughed and pulled him closer. He lifted her and swirled her around. Happiness filled him so much he almost didn't recognize the emotion. Aye, he'd been content in the past, but never filled with . . . joy.

He cupped her face with his hands and soaked in the sight of her. He'd missed her beyond measure. And God she was lovely.

"I like this better," he said as he shifted his fingers through her auburn tresses.

She tipped up her chin at him. "Me too."

He captured her lips in a long, searing kiss. The rain washed over them as each grappled to get closer, tighter against each other. Her mouth opened to accept him as he circled his tongue around hers. He splayed his hand against her back, supporting her, loving the feel of her beneath his touch. Their bodies melded into one. Her every curve was cradled against him, incensing him with desire.

Martine caressed the back of his neck, warming his skin ah, he loved her touch, soft as a feather, then more insistent.

He raked his gaze over her. She wore red from head to toe. Her wedding attire.

His heart nearly stopped. "Please tell me you didn't wed Magor."

"Nay, I did not."

Never had he been so relieved. "Come with me."

She glanced at the woods beyond the narrow stream as she bit her lip. He could sense her wavering and pressed on. "We can leave Ireland. No one will look for us."

Anguish creased her beautiful face. "My family."

He rested his forehead against hers. "We can create our own."

"I am Rom."

"You are English," he said fiercely.

"Anya," she whispered as tears shimmered anew in her eyes.

Aye, he'd miss her as well, but he knew deep down she'd support their union. "She wishes us well, I'm certain."

Martine nodded as she sniffled. "She does wish us well."

His heart pounded as his blood sang through his veins. "You'll stay with me?"

She nodded as a smile filled her face. "I am sorry I deceived you. I couldn't hurt the clan that saved my life."

He kissed her brow. "Rafe shared the story. I understand." He squeezed her against him, just to prove she was real. "What did Magor say?"

She shuddered. "I'm not certain. I left before the ceremony." She pulled back and looked up at him. "I'm surprised we can't hear my brother screaming from here."

"Aye. I'm sure he's angry with you and me."

"No matter. Linka's daughter will replace me. 'Tisn't as if it was a love match. Just a joining of clans." The bitterness in her words caused him to frown.

"I have deceived you as well." His gut clenched as he thought about what he had to share. His life had been filled with hatred and turmoil. He'd hate for any of that to affect the woman he loved.

She looked up at him. Her eyes wide and lovely, filled with compassion and love. "You are innocent. I know it in my heart."

He pulled back. "How long have you known?" Sweat coated his back as he thought of her knowing he was accused of murdering his wife.

"Rafe told me yesterday and I knew you were innocent. I told him as much."

He cradled her cheek with his hand. "My love, I *am* innocent. Sadie Bannon is on her way to the gaol as we speak." He kissed her, drawing her in deep.

As he kissed along her silky jaw she said, "Ask me again."

"What?" he murmured against her neck, gaining a shiver as she gripped onto his shoulders.

"To be your wife," she whispered as he tilted her face up so he could look directly into her eyes.

He grinned. "I want you to be mine. But I have to ensure we will be safe. There are matters I must settle in London. When I do, will you marry me?"

"Aye, Declan Forrester, I'll be yours." But a troubled furrow formed between her brows.

He tipped up her chin. "What is it my love?"

"I have left my clan to be with you. But what are we to do now? I'm no longer accepted by the Rom, and the people of your village will not accept me."

He thought for a moment. They both searched for things that may be impossible to find. Innocence and acceptance. "My love, you will be accepted. I promise you. You will be Lady Forrester."

She rolled her eyes heavenward and he chuckled. Still the doubt in her mind showed through her eyes as they darkened with uncertainty. What he wouldn't do to ease her fears.

He wrapped his arm around her shoulders and together they walked back to Riverton. There he'd prepare for their departure to London. If they made haste, they'd be fast on Finn's heels.

"I need to find out why I was imprisoned, Martine." God, he hoped this wouldn't change her mind. "Without knowing who worked against me, we'll never be safe, and I wouldn't do that to you or our children."

She grasped his hand. "Declan, I will stand by you. I will help you."

What had he done to deserve such devotion? He swung her into an embrace. "I love you. When I thought I'd never see you again, it nearly killed me."

Tears shimmered in her eyes, making them glisten like precious brilliant stones. "Aye, and I love you."

She narrowed her gaze and pointed to the north. "What is that?" Martine asked.

"Riverton," he said with little emotion. While his life in Ireland had saved him from a terrible fate, now he would be tied to something owned by Ettenborough.

Her eyes widened as she gasped. "Your estate? You've lost everything."

"Nay," he said as he shook his head. "All I need is here in my arms."

They stayed in the barn, refusing the comfort and speculation of the villagers. The night air meshed with ash and loam as it curled around them with the moistness known to Ireland. Martine snuggled next to him, her shallow breaths telling him she was asleep.

He'd have to talk of his imprisonment—of that he was certain. And if she forgave him, forgave his numerous sins, then he'd be a happy man. Declan had no doubt the priest in London would wed them once he learned all of his past.

Would she have him, he worried? Could she forsake the fact that he'd been imprisoned and truly was a murderer?

He pulled his arm out from beneath her and laid her sleeping form back onto the blanket. The cushion of straw helped ease the harshness of the ground, but his body still betrayed him with stiffness. Declan stretched as he walked out of the barn and into the night. His back ached as it had since prison. Another souvenir he had to remind himself of his hell on earth.

He continued toward the house, now a pile of ashes and charred boards. Nothing was left of his life at Riverton. 'Twas as he wished it, yet he'd never thought it would be so unbelievably final.

And Abigail. How had she felt when Sadie had drawn the knife across her throat? Knowing the woman she claimed as friend had turned into a foe. His stomach clenched as he thought of his wife. He kicked a smoking board as he drew his fingers through his hair. Damn, he still didn't have the answers, only a few explanations, but still gaping holes remained. It nagged him so, the fear of the unknown. And maybe the fact he might not want to know the past and how it affected him now and in the future.

Declan turned toward the direction of the village. Candlelight flickered in some windows, while others remained as dark as the night. He rubbed the back of his neck, wanting to ride to the magistrate and demand he give him all the answers he sought.

"Declan?"

Martine wrapped her arms around him from behind. He caressed her hands clasped about his waist. Her head rested against his back and the very essence of her, rose and lavender, immediately calmed him.

"I'm sorry I woke you."

"You didn't," she said. "I missed you, 'tis all."

He pulled her around to face him and tipped her chin up. The moon haloed her face with an amber glow, etching her beauty so lovingly, it took his breath away. "I have something to tell you."

She tensed. How could she not? So much had already happened and now he was going to add to the turmoil. Declan butted his forehead against Martine's and sighed. He waited a moment, reveling in her presence and how he loved her.

"You know I was in prison."

She pulled back and looked deeply into his eyes. "Aye." Confusion filled her gaze, yet she remained silent.

He inhaled, then spoke. "I was in Newgate in London. I spent five years in hell until Abigail's father wagered for my release."

Tension shifted through her body. "Why?" she said with a raspy voice.

He shrugged, sorrow filling him as the pain of his time in prison resonated. "I don't know."

Her brow rose in question. "How can that be?"

He clasped her hand and they began to walk toward the barn. "It has to do with my father, Ettenborough, and a man named Broderick. I have been searching for the truth for years."

She clung tighter to him. "Oh, Declan, how you have suffered."

The concern, not pity, flowed through her words. Och, he hated to upset her further, but he must tell her everything. "Martine," he began, "I am not proud of my behavior, to be sure. But life in prison—"

She placed her finger over his lips, silencing him. "You don't need to tell me more."

He shook his head. "Nay. I must tell you everything. I want you to be certain you want to marry me."

A smile filled her face and humor glimmered in her brown eyes, lightening them to cognac. "I don't scare that easily, Lord Forrester."

He scoffed and hugged her tighter. "Just Declan."

"Och, the shame of it all. And me wanting to be a lady all these years."

Her laughter was contagious and he found himself chuckling along with her. Declan swooped her into his arms and captured her lips with a deep kiss. She infused him with goodness and he greedily took it from her.

A sobering thought stopped him. She was a lady. 'Twas the truth of it. Would she want to seek her inheritance? Become ensconced in the *ton*. God save him if she did.

"Martine, your family—do you want to see them?"

Shadows darkened her gaze. "Nay," she said barely above a whisper. "They are not my family."

"But your inheritance—"

She gave an angry shake of her head. "Nay, I have no interest in the money."

God, she was a unique woman. "I love you."

She grinned, an expression that chased away the shadows, hurt and pain. "Aye, and I love you."

A horse neighed, startling them from their embrace.

"It seems as if the big mon has found a way to distract himself."

Nate swung down from his horse and patted Declan on his back. Lange and Pierce did the same. Matthew stayed astride, his gregarious smile visible even in the darkness.

"We've been waiting for the dust to clear, so to speak," Pierce said as he hugged Declan. "Oh, sorry, m'lord." He swept Declan's shirt free of wrinkles as he was wont to do when he worked in the house. "Grand. All set now."

Declan chuckled and patted his valet. "Not to worry, Pierce."

He bobbed his head as the other men stared at Martine.

They were huge, all except the one he called Pierce. Rough and a bit ragged, she witnessed camaraderie among them that made Declan seem less the solitary man. She liked the warmth, the softening of his stance.

She watched silently as the men inspected her. Wariness, some primal predatory reaction, she supposed. Declan was their leader after all and here she was distracting him.

"This is Martine," Declan finally said. The men tipped their heads toward her. Only one reached out to take her hand.

She wondered if Declan had purposely left out her surname. Petrulengo was Rom. Was he acting as if she wasn't Rom? Did he think if he didn't mention it, others would accept her?

Not that the men would run into many a lass called Martine.

"I'm Nate," the man with a reddish mop of hair said. She could discern he was from Scotland; his brogue was thick, yet friendly.

She accepted his hand, trying not to be intimidated by the brawn of the man.

Declan stepped closer and eased an arm around her shoulder. "Where is Finn?"

"He sent us back in case ye decided to follow him."

He shook his head. "The bastard took off before the sun rose."

"Don't be vexed," Nate said. "He did what was best. Broderick wouldna speak if ye were there as well."

Declan grunted. Martine stifled laughter at the disgruntled look on his face. He looked toward her, and her heart turned as his ire melted into a charming grin. "Men," he said, "I'll speak with you in the morn. As you can see, the house is gone. Make yourselves comfortable in the barn or in the village at the pub."

"Aye, the pub will suit us." Nate mounted his horse and saluted Declan before leading the animal and the men toward the village.

She was sad to see them go. She wanted to learn as much about Declan as possible and it appeared as if these men were a huge chunk of his life. One he hadn't shared with her. Pah. Men weren't chatters like women. They didn't gossip around the dinner pot or mending circle. He'd tell her, of that she was certain.

After all the men had mounted their horses and left the estate, Declan led her into the barn. He adjusted the blanket that served as a makeshift bed and beckoned her to lie upon it. She fell into the straw that made the mattress and sunk into the heat of him. The sheer size of him against her made her feel safe. Martine blessed her luck and snuggled even closer. A possessive arm wrapped around her. Safe, lovingly, and perfect.

It was as if Declan had taken a key and, with the slightest twist, opened her heart and mind. He gave her the courage, or at least made her aware she was brave enough, to leave the Rom. 'Twas perhaps the hardest decision she'd ever made. And she still missed her grandmother with a fierceness that overshadowed her current happiness.

Declan kissed her brow and whispered goodnight. She sighed, content to be in his arms, and fell asleep to the rhythm of his breathing as if it paced her heart.

Chapter 17

In the distance a cock crowed. Martine rubbed the sleep from her eyes and groaned as she sat up. She quickly inspected the barn and Declan was nowhere to be found. She rose and swept her skirt free of straw.

The acrid scent of ashes still lathed the air, oppressively so. Martine frowned as she searched the yard for Declan. Had he already gone to meet with his men? Surely he'd tell her. Her heart began to race as she ran behind the ruin of the house, then to the side garden. No horses, no men, no Declan.

She ran back to the stables, panicked and out of breath. Tears clogged the back of her throat as she gazed over the horizon. The empty landscape hastened her fear.

Had his past returned? Had they taken him from her?

Had he left her? Did he realize she'd never be accepted? No matter she wasn't of Rom blood, she'd lived with them, adopted their traditions, embraced their way of life. He must have determined she'd be too much trouble.

Dear God, what was she to do now?

"What news did you bring?" Declan paced the small room on the second floor of the pub. Nate, Lange, Matthew, and Pierce all gathered at the table breaking their fast and telling of their travels.

Nate shrugged. "Randolph didn't reveal much, the bastard. All he said was tae make sure ye dinna follow him. He was going to break Broderick and force him to tell all."

Declan raked his fingers through his hair. "There has to be more to it, man." Frustration had him refusing the coffee that Lange offered.

"We must go to London."

Nate nodded. "Aye, 'tis his plan, ye big *amandon*. He knew ye wouldna be able to stay here."

"And what of your lady?" Matthew asked. "Will she be going with us?"

Declan pinned the young man with a glare. "And why wouldn't she be? She's to be my wife."

Nate put his hand on Matthew's arm. "Och, now, Declan. The lad meant no harm. 'Tis just concern for her safety."

Matthew nodded his head. "Aye, that's it."

He looked out the window, toward Riverton, and thought of all he'd lost in his life and how, at this moment, it didn't matter. He had Martine. She didn't care he'd been to prison. Nay, she loved him regardless, and that was the gift she'd given him.

"I'll return later."

The men made some disparaging remarks, in good humor of course. He rode Kindred back to Riverton as if his life depended on it.

"Martine!" he called as he entered the yard at a fast canter. He leapt off his horse's back and just released the reins. Kindred snorted as he began to eat the ample grass before him.

He ran into the barn. Weeping drew him to the stall they'd slept in the night before. Martine sat, knees drawn toward her chest.

"Martine," he said as he wrapped his arms around her. "What happened?"

She looked to him, her eyes widened like those of a startled doe. "*Declan*." She clutched his hand. "I thought they'd taken you, and then I thought you'd left me."

"Nay, my love," he said as he kissed her. "I was meeting with my men. I left a note."

Her eyes widened as he reached by the blanket and retrieved the note.

She shook her head and a crooked grin pulled at her mouth. "I kept thinking," she said between tears, "that I'd have to go back and marry Magor."

"Never," he growled. No man but him would ever have her. He tipped up her chin. "Tell me. What made you come to Riverton?"

She wiped at her tears with the back of her hand. She inhaled and quickly tipped her head to the side. "My grandmother brought my wedding dress to my wagon."

She stopped and looked at him. Her pleading gaze almost stopped him from probing further. Curiosity and the basic need to know won out as he questioned her once again. "I need to know you came to me of your own accord."

"Pah, it would be no other way." A hint of laughter eased some of his worry. "'Tis red," she said as she fingered the material of her skirt.

"Isn't that the custom?" Declan attempted to hold in his chuckle but failed.

Martine playfully slapped at him. "'Tis tradition if you're still a maiden. All brides long to wear red." She wiped the corner of her eye free of tears. "Anya asked me if I could wear it or had I lost the right."

Declan sobered. Anya, who had once championed him, had forced Martine's hand in the matter of her honor.

She waved at him as if reading his thoughts. "She knew before I could tell her. I've no doubt of that. And I couldn't lie to her."

He gripped her shoulders. "Look at me," he demanded. "We have nothing to be ashamed of. We *love* each other. And we'll be married." He prayed soon because it would mean he'd discovered why he was sent to prison.

She caressed his face with her hands. "I couldn't stay and wed Magor. I know I've left my brother in a horrid position.

I'll never see my grandmother again, even if I wanted to. It wouldn't be allowed."

He hated the sadness overshadowing her features. "I understand your sacrifice." How he wanted to challenge Rafe for the position he'd forced on Martine. 'Twas his actions and decisions forcing tears to swim in her gaze.

"Nay. 'Tis not a sacrifice." She turned away and gnawed on her lip. "It was my choice. I was ready to make it. I needed to make it."

Although her words were softly spoken, they calmed his rising fear that she hadn't come of her own volition.

"I knew I had to find you. I would have searched all through Ireland to find you."

He smiled at her honesty. "'Tis lucky I was still at Riverton."

She stood and held out her hand to him. "Aye. I knew you were." She playfully slapped at him. "I didn't know your estate had burned to the ground and you'd found the woman who killed your wife."

He stilled, not yet ready to deal with Sadie Bannon and the horror she wrought.

Martine brought her hand to her mouth. "Declan, 'tis sorry I am to have ever mentioned it."

He rose and they walked out of the stable. They'd have to find proper lodgings after they wed, and it was odd he would think that at this moment. "Nay," he said as he shook his head.

She scowled and her fist clenched. "'Tis no matter now."

He called to Kindred. "Aye, you've the right of it. I am no longer suspected of killing my wife. We will travel to London, and there we'll wed." He looked into her eyes, soft brown and full of compassion. "Without knowing who sent me to prison we will never have peace."

A frightened look furrowed her brow and she chewed on her lip once again. "What priest will marry us? I'm Rom."

"You're English." He grabbed the reins from the ground and held them tight.

She scoffed. "I've lived with the Rom longer than anywhere else. The way I talk, the way I dress, all say Rom."

"Father Anthony will marry us," Declan said with conviction. "He's the priest near my home in London."

She looked uncertain, but she accepted his help onto Kindred's back regardless. Declan whispered a prayer as he leapt into the saddle that his absence at mass wouldn't cause the priest to punish him. Of course, a few pounds in the offering cup would go far to soothe the man. Luckily his money was kept safe in a metal box the fire wasn't able to breach. And he had other resources in London.

As they made their way to the village, they drew the attention of those working the fields or herding sheep. Some called to Declan in an attempt to show support. Probably feeling guilty over the day they tried to lynch him. Martine rode stiffly in front of him, her body tense. He patted her hand. "We'll be fine. Don't worry."

Martine looked down at her clothing. "I must clean up."

She still wore her red wedding gown. Declan looked at her and saw nothing but beauty. The gown's full sleeves drew tight at the wrist and lace edged the neckline hiding her ample cleavage. He wouldn't change a thing, but he realized the wrinkles and tears bothered Martine.

He gazed down at her. Even though she'd spent the night in a barn, she looked truly magnificent. The dormant sun flickered through cloud cover and shone over her luminous skin. Her thick hair teased over her shoulders, infused with brandy highlights. He wanted to bury his face in its softness and inhale the scent of her. A swift shot of lust tightened his loins. *Bollocks*, she was lovely.

She tipped her head up to him as a quizzical look raised her brow. "Why are you grinning so?"

"Because you are so beautiful."

She swatted at him. "Pah, don't you think compliments will win me over."

"Do you mean I haven't won you yet? Now I've more work to do." He kissed the tip of her straight nose.

Martine laughed. A musical twinkle that went straight to his heart. Pure, lovely, her. He wiped the back of his neck as he wondered at his winsome thoughts. *Bollocks*, not only was she bewitching, she'd bewitched him.

He steered Kindred farther into the village and straight towards Finnian's Pub. 'Twas the cleanest and friendliest. Details Martine was sure to appreciate. Again, villagers' attention sought them. Instead of the vulnerable woman who'd just ridden past farmers, Martine's spine was straight and her chin thrust a notch higher than usual. He was proud of her.

"Stay here while I arrange for rooms," he directed.

She glanced about the walkway and at the people completing their errands. Her chin trembled a wee bit, then she squared her shoulders and nodded.

Declan walked into the pub and stood in the doorway. He inhaled the aroma of ale and smoke and the underlying scent of stew bubbling in a pot. After surveying the main floor, he almost left in search of something more suitable. Knowing full well that nothing existed, he walked toward the bar area and flipped a coin to the bartender.

"I need two rooms."

The barkeep continued to clean a glass and didn't even glance at the money on the scarred wooden bar. He jerked his head toward the stairs and a withered-looking woman standing at the landing. "She'll see to ye, m'lord."

He knew this would happen. With Abigail gone and Ettenborough back in London, his authority over the villagers and tenants was gone. The man hadn't even looked at him. Lord knew who Ettenborough had decided to put in charge, but he was certain 'twasn't him.

Declan approached the woman who looked more worn than his saddle. She hobbled up the stairs and opened the first door on the left. He entered the room and felt assured 'twas clean and roomy enough for Martine. The second chamber was much of the same and he told the woman he'd take them. "Make sure water is brought up for my lady's bath."

"Reggie won't be likin' that, I tell ye."

Declan ran his fingers through his hair. "I'm paying more than enough for these rooms. Now see to the water."

She headed back down the stairs, talking to herself the entire way. Daft, 'twas no other explanation.

He shrugged and went back down to fetch Martine. While she bathed, he'd visit some shops and purchase new clothing for her to wear as they traveled.

She was still on Kindred when he came back down, eyes wide and bright. Kindred's nostrils flared.

As he exited the pub, he saw what had them so nervous. A few men had surrounded the horse, taunting Martine.

"Aye, look what we have here."

The other men chuckled and moved in closer.

"Quite the beaut." He laughed. "The horse, not the Gypsy."

Rage shot through his veins. "*Step away.*"

The men looked to him.

"I saw her first," one said.

Declan quickly glanced at Martine. She looked to the ground, her face ashen. He must get her to safety, far away from the strangers. "Step away from my betrothed."

Metal scraped as one of the men pulled a knife from its hardened leather sheath.

"Put your weapon away," Declan warned as he reached for Kindred's reins.

He sensed his men arriving before they were visible to the men harassing Martine. With a quick grin, he pulled back and punched the man holding the knife.

The weapon clattered against the rocky road.

"Grrahhh!"

Chaos ensued.

Nate and Pierce flanked one man. Matthew and Lange wrestled another.

Declan threw Kindred's reins to Martine. "Go," he yelled as he turned and punched another ruffian. The man lunged. Declan landed against the ground. He scrambled up, feinted right, and released a punch. The ruffian landed on the ground out cold.

"Lads, 'tis enough."

The magistrate, Connelly, had arrived.

"He punched Paddy, he did."

Declan wiped the back of his neck and released a sigh. He scanned the horizon to see where Martine had fled. *Damn*, he didn't see her.

"The men were harassing my betrothed." He said, no longer caring about the men, his concern solely fixated on Martine.

"We were just being friendly like."

He scoffed and the rest of his men gathered close as a united front of intimidation.

"Gather your friend," Connelly said. "I'll take care of them, m'lord."

The men looked at him and blanched. "We didn't know he was a lord."

The magistrate shoved the men toward the jail, grumbling the entire way.

"Where is Martine?"

Little came around the corner, leading Kindred.

Declan breathed a sigh of relief as his gaze settled on his betrothed. Thank God she wasn't hurt.

She slipped off his steed's back and raced toward him. He held her tight in his embrace and kissed her head as she shook. "You're safe, my love."

She pulled back, tears glistening in her eyes. Deep pools of brown gazed at him, pulled at his heart. Not only fear lingered in her eyes, but anger as well.

"Now do you think London will accept me?" The anger shimmered through her tears, fiery hot. "See how they treat your Gypsy fiancé? English women do not have tanned skin. They do not speak with my accent. They are not called Martine. They will all know I am Rom."

He cupped her cheek. "You will be my wife. A few ill-mannered ruffians won't change that." He ran his thumb over her lips. "I love you."

She snuggled into his hand. But he saw the doubt that flared in her eyes, the slight flare of her nose. It killed him to see her so uncertain, so fearful.

"They will never accept me. How can I do that to you? To us?"

Dread punched him in the gut. He kissed her forehead. "I have faith in us."

She shook her head while tears raced down her face.

"A bath is being drawn for you, m'lady."

A small smile quirked her mouth, even as tension tightened her shoulders. "Och, thank you. I feel as if I hadn't bathed in months."

Declan chuckled. "This way." He nodded thank you to his men. They saluted and went about their business. He'd have to check with the magistrate to ensure the men were sent on their way.

As they entered the pub, the establishment went silent. Martine ducked her gaze, knowing full well she was the cause of the silence. Dear God, it shamed her to be treated as those men treated her, to be glared at by the people in the pub.

"Ye can be staying. But her," the barkeep said as he pointed at her, "will have to leave."

Declan drew up and glared at the man. "Tell me, old man, do you wish to die today?"

The man blanched and the lump in his throat bobbed up

and down. His gazed raked over Martine in her red dress. "I'll not have a damn Gypsy in me pub."

Declan rested his elbow on the bar and lifted his boot onto the brass footrest. "You'll provide a room for my betrothed." He spoke low but with an undisguised growl. "Do we understand each other, old man?"

The barkeep nodded and picked up a glass. He must have decided Declan needed reassurance, because the glass was soon filled with frothy ale.

Never had she felt so humiliated. She felt rooted to the dusty, wooden planks of the floor, unable to force herself forward or back.

Surely Declan would see the errors of his ways and decide he couldn't marry someone who would never be accepted into his society. She felt the interest of every man in the pub, disgust and mistrust. No matter she wasn't truly a Gypsy. The villagers didn't know she was English—they saw only the brightly colored clothing, tanned skin and heard her accent, thick and foreign.

They saw Rom.

Martine tugged on Declan's elbow. "Let's leave." The begging tone of her voice shamed her. Where did her courage flee to? Even more degrading was the fact the barkeep and everyone in the pub seemed to agree with her.

He took a long draw from the ale. "Nay. Go and bathe." He drummed his fingers on the bar. "I'll purchase a traveling costume."

He placed his hand at the small of her back, offering an encourage smile. "Go, 'tis safe."

She tried to smile at him, but she knew her mouth didn't form more than a straight line. With trembling fingers, she gripped the railing to the stairs and began walking up one step at a time. She could feel the scrutiny of the pub's patrons as if they were burning holes through her back with their intense stares.

Just as she also knew Declan was there and wouldn't allow harm to come to her.

As she reached the door, she heard Declan leave and wanted to run back down the stairs and cling to him. No, she chastised herself, I'm a Petrulengo, or at least was raised as one. Rise above. Martine straightened her spine and continued through the door, refocused and determined not to allow the villagers to strip her of her dignity.

The chamber was clean and warmed by a small fire in the hearth. A small bath sat in the center and beckoned to her like a sweet. She shut the door and began to undress. When she spied a linen towel and a chunk of soap, she almost squealed with glee.

A knock on the door stilled her actions. Cautiously she put her ear to the wood. "Who's there?"

"'Tis me, m'lady. Ruth, the chamber maid."

Martine sighed, rebuttoned her blouse, and opened the door. "Come in."

The stooped woman struggled with a steaming bucket of water.

"Let me help you." Martine relieved Ruth of the cumbersome bucket and set it on a stool near the tub.

The woman ducked her head. "'Tis for rinsing."

Martine touched her arm and said, "Thank you for bringing the water. I've been dreaming of a bath for several days."

"Aye, 'tis been quite the time ye had at Riverton. That crazy Sadie is being taken care of, more's the pity. She was a fine tipper, that one."

Not knowing how to reply, Martine absently straightened the coverlet on the bed. She didn't want to talk about Lady Bannon. She wanted to forget the loathsome acts the woman had perpetrated.

"Listen to me chatting like a hen. Me Joseph always says I don't ken when to quit."

Martine smiled. "No matter. I'll take my bath now."

The older woman bobbed her head and ducked out of the room. Before she closed the door, she said, "I'll be sending a meal up for you and the fine lord."

"Thank you." She didn't know why, but a nervous tremor clenched her stomach. She was to be married to Declan. Something she never hoped to dream of and now it was coming true. Oh to have her grandmother here to witness the event. Martine rubbed her eyes to stop the winsome tears clogging her vision. She sniffled and then began to undress once again. With a second thought, she put a spindly-back chair beneath the doorknob to ensure there would be no more interruptions.

She slipped into the tub and sighed. 'Twas glorious. The heat, scented soap, and just getting the grime from her body. She nearly fell asleep she soaked so long. After lathering her hair, she rinsed with clean water and began drying off.

"Martine," a voiced called between banging on the door. "Let me in."

She wrapped the towel around her still-damp body and removed the chair from before the door. "'Tis open," she called as she moved into the protective shadows of the room.

Declan entered with packages overloading his arms. "I've bought the stores out."

"Aye, I can see." His generosity warmed her. Pah, what sentimentality. Still, the girlish side of her nature was thrilled to be wearing stylish clothing. Her brother would seethe if he saw her in the dress of the Irish. And since she was still peevish when it came to him, it brought a wee bit of satisfaction that she'd done as she pleased instead of bowing to Rafe's wishes.

"Come closer," he said as he crooked his finger at her. "I have another surprise."

Curious, Martine came forward as she attempted to guess what his surprise might be. Not that he needed to give more to her. He'd already saved her from a hellish marriage and made her heart fuller than she'd ever imagined. He set down the packages and pulled her into his chest. She caught her breath, then released it as she looked into his loving eyes. They darkened to a deep midnight blue as his gaze roamed over her face.

Declan smoothed her hair back and his fingers tangled into the wet curls. He tugged her head back and kissed her thoroughly. She returned the kiss in kind as heat coiled within the pit of her stomach. She sank further into his embrace and wrapped her arms around his neck. As she did so, the towel slipped to the floor in a puddle at her feet. Cool air hit her skin as internal heat surged within with a provocative decadence. Declan's hands roamed her body, a soft touch with slightly abrasive hands. Her heart beat fast against her chest, pushing her to open her mouth to his demanding tongue.

"No," he said breathlessly. "After we wed." He rested his forehead on hers. His hand slipped behind her neck, warm and protective.

"You're a good man, Declan Forrester." She rose up on her tiptoes and gently kissed him on the lips. "'Tis why I'm marrying you."

His mouth tilted into a cocky grin and then he started opening all of the packages. "This," he said while holding up a lovely rose-colored skirt, "is for you."

She accepted the skirt and held it up to herself to check the fit, not caring a whit she was naked. She wasn't surprised when it appeared to be the perfect length. He followed suit with several blouses, waistcoats, and under garments.

With a twinkle in his eye, he said, "I've saved the best for last." He opened a large box and unfolded a deep sapphire blue gown.

The luxurious fabric tempted her fingers and she slid them down the silk. He held it up and mockingly pretended to waltz around the room with the gown draped before him.

Martine laughed and hugged him. "'Tis elegant, to be sure. And such a grand shade of blue to match your eyes."

"'Tis your wedding dress."

"Blue?" she said as she caressed the fabric once again.

He cocked a brow. "You were going to wear a red dress, were you not?"

She shrugged. "Aye, I was." 'Twas true, but Martine wasn't sure how she was feeling. Homesickness. That was the answer. She tipped up her face and said, "I'll take my dress, if you please."

Declan handled it to her. As she stepped to retrieve it, he wrapped his arms around her and just stared into her eyes. "I've another gift."

She swatted at him. Never had she had this much attention before—the gifts, his loving words. "You'll spoil me."

"'Tis my right." He reached into his pocket and took out a slim box.

Martine glanced at him, then back at the box. She untied the white ribbon and opened the lid. A golden band, etched with scrolling filigree, nestled in silk and sparkled with a large red stone. She touched the cool metal as she marveled at the ring's beauty. Anticipation swirled within her stomach and tears overflowed her lashes. 'Twas the most precious item she'd ever seen.

Declan lifted the ring from the box and went down on one knee. She gasped as he slipped the ring on her finger. "Be mine forever, Martine. Tell me you will."

She brought her free hand to her chest and said, "Aye, I will."

He stayed silent, his firm jaw making his face appear hard as granite.

"Declan, is something wrong?" Panic surged through her. Did he change his mind?

"Nay." His voice rasped the word. "I'm proud to have you as my wife." He lifted from his kneeling position and brought her hand to his lips. "You're my treasure, my life."

Her heart missed a beat at the vehemence of his words. Never had she felt so wanted and accepted.

"Get dressed, woman. You're too tempting to be sure."

She nodded, too touched for words. She pledged she'd never shame him, never allow those in London to know she was Rom.

From this day forward, she was English.

Chapter 18

She watched Declan rise and begin to dress and ready for their departure to England. Och, her head hurt as she thought of the voyage and then landing in a land so foreign to her. No matter, her betrothed's body garnered her attention as he shucked his clothing unaware of her perusal. He was an excellent example of manhood. Broader of shoulder than most Rom men, taller, and with a rugged handsomeness that pleased her beyond comparison. His muscles rippled and bunched as he moved, strong, powerful. Pah, she was like a love-sick cow.

The only sour note was the band of scars across his back. Stark white against his tanned skin, they stood out horribly. It sickened her to think of the pain he endured.

He turned and noticed her watching. A cocksure grin creased his face, then concern shone as he approached. "Why are you troubled, my love?" He knelt beside her and pulled her into his arms.

She shook her head. "'Twas nothing," she said softly as she dressed.

Doubt in his eyes told her he didn't believe her. "Right. If you wish to tell me later, feel free."

Martine rested her hand on his forearm. "Tell me of your time in prison."

He looked at her, his gaze unreadable, as if he shuttered any emotion from her. He sighed, then uttered a curse. "'Tisn't pretty." He pulled on his breeches, yet remained shirtless.

"I know," she said softly as she ran a finger along his back.

Declan made himself comfortable by leaning back on his elbows as he lay beside Martine. He stared at the ceiling, wishing she'd change her mind about learning of his horrid past. The shame of it all returned to him, quick and painful. He grimaced at remembering his time in prison, the smell of rotting flesh. The value of life so poor that many killed for a meager bowl of gruel.

He'd killed for a meager bowl of gruel.

Once again he looked to Martine. The early morning light caressed her, making her more lovely than he'd ever imagined. She sat patiently, her large eyes filled with compassion. He knew he had to tell her, but the urge to tuck the toxic memories away tempted him.

"They came for me. My father's colleagues and the magistrate."

She nodded her encouragement and gave a slight smile. God, he loved this woman.

He looked out the window and watched a bank of clouds shift its shape through the sky. The distraction failed. He leaned forward and draped his arm over a bent knee. "They arrested me. Treason, they said." He shrugged. "But 'twas a lie."

She leaned up. Concern narrowed her eyes. "And your father? What did he do?"

Declan gave a bitter laugh. "He sat in his chair and watched." It felt odd talking to her about his past. As if he were talking about someone other than himself. Yet the more he spoke, the more his soul felt purged of its demons.

Martine gasped. "He didn't try to save you?"

"Nay." The word dragged out of him like a knife through a fish's gullet.

Tears glistened in her eyes. Bright, sympathetic. He was certain she was hurting nearly as much as he was.

With a wry grin, he said, "If it eases your heart any, he died after my trial."

The tears fell, racing down her cheeks in shiny rivulets. "And your mother?"

Darkness consumed him. "I barely knew her."

She gasped. "Oh, Declan."

Her sympathy almost undid him. Instead of succumbing to his desire to rage about his past, he inhaled and continued to speak. "When she died, my father became my enemy."

"I barely remember my mother or father," she said with a hitch in her voice. "My past is a faded memory."

He reached for her hand. "I know, lass. I know."

She gave a sad smile, one filled with memories and hope. "I remember bits and pieces. My mother's hair was almost the same color as mine. My father was tall with a grayish beard. Sometimes I hear a voice that I'm certain is his. Wishful, I know."

He brushed away the tears on her cheeks. "We're a damn sorry lot."

"Tell me more," she urged.

He shrugged. "I lived in the hell of prison all the while wanting to die. Then Lord Ettenborough arranged for me to leave."

She fingered his hand, tracing his thumb, along his palm and around his wrist. He knew she meant to soothe him, but the soft movements inflamed him.

"And the marks on your back?"

Desire doused, he answered her. "In prison, 'twas the guards' duty to keep us in our place. Or, for the thrill of it, they'd drag us, one by one, into the yard and beat us for sport." She was too gentle of a woman to hear the other harsh realities of prison life. "Ettenborough handed me a gift."

She nodded and said with a soft voice, "Aye, and to him we can be grateful."

Declan grunted. He held no sympathy for Ettenborough.

"Truly. If he hadn't found you, you would have never have found me."

He slipped his hand behind her head and pulled her forward. As he gazed into her eyes, he pondered her arrival in his life. Luck, fate—no matter. She'd saved him from a life of loneliness. He glanced at her full lips before he lowered his head and kissed her. They were pliant, giving and demanding. As each moment passed, blood traveled faster and faster through him, igniting a fervor to have her and have her now.

A knock sounded at the door.

"*Bollocks*." He rose and opened it.

"I was told ye'd be here."

"'Tis a bit early, Nate."

"Aye, well," he said sheepishly. "The men are restless, and full of spit and vinegar. Could we be having some training?"

Declan chuckled. "Aye. Go to the estate. I'll meet you there." He smiled apologetically.

"Go. Play with your men," she said with a smile.

He quickly kissed her, grabbed his shirt, and turned to Nate. "Aye, you've asked for it, lad. Now let's see what your lazy carcass can do."

Nate laughed and slapped him on the back. "'Tis good to be back, ye ken?"

He looked over his shoulder at Martine, taking in her womanly curves.

Aye, 'twould never be dull with his Martine. His Gypsy brought out the goodness in him and had a passionate fire that lit her from within.

But would she be able to live with his sins, the sins of his past and those of his father?

When they arrived in London, would her faith in him unravel as his past became clear? He prayed to God no, but his heart worried it would be yes.

Sadie lounged in a chair by the hearth and twirled a lock of her hair. Trenmore stood behind her, driving her to insanity with his solicitous manners and continuous attention. She'd done nothing wrong, to be sure. Didn't Abigail deserve to be dead with the way she had neglected such a fine man as Declan Forrester? Aye, her friend had ensured misery wherever she went and Sadie's heart broke at the how Abigail treated her husband.

"Would you like a bit of tea?"

She rolled her eyes. "Nay, Trenmore. I'm drowning in tea."

He patted her arm. "Now, now, my dear. No need to be upsetting yerself."

She rose and paced to an open window. The day blazed with a bright afternoon sun. How she wished to be outdoors and out of her prison. Trenmore had assured the magistrate he'd keep her secure in her home. And blast him if the man didn't hold true to his promise.

The green landscape taunted her. Och, how she wanted to go to the village, buy a hat or some ribbons, hear some gossip. No doubt the gossips were a wee bit busy with the news she'd created.

"My dear, you'll catch yer death. Come away from the window."

"Aye, Trenmore," she said sweetly. "'Tis a brisk day."

She sat on the chair and accepted the throw. Aye, Trenmore was handsome, quite a catch in the midst of County Kildare. However, she had a more comely suitor in mind. Trenmore's constant attention smothered her and the way he picked his teeth after a meal churned her stomach. Sadie covered herself with the woolen blanket, feigning compliance.

He leaned over the hearth and added a brick of peat and some brambles to the fire.

Sadie leapt from the chair and grabbed the poker. In one swift motion, she struck him on the head. He landed in a heap on the stone hearth with a guttural oath. Blood poured from the small hole in his head. A hiss passed his lips as his body stopped twitching.

"Well," she said aloud, "that didn't take long at all, at all."

Chapter 19

"How could this happen?" Declan paced in front of the magistrate's desk, seething with anger, still muddied from training his men.

Connelly's ashen face didn't soothe his temper in the least. "I'm sorry Lord Forrester. Grey assured me he had the situation well in hand."

"You trusted her lover to watch over her?" Declan raked his fingers through his hair. Sadie Bannon had escaped. Worse, she had killed again. How could he protect Martine without knowing where the damn woman was? His men were watching the pub, stationed at each entrance to ensure her safety. He pinched the bridge of his nose while he contemplated wringing Connelly's worthless neck. "Is there any sign of where she has gone?"

The magistrate shook his head and cast his gaze to his desk. He shuffled some papers and lifted his shoulders in a helpless shrug. "I'll be alerting the villagers."

Declan threw up his hands. "Aye, and I'm certain she'll be wandering down main street for all and sundry to see."

Connelly stood and pulled his posture into one with gumption. "I can protect you."

Declan cocked a brow. "I've seen how you've protected mine so far. I'm not impressed with your measly efforts."

He sputtered, yet no reply escaped the man's mouth. For that Declan was grateful. He'd hate to beat the hapless man if he spoke.

"I'll see to my own. Of that be sure." Declan left the small jail.

"See here, don't be taking the law into your own hands," he yelled.

Declan ignored the man. He had to ensure Martine was safe. No other purpose mattered.

Frustrated and madder than hell, Declan silently paced past villagers. He was in no mood for chit chat and the solicitous nature of the inhabitants of the village. Even preparing for their departure with his men hadn't quelled his unease at Sadie's escape.

The pub bustled with the afternoon crowd, a meager crew of regulars that would eat and drink their day away without an ounce of guilt. He cast a quick glance to ensure no trouble lay in the shadows.

"Barkeep," he yelled. "Send dinner up to my rooms." Declan threw a bag of coin on the bar. "Make sure it's your best."

One last meal before they departed. It had taken longer than he'd planned to ready his men and their steeds. They were now two hours past departure time and it festered in his jaw.

He pounded up the stairs. Where was Little? He was not to leave the door. Outside their chamber, he attempted to settle his temper. Declan scrubbed his hand over his face and inhaled as he turned the knob. "Martine, I've had dinner sent up."

He stopped in his tracks.

His wife sat in a chair with ropes binding her wrists and legs and a rag stuffed in her mouth. He rushed to kneel before the chair and began untying her. "Stop struggling, I can't get the knots."

Panic filled her gaze as she shook her head.

Dear God, he'd failed to protect her. "'Twill be just moment, lass. Sit still."

"Cease," a voice behind him said.

Declan shut his eyes and sighed. What a fool he'd been. "Welcome, Sadie," he said as he stood. He positioned himself between the two women.

With a crazed gleam in her eyes, she advanced from the corner. Her unbound hair snarled around her face and her clothes were stained with ashes and blood.

He forced a smile on his face. "Why don't you sit and dine with us."

Martine squeaked from behind. He clasped his hands behind his back and then opened his palm in the same manner he remembered she used with the Lurchers. He prayed she understood that he wanted her to remain calm.

"Nay, me love," she cooed. "You and I alone will make our way to my estate."

He schooled his features to mask his fury. Yet his anger chased through his veins. "'Tis sorry I am to be refusing you, but I've plans with my betrothed."

"Your betrothed!" She screeched. "*I'm* to be your wife." She ran forward, her hands ready to claw him. "I'm yer wife. I'm yer wife," she yelled as she battered his chest and sunk her nails into his face. "I saw you with her—the Gypsy whore. By the river she bewitched you. Forced you to bed her."

He grappled for her flailing hands. Blood dripped from his face. Finally he pinned her arms to her side, holding her back as much as he could. "Nay, Sadie. I love Martine."

"No!" she screeched as she ripped from his grip and continued her assault.

Declan didn't want to hurt the befuddled woman. But he did want her in jail where she belonged. He grabbed her arms and forcefully pinned them to her sides. "Stop."

Martine grunted from behind. He shifted his gaze to the door and saw the Pub's owner holding a tray laden with food. "Get the magistrate. *Now.*"

The tray clattered onto the floor in a clash of broken china.

The man nodded and turned to leave, shock visible on his unshaven face.

"Wait," Declan called after him. "Untie my bethrothed."

The man came back and skirted around them. He quickly untied Martine and left.

"You despicable, vile woman." She came close to Sadie, her face red with indignation. "You nearly killed me."

"And kill you I will," Sadie yelled back.

Declan almost laughed at the absurdity of the situation.

"Pah," Martine said. "You could barely hurt a fly."

Sadie spat, hitting Declan instead of her intended victim. "Och, 'tis sorry I am, my love."

"No matter." He wished to keep her quiet until Connelly arrived. If Sadie became overly agitated, she may just attempt murder once again.

"Sadie," he said in a soothing voice while he looked pointedly at Martine. "'Tis important you stay calm."

"Calm?" Her eyes widened and the harsh manic tone of her voice set his teeth on edge. The room seemed to be consumed with an evil spirit.

Declan tightened his grip and nodded to Martine to step back. An angry glare still hovered in her eyes, but she complied.

"How did you get in the room, Sadie?" he said in a deceptively calm voice.

She giggled. "Your man Little ordered tea. And I brought it to him with some of the same drug I gave you." She appeared pleased with herself and although he wanted to throttle her, it was more important she went to jail.

"*Forrester*," Connelly yelled as he bound into the room. Sadie shoved against Declan, attempting to twist out of his grip. He held his position, thwarting her efforts.

"Sadie Bannon." Connelly wiped his brow and whistled under his breath. "You'll be coming with me."

"I'll help you," Declan said. "She may try to escape again. Truth be told, she's a stronger lass than I thought." He couldn't help but smile when Martine scoffed.

"My love, don't let this *eejit* hurt me," Sadie whined.

Connelly grabbed Sadie and forcefully dragged her from the room.

"*My love*," she screamed. "Come to me, my love."

"Don't move an inch," Martine warned.

He turned toward her. "I need to make sure she goes behind bars."

She tipped her head. "I know." Refusing to meet his gaze, she continued with a shaky voice. "She meant to kill me, Declan."

He pulled Martine into his arms and kissed the top of her head. Holding her stilled his hands from shaking. He'd almost lost her. What would he have done without her? "I know. I know," he said into her freshly washed hair. He could barely catch his breath over the thought of her in danger. "We leave soon."

"Aye, in London we'll be safe."

Declan didn't have the heart to tell her that may be far from the truth. If he couldn't keep her safe in the small village, how would he in London? He fleetingly thought of seeking Rafe's help in keeping her in Ireland as he went to secure his innocence. He dismissed the thought, knowing she'd refuse.

He kissed her once again. "My men are downstairs. Don't open the door to anyone but me."

She nodded and he headed out the door. At the threshold, he stilled and looked back at her. She stood proud. Proud and lovely. He smiled and left.

What a sight it would be to see Sadie Bannon behind bars at last.

Declan strode into the small village jail as if he owned the place. Actually, he did. He fleetingly wondered if he was still lord over Riverton and determined not to allow the good people of the town to suffer because of the machinations of Ettenbourgh.

"Now, Forrester," Connelly said as he held up his hand. "I'll be taking care of me guest."

"As you did before?" He leaned against the door jam, trying to remain calm when he was anything but. Truth be told, he was both relieved she was captured and damn furious. "Seems to me, you've a need to restrain your prisoners better."

Connelly dipped a fat scone into his tea. "You've the right of it." He took a huge bite. "Thought I could trust Grey."

Declan scoffed.

"Is that you, my love?"

He ignored Sadie's question as he placed his hands on Connelly's desk. Although he'd rather smash his fist in the incompetent magistrate's face. "Keep her here, or die trying."

Declan turned and left the building as Sadie screeched his name over and over.

In front of the pub he waited until he was calm before he entered. Still agitated after a few breaths, Declan walked the length of the street as he rubbed the back of his neck.

Truly the last few days had been exhilarating and treacherous at the same time. He entered the pub and went to their chamber.

"Open up, Martine. 'Tis me."

The door crept open and his wife peaked out. "Pah. 'Tis about time. I've been pacing forever."

Just being near her calmed him. He grabbed her and held tight. She pulled back and searched his face. "Is all well, then?" she said as she brushed a piece of his hair aside.

He nodded and enjoyed the feel of her against his body. 'Twas a perfect fit and one he'd never tire of. "No worries. Sadie is in jail and Connelly is on guard."

"Ha," she scoffed. "That one is as lazy as they come."

Declan frowned. "How do you know that?"

She smiled a purely feminine grin as humor lit her gaze. "'Tis a Gypsy's job to know the ways of the local magistrate."

He laughed, cleansing his soul of the day's bitterness. "I've had the cook prepare another meal. Due to all of the delays, we'll leave on the morrow." Declan kissed her and took her hand. He led her to the bed and bade her to sit.

A knock rapped on the door. Declan put a finger to his lips to silent Martine as he opened the door a notch. The maid held a tray with the agreed upon evening meal. His stomach rumbled at the smell of roasted lamb and mash, and he allowed her to enter.

She made haste as she deposited the tray and gave a quick glance at Martine. Only when Martine smiled and nodded, the maid left.

He'd have to watch her in London or she'd have the king wrapped around her finger.

As day broke, a freshness, a renewing spirit energized the group as they saddled their horses and packed provisions. Declan had risen early, anxious to leave Kilkenny and Sadie. He'd miss the estate and his time with Abigail, but it was part of his past and the path his life had followed. Now he had a new path, one filled with love and joy and the potential to solve the mystery of his past.

He allowed Martine to sleep as he made preparations, knowing their trip would be a harsh one. Although she was used to traveling Ireland's countryside, the speed in which they would need to travel would far exceed that of a caravan. And she'd be on horseback, not tucked away in a wagon.

"'Twill be hard for her," Nate said from behind. "We'll need to be riding slower than our usual pace."

"Aye."

His friend rested his hand on his shoulder. "She could stay here."

"Nay," Declan said with more vehemence than needed. "She travels with us."

Nate moved to his own steed and placed a laden pack behind the saddle. They continued working in silence until all was complete. The rest of the men ambled in after they broke their fast and quickly readied their horses.

"M'lord," Little said, "I will ride by my lady. We may slow you down, but you will know she will be well cared for."

Declan inhaled, then released the breath. The man felt guilty of Sadie's trickery no matter how much Declan had tried to tell him otherwise. "I'm entrusting Martine in your care. And I know you'd never let me down."

Pride lifted the man's shoulders and a twinkle appeared in his brown eyes. "As if she were my own, m'lord."

Declan stood and looked at the group of men he'd be leading into uncertain danger.

"If anyone would like to back out," he began, "I'd understand."

"Are ye daft, mon?" Nate said.

Matthew spit, then shook his head. "I'll be staying with you."

Declan felt a security he'd never known. He knew it was mostly because he'd found Martine, but his men's loyalty meant a great deal as well. He looked to the others who'd remained silent. Och, he couldn't blame them, to be sure.

"I've pledged to watch over my lady, and that I'll do." Little chuckled. "And if I can lend my hand to kick some arse, so be it."

"I can't believe you'd think we would step away after all of this time."

Declan looked to Lange and Rufus. Each man scowled and he assumed they were as displeased as the rest. He sighed. "There's danger ahead. I can't guarantee our result. That's the truth of it."

"Och, mon, we knew that coming in," Nate said.

The rest of the men shook their heads in agreement.

Lange patted his shoulder. "'Tis settled then. Yer stuck with this mangy lot."

Pierce ran into the barn, out of breath and barely dressed. "Are we set to leave?"

The group chuckled. Declan mentally rolled his eyes at the disheveled butler. "You're just in time."

"Right. Well, let me just ready my horse."

Declan nodded. "I'll see to Martine."

She appeared drawn at the daunting trip before them, but true to her spirit, she rode as hard as the rest of them. They'd have to book passage in Dublin, but Declan knew 'twould only be a matter of time before he stood on English soil again.

Closer to solving the mystery that tore his life to shreds.

Chapter 20

The closer to Dublin they traveled, the more nervous Martine became. Pah, 'tis just a small trip across the water. Yet the last time she'd traveled across it, she'd been consumed by grief and in the midst of a Gypsy tribe. As a woman, she'd have to be brave, not the little girl in her with her memories tucked neatly away, threatening to emerge.

Declan kept a watchful eye on her, and Little as well, the sweet man. When they arrived in the crush of Dublin, their horses were dwarfed by the busy city. Martine held a hand against her stomach, hoping to quell the nervous quake that gripped it.

So many sites and smells surrounded them—throngs of people, food cooking along with rubbish, and something she only associated with Dublin. The harsh volume of a crowded place hurt her ears. Urchins and the wealthy strode along the same wooden walkways, although the urchins appeared to be shadowing their betters, maybe in hope of gleaning a few pounds. Their poor dirty faces and ragged clothing broke her heart. How she wanted to gather them in her arms and give them a big hug.

Declan led the way toward a large inn with a clean walkway and potted impatiens flanking the door. Would she receive the same welcome she had in Kilkenny? Would the proprietor turn them away because she spoke like a Gypsy? All it would take is one person knowing her past and then all would know.

"Nate, you and Matthew can bring the horses to the nearest stable." The men gathered the reins and did as they were told.

"Lange, Rufus, and Pierce, go to the pubs and listen for talk of Randolph. If he's in Dublin, 'twill be causing a stir."

Martine watched the men disperse, curious but too tired to ask any questions. She slid into Declan's waiting arms, relieved to be off a horse and secure in his embrace. "Food, I need food," she whispered into the crook of his neck.

She felt his throaty chuckle as well as heard it. "Aye, lass. I'll feed you."

He carried her into the inn. She blushed at the stares they garnered and felt shabby with her dirty traveling skirt and blouse. She'd long taken off her jacket, too heated by the sun to tolerate its weight. Dust from the trail coated her hair, skin, and clothing.

"Declan, put me down," she protested.

"And what kind of gentleman would I be if I did that?" He grinned a sexy, all knowing smile and refused to let her go. "I'll need four rooms," he said to the man behind the desk.

Martine had to bite her lip to keep from laughing at the pinched-nosed man. He peered through spectacles and rapidly tapped his quill against the guest registry.

"Four, ye say." His gaze bounced between Declan and herself. She held her breath waiting for him to turn them out.

"Aye."

He took another glance that did its best to show he wasn't pleased with the scene in the lobby. "I can give you three large and one small. 'Tis all I have."

"I'll take them." Declan set her down and reached into his pocket for money.

The man noisily cleared his throat. "Will ye be needing baths and a meal as well?"

"That would be lovely," Martine answered. She disliked the way the man appeared to dismiss her. Aye, she wanted to shout, *I'm Rom. No need to act as if I have the plague.* "Please have them sent up right away."

"Aye, Madame."

Martine tipped her chin up a notch and stared at the

man. Obviously flustered, the man looked to the registry and asked for their name.

"Forrester," was all Declan said, and she felt his tension as if it were her own.

"Yes, weel. Neill will show ye to yer rooms."

They followed a lad whose uniform would fit better on a boy twice his size. Freckles covered his face and red hair stuck out in alarming angles beneath his cap. He bowed to them and picked up their satchels.

"Be sure to give my men their rooms when they arrive," Declan all but growled.

The innkeeper nodded and pulled at the collar of his starched shirt.

She elbowed him in the ribs. "You frightened him."

"Och, that hurt." He motioned her to precede him on the stairs. "'Twas deserved, to be sure. The man looked down his nose at us."

"When you travel with a Gypsy, 'tis the welcome you will receive," she said over her shoulder. "But you didn't help his opinion of us, now did you?"

"You're English." He shrugged and eased her into their room, which the baggage boy had opened.

She furrowed her brow. Did he think stating she was English would suddenly turn her skin pale and grace her with a clipped accent? The accent of the Rom had been deeply ingrained in her speech and she didn't know if she could learn to speak differently. She worried he'd deny the truth of the matter. Gypsies were not acceptable company for anyone of the *ton*.

She entered the room. "Ah," she said as she slipped off her shoes and sat on the luxuriously covered bed. Two winged-back chairs nestled near the windows with tea set out on the small table before them. "Tea!"

"There's your food." Declan rummaged through his bag

and took out clean clothing. He followed suit with Martine's bag and did the same.

'Twas incredibly sweet, the way he laid out a gown and her undergarments. She leaned back in the chair, enjoying the cushion after so many hours on horseback. The tea felt wonderful on her throat, and the scones and clotted cream helped sate her hunger.

"Would you care for some?"

Declan smiled at her and said, "Nay, I think you'll need it all."

She winked. "I'm willing to share."

He cocked his brow and pointed to the plate. All the scones were gone and crumbles lay in their place.

Martine laughed. "Some gentleman you are, making me feel like a glutton."

After he set her bag down, he walked over to the windows, slow, like a cat ready to pounce. He placed his hands on the side of the chair and leaned in for a kiss. "You taste like cream." Declan brought up his hand and cradled her face. She leaned into the warmth and sighed.

She looked at his chest. "Tell me about Randolph."

He pulled away, physically, emotionally. She watched him turn toward the chest of drawers and methodically put his things away. "There's nothing to tell. We grew up together."

"Why are your men looking for him?" She rose and walked to him. "What aren't you telling me?" Martine asked as she placed her hand on his shoulder. She tried not to be insulted when he flinched. Regardless, she kept her hand there to remind him of her love.

"Finn Randolph was my only friend." His voiced rasped sadly. "He's always shown loyalty to me, unlike so many others."

"He sounds special." It hurt her to see he was so obviously pained. His knuckles whitened as his grip tightened on a pair of trousers. She removed the garment and took his hand in hers.

Martine led him to the bed and sat him down. She crouched before him, placed her hands on his strong thighs, and looked into his troubled eyes. They darkened like the pit of the sky in the midst of a hardy storm. Absentmindedly, Martine ran her hands up and down Declan's legs. They tensed, then relaxed. "Please, Declan, I can sense your heart is troubled."

His mouth rose into a wry grin. "*Bitti chovexani.*"

Her hands fell to her side. "I'm *not* a little witch."

Declan tangled his fingers into her hair, loosening the knot at the base of her neck. "I know," he said with such great weariness. "Perhaps if you were, you'd be able to help me."

"I can help you," she implored. "If you share with me, I know I can help."

Her heart broke when his shoulders sagged. "Aye, 'tis the truth of it." He lifted her up beside him. "Finn worked at my father's estate, in the stable, kitchen, wherever he was needed."

Martine nodded. "Resourceful."

He smirked. "You have no idea."

She nudged him. "Go on."

He shrugged. "After my mother died, my father became very political. At least that is what I was told by the servants. My mother died when I was a wee lad." He stopped speaking and gazed forward, pensive in thought.

Declan shuddered inside. How could he tell her the details of his time in prison? She'd run and never stop. Yet there she sat, beside him in mind, spirit, and body. He rubbed his eyes, weary from their travels and tired beyond reason.

"I spoke with my father. He pretended I didn't exist. At meals he looked right through me." Declan felt as if he'd gone back in time, trying to engage his father in conversation across the finely set dining table. Each time he tried his father would methodically raise his fork from his plate to his mouth. Never did he respond, he thought, as he clenched his fist. Martine unfurled his fingers and weaved her fingers within his. They were long, soothing, warm. He squeezed and continued. "This went on for years. Then one day the magistrate arrived and arrested me." He shook his head as he pinched his nose. "When they arrived to take me to prison, he said to trust him. *Trust him.*"

Anger swirled though his mind, heating his body with indignation. Damn, he loathed the memories that were still as sharp as a knife. He ran his fingers through his hair with frustration. His body was strung as tight as a bow, despite Martine's steady presence. "For one fleeting moment, I thought he cared for me and I went with the men."

"They took you to prison?"

He shook his head. "Nay. I had a trial first."

She stood and paced before him. "Why? What crime did you commit? Did Finn do something and blame you?"

Declan stared at her in surprise, then released a bitter laugh. "Finn would rather die than turn me over to a noble."

His wife furrowed her lovely brow. Confusion weighted her gaze.

"Finn's father was a very important man in London. His mother was a servant."

"Oh."

His smile was sincere. "Aye, oh."

"I fought the men as well as I could. But there was one of me and four of them. And in the courtyard . . . about twenty soldiers."

Martine stopped pacing and hit her chin with the tip of her finger. "Who were these men?"

He threw up his hands. "At the time, I didn't know. But now I know they belonged to a secret political society."

"Pah. What could politics have to do with you going to prison?" She stood glaring at him, her face a study of thoughtfulness right along with fury and sympathy.

"In London, politics was and still is everything," he said with a droll tone. Of course she wouldn't know how it worked. The Gypsies only knew that magistrates hunted them and made certain they were killed or locked away indefinitely. "And in English politics, money will open doors, bribe judges, and ensure someone is locked away."

"Why were you in England? You're Irish."

"My mother was English and my father wanted her to be happy. That meant living in England." And that was why Declan had purposely lived in Ireland—Abigail loved Ireland and wanted to be rid of England. God, the irony of the situation wasn't lost on him.

She nodded.

He cleared his throat, wishing he could erase the memories. "After my mock trial, as I now know it to be, I was sent to rot away."

Tears flooded her eyes and trickled over her dark lashes. "Oh, Declan. How horrid it must have been."

"Aye," was all he could manage. The smell of prison wafted by his nose as the screeches of inmates pierced the air. He wanted to fist his hands over his ears to block away the torturous sounds.

Martine clutched his face between her hands. Tears coursed down her face in fast rivulets. His eyes blurred with unspent tears. God, he hated the weakness.

"Let me in, Declan. Let my love heal you."

He nodded, gently gripped her arms, and crushed his mouth against hers. They tumbled onto the bed, a tangle of limbs clamoring to get as close as possible. Declan ripped her clothing off as a primal need drove him to devour her. She pulled back, passion radiating in her expressive eyes, then he captured her lips once again as he fondled her breasts. Martine writhed and moaned, spurring him into a heated frenzy.

Declan needed to be in her. Quickly. He pulled her over him until she rode him and he couldn't tell where he ended and Martine began as they moved as one. She was so hot, tight. He bathed in her as she moved her hips torturously. Declan teased her nipple with his tongue. Then he lapped the other. Pleased with her increased rhythm, he repeatedly suckled her breasts until he could hold back no more. In one swift motion, he gripped her hips and rolled them over so he was on top, still joined, still thrusting.

Martine wrapped her long legs around his waist, drawing him deeper than he could ever imagine. Still, they fought to be closer, deeper.

"Please, Declan," she whispered through parted lips.

"Aye, my love." He plunged into her. She bucked off the bed—her hands gripping at the bedding.

He watched satisfaction flow over her face. Peaceful. Beautiful. He buried himself one last time, reaching the pinnacle of fulfillment as never before.

Well sated, he collapsed upon her, chuckling as their breaths came in exhausted spurts. He leaned to the side. Martine's eyes remained closed, but he knew she was still awake. He trailed his finger along her forehead, over the length of her nose and across her lips. She finally opened her eyes.

"That was . . ."

"I know," he said as he leaned down and kissed the perfect peak of her nose. "I know."

They slept, still entangled, unclothed, yet incredibly sated and content. Never had he ever felt this close to another person. The perfection of the moment hovered around them as if protecting them from the harsh reality outside their door.

Declan knew that nothing could possibly surpass what they shared. Even if the truth were revealed, they'd have this afternoon and the bliss of their lovemaking.

He hoped with one last fleeting thought that his bairn grew within her. 'Twould be a divine example of their struggles and how their love overcame them.

They woke to sun streaming into the room and an insistent knock on the door.

"*Bollocks*," Declan muttered as he eased Martine's body from atop his. "Coming." He pulled on his britches and covered Martine with a blanket.

He opened the door and leaned against the jam to further protect her privacy. Nate and Pierce stood in the hall with sheepish expressions on their faces.

"We hate to disturb ye, but Randolph hasna been in Dublin for several days."

"Damn."

Pierce jumped at his outburst.

"We'll be going to London?"

"Aye, go to the docks and book passage. You know the ship." Declan knew Nate was familiar with the vessel from which he wanted passage purchased. "Martine bunks with me."

"Of course, m'lord," Pierce sputtered. "We wouldn't do otherwise, to be sure."

"Grand. Now leave me be until it's time to sail."

Pierce trotted down the hall. Nate remained and gave a crooked grin. "She appears to agree with ye, lad."

"That's enough out of you, you *eejit*." He shut the door and smiled. Aye, Martine did agree with him. Together for love. There his beautiful woman lay, snuggled in the bed. 'Twas Martine who saved him with her love and acceptance.

She stretched and yawned.

He pounced on the bed. "Wake up. 'Tis time to break our fast."

She grinned, a sleepy little moue. "Aye, I'm starving."

He kissed her then rose from the bed before he started something that would make them miss their voyage. "'Tis time to shop for you."

She scoffed and pulled a face. "You bought half of Riverton for me already."

He looked pointedly at her. A woman who didn't want to buy gowns and hats and whatever else they bought? How lucky was he? "I've a right to spoil you."

She sighed and tossed off the covers. He nearly jumped back into bed and feasted on her naked body.

"Now, now, I see that wicked gleam in your eye. We've shopping to do."

He tapped her chin. "I thought you didn't want to be spoiled."

Martine waved at him. "Not for me, for you," she said with a pointed look.

"Me?" His entire plan had backfired. He just wanted to give what she'd been lacking and now he was going to be subjected to the endless bore of shopping for himself. At least by purchasing items for her, he could enjoy her pleasure.

"Come on with you, get dressed."

Declan obeyed, somehow feeling as if he were ten and on his way to be fitted for his first suit.

Chapter 21

After an endless morning of selecting trousers and suit coats, Declan had endured enough. He insisted Martine select something for herself.

"Look," he said as he pointed across the road. "There's a quaint shop."

Kane's Millinery, the sign read. "Would you be pleased with a hat?"

She flushed and looked to the walkway.

Declan stopped and tipped up her chin. "What's troubling you?" She bit her lip and his heart careened. "You can tell me."

"It's just the woman all have fair skin. And mine," she said as she touched her cheek. "Is tanned."

He wrapped his arms around her and kissed the top of her head. "My sweet, sweet, Gypsy."

A frown tipped her mouth downward as she furtively glanced up and down the walkway. "Please do not call me that."

He cocked his brow. She met his gaze, her eyes pleading. "I'm English. If others know me as a Gypsy, they'll never accept me. And in doing that, they'll never accept you—us."

He tangled his hands in her hair, touched she was concerned with his image more than her own. She was unique, and he thanked God for it every day. "Don't worry about me. If I have you, that's enough."

She smiled, but he saw doubt in her expressive eyes. "Let's go see about a hat for you."

As they entered the store, a bell tinkled. A woman came into the shop from behind a velvet curtain. Martine looked around the shop and smiled. He was enthralled by her reaction at the little shop, its neatness, and the variety of lovely hats stacked on the shelves.

"May I help you?"

"Aye," Declan said as he grasped Martine's hand. "We need a few hats."

"You've come to the right place." The auburn-hair woman walked from behind the counter and stood in front of her. He held tight as Martine tried to back away. She cast her gaze to him and he nodded encouragingly.

The woman tapped her lip. "I've just the thing."

Declan stood back as the woman whisked Martine to the other side of the shop. Martine kept looking over her shoulder at him. He just smiled and watched her.

"Now this will accentuate your lovely eyes."

He watched as Martine spoke with the woman. The uncertainty she exhibited on the walkway remained. It broke his heart for her to struggle, be concerned about her heritage. Perhaps she'd relax on the voyage after she spent more time away from her clan. She glanced over at him, the line of her jaw tight. He hoped she'd begin to enjoy shopping for herself.

"'Tis time to try it on." The woman grabbed her hand and led her to a mirror. "I'm Bronwyn McKenna. Are you new to Dublin?"

"Aye, we just arrived yesterday."

The woman smiled. "Ah, I thought so. Your accent gave you away."

Martine dropped the hat on the small table before the mirror.

Declan came forward. "We were just passing through on our way to London. I'm Declan Forrester and this is my betrothed Martine."

"Grand. Now, you may need an evening hat. Let me see," she said as she surveyed the shop. "Yes, 'tis perfect." She selected a sapphire velvet hat that had intricate lace draped over the top and hung off the front. The lace was dyed the exact color of the velvet and was extraordinarily fine.

Martine put it on and pulled the lace over her face.

"'Tis perfect," Declan and the woman said in unison.

She flushed at the attention and removed the hat. Somehow the shop seemed to calm her and she was able to focus on the task at hand. Declan surmised 'twas the warm attitude of the proprietress.

"Your shop is lovely," Martine said, as if trying to make up for her previous blunder.

"Thank you. I'm usually not here in the afternoon, but one of my girls was ill and needed me to fill in."

Martine fingered the lace of the hat. "Do you make all of the hats?"

"My partner Caitlin and I make all the products as well as teach young women in need to make lace and hats."

"'Tis a fine business," Declan said. "We'll take both of the hats."

"Excellent."

After they purchased the hats, they bid farewell.

"If you're ever in Dublin again, please stop by," she called after them.

"To be sure," Declan assured her.

They strolled down the walkway, hand in hand as Declan balanced their purchases with his free one. "She was a nice woman."

"Aye."

"She runs her own shop. Can you imagine?"

"Many women do," he replied.

She looked at him in surprise. "Aye, I suppose they do."

Declan laughed and patted her hand. "'Tis time to return to the inn and see Nate about our voyage."

'Twas obvious she forced a smile. He furrowed his brow as he tried to think of a way to make her understand all would be well in London. As they made their way back to the inn, she stared forward as if she loathed to see if anyone reacted negatively to her—as if they'd recognize she was Rom and would point it out to all who could hear.

He swore he'd protect no matter what others thought.

Or he'd die trying.

Martine clutched her stomach as she once again heaved into a bucket. The choppy waves refused to cease. She leaned against the headboard of the bed and placed a cool cloth on her forehead. Declan had left to conference with his men, thank the Lord. She loathed for him to see her in such a dreadful condition.

And the stateroom did little to ease her discomfort. The bed and chair filled the room with just a narrow space to walk through and open the door. Their clothing stayed in their bags, horribly wrinkled and in need of washing.

Pah. How long was this trip to last? It appeared endless, much more so than she remembered. The Rom had traveled from England to Ireland when she was so young she had no concept of time.

Declan peeked his head into the room. "Feeling any better?"

"Nay," she mumbled as she wiped her sweaty brow.

He came in and sat upon the end of the bed. "'Twill be two more days if this weather holds." Declan pushed her hair behind her ear and caressed her face. "Green or no, you're still lovely."

With as much energy as she could summon, Martine swatted at him.

"'Tis the truth of it," he said with a crooked grin. "Try to rest and I'll bring some broth."

When she groaned, he kissed her brow.

"And once we are in London?"

"Depends on how you are feeling, to be sure." He shrugged.

She bit her lip. "I don't want to slow you down."

His expression was inscrutable. "You won't."

"But—"

Declan put his fingers on her lips. "Shhh. Rest. We'll talk later."

He left the room after one more quick kiss. Och, he was a treasure. She closed her eyes and tried to sleep. Her stomach protested and Martine grimaced at the tears threatening to overflow her tired eyes. Instead of submitting to her errant emotions, she began planning for their future. A home, small and tidy. Children, at least a half dozen. And love, until they met their maker.

Children. How she missed her students.

She touched her stomach, envisioned it plump with Declan's child. Aye, to have his child would be the best of things.

Hope flared within her and it was that hope she'd cling to as they made their way to London.

Chapter 22

"We need to prepare," Declan stated. "Our welcome in England may be less than pleasant." He scanned the faces of his men crammed in such a small room deep in the middle of the ship. Stern, resolved. 'Twas lucky he had such support.

"Aye," Nate agreed. "We found as much when we landed before. The natives didna enjoy our presence."

The normally silent Rufus slammed his fist against the table. "*Bollocks*. They hated us."

Declan grinned, fueled by the challenge, the prospect of ending the torment of his being. To solve the mystery of his imprisonment had driven him to this day and he vowed to be victorious against the hidden nemesis. Getting back to the matter at hand, he said, "Since there was little word of Finn in Dublin, our first job will be to find him. This mystery has gone on for too long."

Little voiced his opinion. "'Twill be like finding a needle in a haystack."

He turned to Little and glared. "Aye, old man. And I've no doubt you'll be up to the task."

His butler chuckled and nodded.

"'Tis all for now. Go. Rest. I've Martine to attend to."

Pierce fumbled in his pocket. "M'lord? I've a few pieces of willow bark and some chamomile leaves. 'Twill help her stomach."

"Thank you." He left and headed directly to his room. He quickened his pace, eager to rid himself of the ideal of revenge in Martine's presence. How she steadied him. 'Twas odd, in a manner of speaking, that he found love at all. Never experiencing any in the past, he'd been accepting of the fact he may be fated to be without.

Martine was tucked beneath the covers, her lush body curled into a ball. He ran a finger down her cheek, over her jaw, and along her graceful neck. Tempted as he was, he allowed her to sleep and sat in the chair nestled into the corner. Kicking his feet on the end of the bed, he leaned his head against the wall and gazed upon her.

He'd do anything to keep her safe, away from the venom he knew lay in London. Yet selfishly, he wanted her near, needed her near.

She stirred and he rose and burrowed behind her. As he wrapped his arm around her shoulder, she stilled and sighed.

Aye, 'twas contentment, nay fulfilled he felt, to be sure. He inhaled the scent of her hair and rested his face as close to her as possible. He felt her chest rise and fall and allowed it to lull him to sleep. In the morning, they'd be one more day closer to London, and one more day closer to victory or ruin.

Martine clung to the chamber as her sickness lasted from morn to night. 'Twas disconcerting, the trouble her normally reliable stomach was causing. After three days on the rocking and rolling ship, she'd consumed only sips of broth and a soothing tea. Regretfully, its calming effects were short lived. Once the wind kicked up the waves, her stomach rebelled once again.

"'Twill be just a little longer, my love."

Although her eyes remained closed, Martine heard him and gave a slight grin. His fingers felt lovely as they smoothed her hair and brushed against her skin.

"How would you like a bath?"

Her eyes popped open. "Truly?"

Chuckling, Declan pulled back the covers and helped her out of bed. "Truly."

He led her to the captain's cabin and rapped on the door. "Enter," a gruff voice called.

Although she felt like death, she looked forward to soaking in a bath, so she entered.

The richly appointed chamber contrasted greatly from the rest of the ship. Tapestries, plush rugs, and the most elaborate velvet dressings for the huge four-poster bed were only a fraction of what occupied the room. Jeweled trunks stacked in the corner looked as if they would topple at any given moment. And in the center of it all, at long table dressed for dinner with royalty, sat the captain, fork raised with a thick slick of mutton from the smell of it.

"So here's yer woman, Forrester. Thought she was a myth. Come, join me." He waved toward the table and poured a healthy glass of wine for himself.

Martine smiled at the magnitude of the man. A pirate by the looks of it, and a wealthy one at that. Gold glittered on his fingers and ears. A rich velvet doublet and waistcoat stretched over his broad shoulders and wide form. And a mass of black hair was tied back into a queue.

"May I present my betrothed, Martine." Declan pulled out a chair and bade her to sit.

Again he failed to mention her surname. Was he doing it for her or him? Was Declan ashamed she was Rom? She so wanted to ask him, but was afraid of the answer. If he said no, would she believe him? And if he said yes, she couldn't marry him. God, she prayed it was to protect her.

"Pleasure. Pleasure." He flashed a toothy grin.

She felt her queasiness subside as she rested against the back of the chair. Even the thought of eating began to appeal to her.

"Please," the captain said between bites. "Help yerselves."

Declan selected tatties and mutton. He ladled soup into a bowl for her and gave her a small glass of wine. "Be careful. You've had nothing to eat in quite a while."

She smiled at his concern and sipped the soup. She was much more interested in the captain. A robust man, he talked with an unfamiliar accent, thick with brogue and an underlying twang of an unknown origin.

He squinted at her and said, "Bloody hell, Forrester, she's a beaut." He winked, and she felt a blush stain the crest of her cheeks at his audacious comment.

Mischief filled Declan's gaze. "Aye, 'tis the truth of it."

She waved a hand. "Pah. I'm dirtier than some of your sailors."

The men laughed and the captain said, "I'm Captain Brooks."

She nodded and sipped her wine. The flavorful spirit eased down her throat and settled into her stomach. Pleased her body didn't rebel, she took another sip.

Brooks regarded her intently. "A bath ye'll have, milady. And I've some gowns that would suit ye."

Although tempted, Martine held up her hand. "I couldn't possibly." Och, it cost her, especially since her new clothing was secured below deck and out of her reach.

"Ha," he said with a wave of his hand. "Insult me and no bath for ye."

She blanched, disgusted with her filthy hair and skin. "'Twould be my pleasure to accept."

"That's the way tae be, milady." He thunked down his glass and wine sloshed over the rim and onto the table. He stood and went over to the trunks. He lifted the massive objects as if they weighed as little as a feather. Opening one, vibrant fabrics slipped over the sides.

Not able to restrain her curiosity, Martine rose and looked into the wooden trunk. Heavenly silks and damask made into breathtaking gowns shimmered before her eyes. She reached out to touch one, then quickly pulled back her hand.

Brooks picked up one of the gowns and held it before her. "'Twill suit."

While she enjoyed the captain's jovial attention, she felt

Declan's scrutiny. He sat leisurely with his feet resting on a chair, ankles crossed. But his intense gaze never left her.

The way he watched her sent shivers of pleasure through her and she wished they were in their chamber. She flushed and turned her attention back to the Captain.

Martine fingered the gown and nodded.

The captain laid the gown on top of the trunk.

Declan raised his glass in salute. After a moment, he said, "'Tis time for business, Brooks. Ready my betrothed's bath."

He nodded. "Aye, have one of yer men stand guard. Wouldn't want to be temptin' me own."

Martine shivered and tried to dismiss the oblique remark. The captain pulled a chain near the doorway. In the distance, mixed with the sounds of cresting waves and men shouting orders, a bell tinkled. Brooks then grabbed the bottle of wine and nodded to Declan.

He flashed a reassuring smile and followed the captain. "I'll send Little to watch the door," he called over his shoulder.

After the men had left, a cabin boy entered with steaming buckets stretching each arm. "'Ere's yer water, m'lady."

She moved aside so he could enter. "Thank you."

He set down the buckets and wiped his brow. "I'll be getting the tub." The young boy went to the corner and whipped back an oilcloth. Beneath the cloth was the largest tub she'd ever seen. She could barely hide her excitement. As the tub slowly filled with bucket after bucket of water, she told the boy to set the last bucket for rinsing and bade him to leave. She peeked out the door to ensure Little was at his post, then closed and secured the door to intruders.

'Twas heaven, the hot water soaking the dirt from her body. Tension eased from her as she lathered the scented soap the captain had left on a chair along with a linen towel.

As she bathed, she inspected her surroundings once again. How did her husband know such a man enough to do business? Was the captain the reason Declan seemed to have ample funds? The more time she spent with her husband, Martine realized how little she knew him. Surely, once they reached London answers would be given.

She soaped her hair and rinsed with the cumbersome bucket. Satisfied she was as clean as possible, she lifted from the now tepid water and dried off. She still walked a little slowly, gripping her stomach when it rumbled.

Martine picked up the peacock blue gown with white lace trimming and gold stitches. A matching pair of slippers were found beneath, along with under garments.

'Twould be suitable to wear as they departed to ship. After she twisted her hair into a knot at the base of her neck, Martine opened the door.

A piteous whimper passed her lips when Declan turned around and startled her.

"Clean as a whistle, I'd say." He captured her in his arms and nuzzled her neck. "Hmmm."

Martine squirmed against him. He trailed kisses up her neck, over her chin, and then finally captured her mouth with searing heat, spurring her heartbeat.

"Declan," she whispered. "We're in the captain's cabin."

He lifted his head and looked chagrinned. "Och, that's the truth of it." He led her out of the chamber as he flashed her a smile full of promise and raw with lust. She shivered at the invitation his gaze extended, pleased with his humor.

They strolled to their cabin, hand in hand, heat simmering between them as each step led them closer to making love. The breeze off the water hinted at fish and brine as it mingled with the crisp blue day blessed with sunshine.

"You look lovely," he said as his gaze slid slowly over her.

Humor laced his tone, so she tilted her chin up and replied, "Aye, 'tis lovely, isn't it?"

He grinned and nodded. "You seem to have found your sea legs, my love."

She nodded to one of the crew as they passed. "Aye, just in time to land, I'd say."

His jaw pulsed and his blue eyes deepened with what she knew was desire. He pulled her hard against him and kissed her hungrily. Martine felt it to her toes as excitement and passion surged through her body.

She was no longer aware of the austere ship's deck, the sailors watching or completing their tasks. Declan's hard body imprinted on her own so deeply she found it hard to breath.

"To our cabin, my love."

She nodded and followed his lead. They reached the cabin quickly, prodded by their desire to be in one another's arms.

He secured the door, shifted her so she leaned against it, then crushed her against him. He splayed his hands on the hard wood and just devoured her lips. She started removing his clothing, and all the while their mouths never parted. He loosened her stays, practically tearing the gown from her. They tumbled onto the small bed and began the dance that had become their own as their love flowed from one another in nips and caresses and panting breaths.

The evening rang in as barely audible shouts in the distance announced their arrival in London. Martine ignored the shouts as the crest of desire rode through her body in a wave of unrestrained passion. Together they coaxed physical and emotional responses from each other as their bodies merged into one. She touched every part of his body, loving the twitch and strain of his muscles, the hiss when she touched a particularly sensitive spot. Ah, she loved when he nuzzled her neck, nipped along her jaw. Sweat sheened their bodies and Declan lapped along her shoulder, between the valley of her breasts, tickled along her navel.

"You taste delicious," Declan murmured against her skin, his breath hot and moist.

She laughed and he pulled up. His knuckles grazed along her cheek. "God, Martine you are so beautiful."

"Ah, my handsome man."

They plunged into the passion, the love surrounding them, until at last climax was reached as they called each other's name.

Declan collapsed beside her. "You'll be the death of me," he said as he traced her jaw with his forefinger. "'Twill be a blessed way to go."

She chuckled and snuggled into his arms. "We've arrived."

"Aye, that we have." He voice was sleepy.

"In London."

She felt him tense as muscles in his arms flexed tightly. He lifted from the bed, the moment lost. Bitter awareness came painfully to her. She wished they'd never come but knew peace would remain elusive to him if they did not. He retrieved her gown from the floor and laid it upon the foot of the bed. He avoided her gaze, obviously lost in his own thoughts, which she knew were anything but pleasant by the scowl on his face. Sighing, she began dressing, truly unsettled at the uncomfortable silence after such shared passion.

They left their cabin and the ship unhindered, Martine aware of Declan's men walking silently behind them. She tried to prod him into conversation, all to no avail.

"Nate and Lange, secure a carriage for Martine to be taken to the townhouse."

Townhouse? Was he not going with her? Hurt and anger blurred her vision as she tried to assimilate herself to the busy and dirty docks. At the end of the plank, Declan brought her hand to his lips. "You'll be taken to my home. Feel free to make yourself comfortable. 'Tis ours now."

She glowered at him, but he failed to acknowledge her displeasure. She thought he would at least bring her to their home. They'd enter together and he'd introduce her to his staff. But now—now she'd be alone.

Little and Pierce flanked her as they escorted her to the waiting carriage. She allowed one last look at the ship and witnessed Declan and his men in deep conversation with Captain Brooks. The man handed Declan a large bag and they shook hands. What sort of dealings did her husband have with this man, she wondered, fearful and curious at once?

"My lady," Little said as he interrupted her fury. "Your carriage awaits."

She knew he meant to bring levity to the moment, but she flashed him a frowning glance regardless. When Pierce offered his hand to assist her, she slapped it away in aggravation. *Pah, I'm being a child.* But hurt at Declan's dismissal stung her eyes as she battled to blink away the tears. Here she was in a strange country, feeling so alone. She'd left her family, abandoned them for the man she loved. And it felt as if she was abandoned by Declan.

Wordlessly she entered the carriage and ignored the scenery of London as they traveled down the crowded roadways.

Chapter 23

"Does she know?"

Declan shook his head as he watched the carriage meander down the cobbled road.

Nate tugged at his chin. "'Tisn't wise, lad."

Bollocks. His heart urged him to chase after her as his mind told him to stay on the ship. It must be this way. Brooks had valuable information and he needed to conduct business with the colorful man. "'Tis necessary for now."

His friend gripped his shoulder. "That's tae be determined."

Declan shrugged off the hand and the ominous warning. He felt grief enough as it was, and he didn't need constant reminders of what lay ahead. It rendered him unworthy of her love and devotion, her true loyalty as she left all she'd known for him and with nothing promised.

"Forrester," Brooks called in his booming voice. "'Tis news of Randolph."

Finally. A flicker of hope remained that he'd settle his past so he could then focus on the future. "Where is he?"

Brooks tugged at his earring, and cocked an arrogant brow. "That'll come. First, we've business. Yer fortune has grown faster than I can earn it for ye. 'Tis time for a larger cut, I'd say."

Declan grinned. "Greedy bastard."

The captain laughed uproariously. "To be sure, lad, to be sure."

They conducted their business in the captain's cabin with a bounty of wine and ale and bawdy comments. Declan remained reserved as his men, along with the captain's trusted few, congregated at the table and deals were cut. He blessed his good fortune at finding Brooks before he left England for Ireland and the foresight to invest in his ventures. Now he'd never have to depend on another such as Ettenborough to make his way in the world. In this venue, he was the boss who directed the men and earned a vast percentage of the take.

Aye, 'twas not the most legal way to conduct business. But this way, the English did not gain from his dealings, and he was assured Brooks didn't take anything that wasn't fairly paid for. What the pirate did on the side, Declan didn't want to know. 'Twas the English's own stupidity to pay inflated prices for the goods he offered under an assumed identity. Silks, spices, coffee, and furnishings all comprised his stock. And his customers were more than willing to pay whatever he demanded. His agent told the customers the products were in demand in France and Italy, which spurred them to buy more.

Declan chuckled.

"Something funny, Forrester?"

"Nay, captain," he said as he drank more wine. 'Twas time to see to Martine, yet to insult Brooks wouldn't be wise.

The pirate lifted up his tankard of ale. "Are ye bored? Or is it a fine lady ye are thinking of, ye bastard?"

Chuckling again, he felt something akin to loneliness even in the midst of his men. Aye, he missed her. Just the idea she was near and he wasn't with her tortured him.

"Weel?" Brooks raised his cup. "To Forrester for finding the loveliest lass I've laid eyes on in quite a while. If only I'd seen her first."

"Och," Nate said. "She'd run from ye for sure."

Silence. Then rumbling laughter as the captain turned as red as a whore's petticoat.

"Bloody hell. Go to her. 'Tis where yer mind is. Randolph will come to you at Broderick's estate tonight. Broderick's gone to the country for a house party and it will be empty save a few staff. Randolph's purchased their compliance."

He waited for a moment, not certain he liked being told what to do by the captain, then stood and left the room. His men followed suit and they made haste to his city home.

The carriage rounded the corner and stopped before a large town home. Several stories high and lovely it was with its white exterior and paned windows. Martine gazed at the building without enthusiasm. Boxwood trees lined the walkway along with small pines acting as a privacy hedge flanking the side. Cold, is what she thought, hard and cold.

Little and Pierce left the carriage and extended a hand to help her out. Slowly she mounted the steps to the black lacquered door with huge brass knockers as if she were being sentenced to her death.

It burst opened and a wee lass of about five bounded down the steps and halted before her.

"And who are you?" the girl asked with her clipped English.

Martine smiled despite her mood. "I'm Martine. And who are you?"

The lass gave a sheepish grin. "I'm Betsy. Me mother is the cook and she'd skin me alive if she knew I was out here."

"Well, we just won't tell her, now will we?"

The girl grinned. "That's the ticket."

They walked into the marbled foyer. The high ceilings were framed with moldings and elegant chandeliers dangled like fancy earbobs. Gilt-framed pictures lined the halls and a velvet settee and mahogany table were the only furnishings. A shiver of uncertainty snaked its way up her spine as she watched the staff line up before the stairwell. Eight. Eight formally garbed maids and she presumed a butler and another man. She gripped her shaking hands so that no one else witnessed her nerves.

"Betsy," a robust woman with raspberry-stained cheeks hissed as she rushed to join the line. "Mind your manners."

The young girl gave her an apologetic glance and skipped to her mother.

The cook bobbed a curtsy. "Sorry, m'lady. Don't know what's gotten into the gel."

She waved a hand. "No apologies are necessary."

"Why, you're not English." The woman pulled up, obviously realizing her guffaw.

Little came forward. "Lord Forrester will arrive in a thrice. The lady of the house, Lady Martine, will make her rounds and assure everything is in order before he arrives."

She stifled a chuckle at the butler's sudden pompous attitude. But the fact that he didn't mention her surname wasn't lost on her. Did Declan tell him not to? Was he trying to hide the fact she was a Gypsy?

As she walked past the staff, each bowed or curtsied and announced their station and name. They seemed to be a pleasant group of people and she was certain they'd get along. At least she hoped all would go well. 'Twould be unusual, staying in such a grand home with people at her beck and call. How could she convince them she could fend for herself?

A maid called Gertie came forward. "Let me show you to your chamber."

She tipped her head and smiled at the maid. "That would be lovely."

She followed, all the while peeking over her shoulder to look at Little and Pierce as she ventured into the unknown. Pah, where was Declan? Did he expect her to survive this on her own? Something so foreign and frightening?

The maid opened a double doorway and stepped back. Her thoughts had distracted her so fully, she'd hadn't noticed they reached the chamber.

She hesitated and then walked in. A canopied bed garnered her attention as did the large fireplace and sitting area before it. Such grandeur. And it all belonged to Declan.

As she walked to the fireplace, she ran her hand along a damask chair. Her steps were soundless against the plush rugs obscuring the dark wooden floor.

"I'll send up your bags, milady."

She nodded as she continued to explore her chamber. 'Twas decidedly feminine. Did Declan expect to sleep elsewhere as many of the wealthy did? Perhaps as her parents—

Pah, 'twasn't time for such distant memories. They were like a dream, faded with age, void of any true emotion. It was another time and one she often thought a fantasy not reality, and she couldn't trouble herself with such ideas now.

"My lady?" Gertie entered the room with two young boys in tow. They each carried two buckets and began filling the copper bath in the small antechamber to the rear of the larger chamber.

"Thank you." She wanted to be alone. Why? She didn't know, but she needed to wrap her thoughts around her surroundings, Declan's absence, and how she was supposed to live as a lady when she was anything but.

Chapter 24

He entered the chamber and stilled. Martine stood before the bank of windows, a silhouette of beauty. He strode across the chamber and came up behind her. After a moment's hesitation, he wrapped his arms around her and kissed the top of her head.

"I'm sorry," he whispered. His heart ached at her silence and the rigid line of her back.

"Why?" she said as she spun to face him.

He tipped his forehead against hers. "I know I have a lot to explain." *Bollocks*, where would he start?

She looked at him, her eyes wide with question and, he knew, hurt. He couldn't make her suffer any longer. "Let's sit."

He led her to the small couch before the fireplace. As she sat, he struck a match and touched the wood. The flames ignited and he stood and leaned a hand on the mantel. With his back to her, he watched the fire lick up the flue. His vision blurred and then he summoned the courage, something he never thought he lacked, and knelt before Martine.

"Why did you leave me to fend for myself?"

He cringed as her voice cracked.

"We are not married and I had to come to your home and be introduced to the staff." She moved away from him.

He scrubbed his hand over his face. "I never thought—"

"Aye, you never thought." Her shoulders trembled.

Declan reached for her, his fingers grazing her back as she rose and stepped away from him. He felt wretched.

She whipped toward him, frustration in her gaze, piercing him with hurt. "And now," she said with a sweep of her hand, "I see all you have. You said you had some money, some holdings. But Declan, you are a very rich man."

"I never meant to deceive you," he said as he gathered her hands in his own.

"Go on," she prodded. Her jaw remained firm, unyielding.

He wiped the back of his neck and cleared his throat. "I'm not poor." Had he purposely deceived her? He wasn't certain. He knew he told her he had holdings, but he didn't think he'd have to go into detail.

"Pah, even I can discern that." She ripped her hands from his and crossed her arms before her chest.

'Twas going to be harder than he thought. He smiled, an expression he felt was warm and contrite.

She rolled her eyes heavenward. "Don't be trying to charm me, Declan Forrester."

His mouth thinned. "'Twas worth a try. Brooks buys goods around the world for my business. I have an agent sell the goods here, in London and even throughout England."

The harsh line of her shoulders softened a wee bit, encouraging him to continue. "I met with him before my wedding to Abigail. I worried that my marriage to Abigail 'twould be another prison, just without the iron bars."

She threw up her hands. "Why didn't you tell me? I thought all we had was in the box buried beneath Riverton."

"I didn't know how. You thought I had nothing and seemed so pleased about it." To him it was enough. And a little piece of him thought the fact that they were rich would just be a bonus.

She nodded. "Aye, I come from nothing. 'Twas comforting that you did as well." Her gaze slid around the room and he shuddered as she cringed.

"I come from nothing as well. I just needed the assurance I had safety. And with Riverton gone, 'twas a good thing I did." He exhaled. "I have my title from my father, but the estate and all of his funds were confiscated by the crown."

She looked up at him and asked, "Captain Brooks is reliable then?"

With a shrug, he answered, "As reliable as a pirate can be. I believe he is honest in respect to my dealings. His own . . . I'm not certain."

"So all of this," she said with a shrug, "is the result."

He gave a sheepish grin. "Can you live with it?"

She laughed, a sweet sound to be sure. Still, she shook her head and cast a doubtful glance in his direction. "Do we have to live in the city?"

He looked to the intricate pattern on the couch. "I've a country home as well."

Her hand flew to her chest. "Och, you truly are a rich man."

Declan felt her tense once again. "Nay, we're rich."

"I do not know how to live like a rich person. I dress myself, wash my own clothing." She gripped her hands, twisted them nervously. "Declan, I hate to wear shoes."

He laughed and pulled her into an embrace. "Then you will never have to wear shoes," he said into her hair. He closed his eyes and inhaled. Aye, he felt like a cad. In his haste to learn more about his holdings and Finn, he'd neglected to think about Martine's feelings. He rubbed his hand along her back, trying to ease her fears.

"Pah," she said against his shoulder. "Then all will know I'm a Gypsy."

He kissed the tip of her nose. "You're my Gypsy."

She swatted at him, somewhat in jest, but there was lingering uncertainty. He felt it—saw it in her eyes.

"And Finn Randolph?"

He rested his hands on his waist. "That's another concern."

She tipped up her chin. "Tell me."

Declan pinched the bridge of his nose. "As I've said, Finn is helping me search out the truth. 'Tis as simple as that. I want to shield you from the danger."

She stiffened. "Danger?"

Gripping her shoulders, he looked pointedly in her eyes. "I'll protect you. You're my betrothed, more than that. *You are my life.*"

"Och, Declan," she whispered as tears sparkled in her eyes.

Now he was making her cry. He wiped a tear that fell from her lashes with the pad of his thumb. "I never wanted to upset you."

She shook her head. "You didn't upset me," she said in a watery voice. "You've made me happy."

Confused, he just nodded. Women were a complicated lot, to be sure. "I need to meet with Finn and it must be done at night."

Her eyes shifted from soft cognac to something darker, filled with concern. "If people know you are here, will you go back to prison?"

His gut clenched and anger raced through his veins. "Nay. They released me to Ettenborough, and 'twas legal enough. I just need to find out why."

She wrapped her hand around his cheek. "Please be careful."

He took her hand and kissed her palm. "To be sure, my love. I have the most important reason in the world to return safely."

After he ensured Martine was settled, Declan met with his men in the study. 'Twas odd, visiting his home for the first time. His agent had once again proven his worth by appointing the home with elegant furnishings and a capable staff.

The study suited him with dark woods, masculine leathers, and a well-stocked bar. The chamber faced the front of the house, allowing him a clear view of any visitor. Strategic for keeping the estate safe.

A few of the men smoked, selecting cigars from a well-stocked humidor. Lange stood by the large hearth, his face displaying no inkling of his thoughts. Rufus, Little, and Nate spoke quietly in the corner, each with a snifter of brandy in their hands.

"What's your displeasure?" he asked Matthew who brooded as he stared glumly into his whiskey.

The youngest of the group scowled. "I want to go tonight."

Bollocks. Matthew was pouting. He didn't have time to placate the young lad—nor the patience. "You're needed here. I want at least two men watching over Martine."

The young lad shrugged and a hint of pride straightened his posture. "If you put it that way, I'll stay."

Like he had any choice in the matter, Declan thought, as he resisted the urge to roll his eyes heavenward.

"We have to ferret out Randolph." Although he spoke with feigned aggravation, he was truly worried about his friend. If Brooks hadn't received word, he'd be scouring the street for Finn. And while Brooks shared the information, Declan didn't put it past the man to provide falsehoods for his own perverse pleasure.

"Och," Pierce exclaimed as he burst into the room, "am I late again?"

All the men chuckled and refocused on Declan.

"Sit, Pierce."

With his face flushed scarlet, he sat and glanced wildly about the room.

Declan looked at his men. A mix of brawn and intelligence, but all fiercely loyal. It worried him, the danger. He held a stake in the mission, these men did not. 'Twas only his pay that provided reward and he worried it wasn't enough. In fact, he planned on a hefty bonus for all of them. "Tonight we will go to Broderick's home."

The men quickly nodded their heads, their faces serious yet eager.

Nate held up his snifter. "Aye, 'tis a sound plan."

"Matthew and Pierce will stay here and guard the house." Declan pointed at the men. "I want to be alerted of any trouble. Matthew, since you know London, you bring me any urgent news."

Matthew paled as if finally realizing the severity of the situation. Pierce, still flushed red, simply nodded and stayed mute.

He glanced out the window and grinned as the streets had darkened. "Let's go."

They rode through the narrow London streets beneath the cloak of darkness. Their journey did not take long as they came to Broderick's home. Light flickered in the front hall, yet the rest of the house remained dark.

Where the Devil was Finn?

After waiting for an hour, Declan cocked a brow at Nate. "Stay here. Lange and I will go in."

"Do ye think 'tis wise?" the Scotsman asked as he rested a hand on Declan's shoulder.

"Aye, my friend." He motioned to Lange to follow him and they snuck around to the rear of the town house. Lange used his street smarts to pick open the locked door. As they eased into what appeared to be a back parlor, Declan rested his hand on the knife sheathed at his waist. They felt their way through the darkened halls. He glanced into each room, looking for a sign of a study or office.

Finding none, he motioned Lange upstairs and searched anew. He entered what appeared to be the lord's chamber. A door in the rear of the room was open. The sound of drawers opening and closing filtered through the room. Declan raised his hand in warning to his comrade and paced forward while unsheathing his knife. Once he entered the small chamber, he grabbed the person from behind and whipped his knife to the other intruder's neck. "Move and you're a dead man."

"Hell, Declan. 'Tis me, Finn."

Declan exhaled and released his friend. Lange sauntered into the room with a crooked grin plastered on his face.

Declan cocked his hip and rested a fist at his waist. "You should have waited for us."

Finn laughed. "Aye, I can see yer vexed, with a knife pointed at my family jewels."

He tipped his head and allowed a quick grin. "Next time you might not be so lucky."

"Och," Finn said as he waved his hand. "As if you'd skewer me."

Moving toward the desk, Declan picked up a pile of papers. "Anything interesting?" His body hummed with nerves and anticipation. The answers were here; he knew it deep within his gut.

"'Tis a muddled mess, to be sure." Finn grabbed another pile and added to Declan's load.

"Lange, go and tell the men all is fine. We'll be out directly."

The man hesitated, then nodded. Assured he was out of hearing distance, Declan narrowed his gaze. "You know I don't want anything revealed until I've seen it myself."

Finn smirked. "Don't get your knickers in a bunch. 'Tis nothing to tell by this mess."

Declan sheathed his knife and surveyed the room once again. Even in the darkness, Declan could tell the proportions were not quite right. One of the walls jutted strangely and was flanked by two large chairs. His pulse quickened as he walked past the desk and nudged aside a small chair and ottoman. Feeling his sweating palms along the wall, he found the crack and knew deep in the pit of his stomach that what he sought was within. Once again grabbing his knife, Declan pried open the panel and released a sigh that had been pent up for the last several years. A gilded trunk sat on a shelf in the hidden space, beckoning his hands to grasp it and run.

Finn peered over his shoulder. "That's the ticket."

Declan grabbed the trunk and held it. Its heavy weight surprised him. For a moment he was at a loss. Here in his hands may be the answers he'd been waiting for. Emotions swirled in his mind, tensed his muscles. He set the trunk on the desk and stared at it.

"Open it," he directed Finn as he stepped back and rubbed his chin.

"Should be your honor." But his friend opened the lid regardless as he cast furtive glances at Declan.

The trunk revealed more papers and a small box within. He reached for the box and removed the lid. Inside was parchment imprinted with his family crest along with what he knew as Ettenborough's and Broderick's. Aye, Broderick was involved—his carriage had been at the estate that fateful day. A fourth crest was still unknown. He touched the surface and knew there were still more questions than answers.

Finn laid his hand on Declan's shoulder. "'Tis time to leave. The butler will be back."

He nodded, yet his feet remained rooted to the floor. The unknown crest plagued him. Who did it belong to? He scoured his memory to the time after he was whisked away and tried to remember any indication of whom the crest belonged. No luck. It was completely foreign to him.

"*Forrester.*"

He turned to Finn who was trying to right the stacks of papers strewn over the desk and the floor. "Right. Let's go."

Randolph led the way down the stairs and back through the kitchen. Declan held the trunk as they left the house and met with the men congregated in a nearby alley. The sound of their approach alerted them and weapons were drawn.

"Easy, men," he called. They quickly sheathed their knives and holstered their guns.

All remained silent as they mounted their horses and made their way back to Declan's town home. Not until they reached the privacy of his study and summoned Matthew and Pierce did he reveal they'd met with mild success.

"I need to go over the papers and determine what is relevant. Little, I'd like you and Rufus to find out whose crest this is." He handed Little the paper with the foreign crest. "Take care. 'Tis the only copy."

His butler handled the parchment as if it were spun glass.

The old man squinted at the crest, then looked to Declan. "I'll get your answers for you, m'lord."

Declan took the trunk and placed it in the safe behind a portrait of some unknown man. He'd asked for the house to be furnished as if it were inhabited all of these months. Obviously, his agent had taken liberties and Declan assumed, knowing the man's humor, meant to poke fun with the numerous portraits and even clothing in the chest of drawers. After he placed the portrait over the safe, he turned to his men. How could he tell them he appreciated their efforts and how they plunged further into the unknown with him? At a loss for words, he rubbed the back of his neck. Aye, he paid them, well he might add, but deep down he knew they stayed with him the entire time at Riverton because of a camaraderie they had forged. And Pierce, poor fumbling Pierce. Declan knew Pierce stayed out of a desire for adventure and to glean something exciting out of his normally staid life. The loyal Little would do nothing else but stand by his side as the old man's past behavior had more than exemplified. *Bollocks*, somehow he'd create a unique family out of the bunch.

"Rest, men. Until I figure this out, there's nothing else to do."

Each physically relaxed and Rufus released a sigh. Nate helped himself to the brandy, blast his greedy hide, and Finn cocked his head at Declan, motioning him to follow into the hallway.

"Ye seem a wee bit confident."

Declan leaned against the door jam. "'Tis nothing I can do until I read through the papers and find the name behind that crest."

"Aye," he said with a shrug. "But I could still be watching Broderick for ye."

He pinched the bridge of his nose. He wanted Broderick watched, 'twas the truth of it, but what if Finn was detected as the double agent? "For now, my friend, you'll enjoy the comfort of my home."

Randolph's eyes widened, then a big smile broke out over his face. "'Tis time ye asked. The inn's atmosphere was beginning to wear on me for sure."

Chuckling, Declan led Finn to the guest chamber. "I'll have some food sent up for you."

"Yer quite the king of the castle, m'lord."

"Ye bastard," he said as he threw Finn a scorching look.

"Would you look at that," Finn said as he pointed out the window. He walked to the bowed window. The view of the street showed a woman strolling along the walkway. Finn raised his hand as if to knock, and Declan shook his head. A proper lady? Doubtful since it was extremely late in the evening and she was without escort. Yet her elaborate gown and the proud tilt of her chin belied a lowly status.

Curious, they continued to watch her as she fretfully glanced over her shoulder. His keen eyesight witnessed her anxiety. Did she need help? A sleek black carriage pulled up beside her. She looked shaken as a man opened the door and dragged her inside. Declan knocked on the window to no avail. Finn ran from the room and out the front of the house. He chased after the carriage as it barreled down the road as if the hounds of hell chased it.

Declan watched him disappear and knew if his friend needed assistance, he'd let him know.

Now, now was the time to find out the mystery. Find out why his father had damned him to hell.

Chapter 25

Declan wanted to sink into Martine's embrace. But her peaceful slumber stopped him from shucking all of his clothing and crawling in beside her.

He rubbed the back of his neck and headed back to his study. There he opened the whiskey and drank straight from the bottle. He sat at his desk, kicked up his feet onto its surface, and glared at the safe hidden behind the painting.

What would the papers reveal? Would he understand? He abruptly stood and tossed the painting aside. The safe mocked him with its secrets. He removed the trunk and set it on the desk. The crest would be revealed on the morrow. He trusted his men to discover the owner. But the mound of paper within the trunk was a tricky web of politics and ramblings he'd most likely need assistance deciphering due to their age and the players involved. He raked his fingers through his hair and wiped his sweaty brow. Grasping a letter opener, he flicked the lid open and stared inside.

Lifting one of the pieces of parchment, he quickly scanned the writing. Political ramblings. He grabbed another and another—more of the same. One glaring similarity was scrawled on all of it, the names of his father, Ettenborough, and Broderick. What did these men have in common? He pulled up a chair and began reading all of the papers. Threads began to make sense in terms of politics, but why these men? They were obviously of different opinions on the matter.

A light knocking interrupted his inspection of the letters. A quick glance at the window revealed it was nearly dawn. He'd spent the entire night reading and piecing together his past.

He allowed Finn to enter. His friend looked ragged.

"Do you prefer the inn to my home?"

His friend smiled that lazy grin he was known for. "Nay. There was an incident last night."

Declan stilled, all humor gone. "An incident?"

Finn walked to the bar and poured a healthy serving of whiskey. "The woman. The carriage snatching her from right before your home."

Declan furrowed his brow and waved the papers from the trunk at Finn. "You make less sense than these papers."

His friend looked pained as he slouched in the leather chair before the desk. He balanced the whiskey on his thigh and leaned his head back. Worried over this uncharacteristic behavior, Declan walked to the front of the desk.

"Tell me, Finn."

He rubbed his eyes. "I followed the carriage."

"'Tisn't unusual for whores to escape their client and then have to be chased down."

"She wasn't whore," Finn growled with conviction.

Declan held up his hands in acquiesce. "Then what happened?"

"Don't you understand?" Randolph asked as he stood before Declan, spilling his whiskey onto the carpet. "The carriage. It had the third crest."

Declan fell back until he rested on the edge of the desk. The third crest? What did all of this mean? "You're certain?"

He threw up his hands. "Och, do ye think I'm not?"

He shook his head as his thoughts swirled. Finally he'd know the owner of the crest. "Nay, I don't."

Fury contorted his friend's face. "She didn't want to go. I'm certain. He just grabbed her."

Declan placed a steadying hand on Finn's shoulder. "We'll find her."

"How? I chased the carriage on foot, and lost it. Then I searched all night."

He sighed, then stiffened his spine. "'Tis time I visited Broderick. He knows the crest."

Finn gave a curt nod. "Aye, 'tis time."

The men left the masculine confines of the study, urged by conviction and the need for answers. They saddled their own horses after Declan waved the stable hand away. Time was of the essence, 'twas the truth of it.

Carriages littered the path to Broderick's home, clogging the roads with hapless women vying to be noticed by a particular suitor. Aggravated by the slow pace, he urged his horse to the walkway and bypassed the congestion.

As they arrived at Broderick's home, a carriage pulled up. The man himself exited, obviously home from his excursion.

They left their horses with the carriage driver, his face a comical mix of confusion and indignation.

"We've business," was all Declan said to the stupefied Broderick as he strode past and entered the home without any further comment.

"I say, Forrester, this is a most intolerable way to conduct business," Broderick said as he entered the foyer. A vibrant hue of red was working its way up the stout man's neck and onto his jowls. When he looked at Finn, fear paled his face.

Declan stopped and turned toward Broderick. "Ah. And putting an innocent man in prison? How civilized is that?"

"Not here," came a curt response.

They followed the man up the stairs and into the study they'd just invaded the night before. Nary a trace of their investigation remained, which must be to the credit of Broderick's staff.

"I see you have tricked me," he directed at Finn.

His friend merely tipped his head and gave a roguish grin.

Declan had the upper hand in the matter. He knew where the papers now resided, and Broderick did not. "So, old man, tell me why I spent five years in hell at your bidding?"

Sputtering, Broderick wiped his brow with a handkerchief and felt for the chair behind him before he sat. "Not just me. Your father and—"

"Who, old man? Who belongs to the other crest?"

Shock, then weary resignation settled on Broderick's face. "How did you learn of the crest?"

Declan shrugged and crossed his arms before his chest. "I've ways."

He waved a hand. "So you know all."

Finn moved to the window and glanced out. A moment's distraction had Declan wondering if his friend was still worried about the abducted woman.

He tipped his head and frowned. "There are a few details we need to clear up."

"Details mean nothing. I'll not have you in my home. Leave before I call the magistrate."

He leaned forward, calmly placed his hands on the hard surface of the desk, his nose a few inches from Broderick's. The man was sweating, big beads dripped down his forehead and onto his cheeks. "Do so, old man, and you'll never know what hit you."

"A man has the right to privacy. And your man here," he said while pointing a fat finger at Finn. "He worked for me."

"Nay," Declan replied with a humorous smile. "He *works* with me."

Broderick sighed and leaned back into the chair. The silence hovered tensely. With a regal wave of his hand, he said, "Ask away. I am too old and weary to keep the charade going."

Randolph turned back toward the room and cocked his brow. "To whom does the crest belong?"

He looked to Finn, his eyes pleading. "If I tell you, will you leave me be?"

The smell of fear permeated the room. "I should kill you for what you did to me," Declan said, his voice lethally calm.

"But, being the gracious man I am, I will allow you to live—if you answer my questions."

Broderick paled, and then nodded so vigorously his jowls shook. "The crest is of the house of Wright."

That name meant nothing to him. Why did this man tarry?

He'd come this far and would not retreat. Declan placed his hands on the arms of the chair in which Broderick sat. "Wright? Who is Wright?"

The man sighed and waved a hand before he rubbed his sweaty brow. "Let me start from the beginning."

Cringing at the man's rotting teeth, Declan stepped away. Anticipation made him edgy as he waited for the man to speak. "Aye, that would be wise."

Broderick stood and began pacing across the length of the small room with his hands clenched behind his back. "Your father, Wright, Ettenborough, and myself once had an alliance in terms of our political beliefs. We were regarded as emanate political leaders." He stopped and tugged at his chin. "Then your father began to speak blasphemy against the crown. He wanted the king dethroned!"

Finn and Declan's gazes met. 'Twould explain the numerous political papers in the trunk.

"After several years, he became more and more vocal. We had to distance ourselves from him and that . . . well, that proved to be his undoing. As each season passed, he ranted more and more. As if trying to tempt the king and have himself thrown into prison or worse."

The air in the room seemed to vanish. Declan removed his leather waistcoat and rolled his shirtsleeves. The timing was right, at least in his memories, as harsh as they were.

Broderick stopped pacing and stared at Declan. A chill ran up his spine at the cold look in the man's rheumy eyes. "That was when your mother left as well."

Did the man just say what Declan thought he did? An icy sweat trickled down his back. "Left? My mother died."

If possible, sympathy flickered in those aged eyes. "Sorry, lad. She left your father for—"

"*Nay.*" He pinched the bridge of his nose, trying to stop from leaping on the man and pummeling him to death. What crazed nonsense he spoke. "My mother is dead. I saw her buried."

Broderick held up his hands. "Just a ruse."

He stepped back against the wall and caught his breath.

"Och, let me get ye a brandy," Finn said. He looked about the room. "I'll get it from the study."

His mother was alive. All these years and she was alive. All of the years he suffered from his father's neglect and then prison. "Why? Where is she?"

"We all loved her," he said wistfully, the shine of reminiscence heavy in his gaze. "From the moment I laid eyes on her, my heart was lost. She was the loveliest woman of our society. Long hair, so black it gleamed. And her eyes, well, they are the same as yours." He allowed a feeble smile. "I loved her more than life itself. She was so lovely and intelligent."

He inhaled as the information became firmly lodged in his brain. His mother was alive. Declan grabbed the man by his collar. "*Where is she?*"

He struggled out of Declan's grasp as his jowls flapped with the effort. "You cannot go to her. I saw her suffer from being scorned and then when you went to prison, she was utterly lost. I cannot bear to see her pained once again."

One quick grab and he had Broderick shoved against the wall. "*Bollocks.* I don't give a damn what you want."

Broderick stuttered. "She . . . she never forgot you. She longed to see you, but knew it was futile to argue with your father. He threatened you, her—"

Declan scowled. "My father, the fool."

A startled look flashed on Broderick's face. "He was a genius. He just did not work well in society and his radical ideas made him fodder for gossip. But she pleaded with him to stop and he couldn't. He forced her to leave and then lied to you. And when you talked about her, he couldn't bear it."

Disgusted, Declan glared at Broderick. God, how? Why? He still didn't understand how his father could cause so much turmoil in their lives over politics. "Aye, a genius. Weel, he had me put in prison long before you ever did. Once my mother died—left, he refused to speak to me. He loathed me."

Broderick sat once again and his shoulders slumped. "You're the image of your mother. You reminded him of what he'd thrown away. He did not want you punished for what he did, but you need to understand. He was very ill."

"Och," Declan said as he threw his hands up. "That explains it then." The pit of his stomach twisted. He swallowed the rising bile.

Finn re-entered the small chamber and handed Declan a whiskey. "Drink up, lad. Ye've earned it."

The whiskey burned down his throat, paving a fiery path to his roiling stomach. He wiped his mouth with the back of his hand. "Thank you."

"Now, what did I miss?" Randolph's jovial tone did nothing to alleviate the tension as thick as London's fog.

Declan scoffed, the sour taste of disloyalty filled his mouth. "My father's a genius and not to blame for my horrid life."

Finn cocked a brow. "Right. Is that all then?"

Declan gave his friend a withering look as he swirled the rest of his brandy. "Nay, Broderick has more to tell."

"What? Oh, yes, more to tell." He leaned into the chair and crossed his legs at the ankles. He looked relaxed, but sweat dotted his brow and his eyes darted furtively between Declan and the door. "Your mother had little choice but to rely on us. We knew the hell she lived in, especially since her political leanings were so different than your father's. And she feared they would both be arrested and then where would you be?"

Where indeed? "Go on."

"She always told us your father made her leave. I always felt he did it to stop the gossip and to save your mother from the shame. And at times, I thought she left of her own accord."

"This makes no sense to me, to be sure." Declan strode to the window and opened it. He stuck his head out and inhaled. Better.

"I know. It is hard for me to even speak of it. I longed to marry her and your father won her heart. My own wife, bless her soul, suffered grievously. She knew," he said softly. "She knew I loved your mother and married her as a second choice."

Damn, he didn't give a damn how Broderick or his wife felt. He rubbed his chest, trying to alleviate the pain, the ache somewhere in the area of his heart. All rational thought fled his mind as he tried to sort out what he had learned so far. Still, nothing made sense.

"And where did she go?"

"Many times she cried on my shoulder that your father would not allow her to see you." He cringed. "That did not bode well with my wife either. I longed to see your father suffer because of it." He pounded on the desk and spittle formed in the corners of his mouth. "It's his fault my wife fell into despair, melancholy, without an ounce of joy in her life. I watched her wither away to nothing. The pain," he choked back a sob, his eyes wide and manic, "the pain I saw in her eyes every day was torturous." Broderick stood and pointed at Declan, his chest puffed up with bravado. "Your father caused too much pain in my life—I wanted you to pay. I was going to ruin you and he was going to help me." He nodded toward Finn. "Apparently, I've been played the fool." He quickly sat, deflated, impotent.

Declan laughed, and 'twas bitter and full of years of pain. "You're insane to think my father was the only one to blame. You are all to blame. And I've already paid, old man."

"Now see here, Forrester."

He ignored Broderick's outburst. "Why did he deny her? He loathed me."

Broderick sat as if deflated of all air. "There had been threats to put him in prison. He promised to stop his ranting. They were supposed to leave him alone, but his illness, it plagued him and made him—made him continue to rage against the crown."

Declan turned from the window and watched Broderick open the top drawer in his desk. He retrieved a portrait and looked at it lovingly. "Here is your mother today."

He accepted the painting. As he looked down, he nearly dropped it. He traced her profile with a shaky finger. Aye, she was lovely and his memories of her returned in vibrant color. Before, he had faded images of her smile, soft laughter, gentle touch. He tucked the small painting in the pocket of his shirt.

"When you were taken, we had no choice. The political statements your father had spoken for so many years had come back to haunt him. Never, never during that time did the threats cease. And your father was going to be tried for treason." Broderick shrugged. "And then he was so ill, he'd never be able to recover from a trial, much less prison. So they agreed you would suit after a large amount of money exchanged hands. If they took you in your father's stead, he'd stop his political ranting." He gave a casual wave of his fingers. "As you know, the exchange of money can allow for many to turn a blind eye."

"Aye, money." He was dumbfounded. He patted his pocket, uncertain where his emotions lay in respect to his mother. But relief she still lived overwhelmed any anger he felt toward her. "Why the mock trial? Was the judge truly a judge?"

"Nay," Broderick said with a raspy voice. Weariness flooded his features as he wiped his brow. "Your mother begged us to intervene. We never told her you'd be tried until after you were already in prison." He lifted his shoulders and sighed. "The only solution was to take you in his stead. And, we never thought you'd survive to find out the truth."

Declan startled when Finn spoke. "Why did you release him?"

"A document proclaiming your father's innocence was conveniently sent to the House of Lords. We never found out who sent them. We did not want any further trouble and Ettenborough's daughter needed a husband. So to Ireland you went." He rummaged in his desk.

"So to Ireland I went," he whispered. How they'd played God with his life. And how he couldn't absorb all he was learning. "Why hasn't my mother contacted me?"

Broderick sighed and laced his fingers over his rotund stomach. "Fear, lad. She believes you will never forgive her."

Would he? He had no idea. "I need to leave."

"Wait," Broderick called after them. "There is more."

How could there possibly be more to tell? He stilled in the doorway and turned toward the man. "Go on."

"The third crest is Wrights." He looked to the window as if loathe to continue. "It is also your mother's crest."

Declan shook his head and Finn released a low whistle. "So Wright won her hand."

The man flushed. "It is not as scandalous as that, Forrester."

A smile appeared before he could stop it. So, Broderick was still enamored with his mother and would defend her to the end it appeared.

"Lillian had no protection, money, or choice, and Wright was widowed and in need of a wife."

"I'll be back," he promised as he turned on his heel and left Broderick's home without a backward glance.

"Your mother?"

"Aye." Declan paced to the window, anger and frustration boiling just beneath the surface.

"Declan?"

He turned to his betrothed.

Tears shimmered in her eyes, making them a deep brown reminded him of Ireland, the rich soil in which he loved to toil. Maybe they should return and all this business with his mother could stay buried in London. Nay, he had to know all, and Martine's sympathy made the anger fester deeper within him.

"You must go to her," she prodded.

Surprised at the vehemence in her voice, he shook his head, tore away from her. "Nay. She left me with him. And then she knew I was in prison and did nothing."

"Pah, Declan. She's your mother, 'tis the truth of it."

A cool shiver went through his veins as he thought about his mother.

"Do you know what I'd do to see my mother once again? How can you throw this chance away?" she said with tears layered in her tone. "I have left my family to be here. You have the opportunity to reunite with your mother—your mother!" Tears trailed down her face unchecked.

He moved to reach out to touch her. His arms fell to his side. *Bollocks.* How did he explain the years of distress, loneliness? If his mother truly loved him, nothing would have stopped her from seeing him.

"'Tis selfish of you to ignore a new beginning." Resentment flashed in her eyes as she fisted her hands at her waist. "What I wouldn't give for one more moment with my mother."

"Your parents died," he snapped, trying not to let her beauty sway him. The way her tipped up chin challenged him was beguiling. "My mother *chose* to stay away. Don't ignore that difference."

Her stance softened and she nodded after a moment. Her chin lowered and her gaze softened. He gripped her hand just to feel the strength of her.

"Aye, but you must go see her." She moved toward him and placed her hand on his chest over his heart. "For this, for us, for you."

He looked at her, heard the pleading in her voice, but he wouldn't do as she asked. His mother had rejected him, pretended to be dead, and allowed him to spend five years in prison. There was no forgiveness for such a heinous crime.

He left her in their chamber and went to the study. He locked the door and went to the desk to reread the letters in the trunk.

She didn't know what he'd endured. Truly, to have both of your parents turn on you 'twas unthinkable, yet it had happened to him.

He gave up on the papers and tossed them on the desk. They corroborated everything Broderick had said. His father had ranted about the unjust king incessantly. They warned him in decree after decree. Yet his father ignored them.

It was no longer a puzzle, he assumed. His father was a coward who wouldn't have survived prison. His mother was disloyal to the family—to him.

His life had been unfair. Hell on earth.

He looked at the portrait of his mother, ran a finger along her face. A face he'd memorized, revered—and now loathed. Grabbing the picture, he threw it across the room. Books toppled. A clock crashed to the floor.

Why didn't he feel any peace? He knew what had sent him to prison. The whys and hows and whos. But the soul-drenching peace he expected evaded him.

"Declan."

He turned toward the door. Toward the only thing that mattered.

She raced into his embrace.

"I'm sorry, my love," he whispered into her hair, hugging her close.

"I am too."

He pulled back and smoothed her hair from her face. "You have nothing to be sorry for."

She smiled and she'd never looked lovelier. "Aye, I shouldn't have pressed you to see your mother."

He released her and pulled her over to the chair before the desk. He leaned on the desk, facing her.

"You are right. I should see her, put the demons behind me—us." Declan crossed his arms before his chest. "Then we can marry."

Her eyes brightened with flashes of brown and golden hues. "I thought you were never going to marry me."

"Why?"

She shrugged and her skin pinkened as she shifted her gaze. "I thought you were ashamed of me."

Cad. He was a cad. Declan knelt before her, tipped up her chin. "Never."

Her eyes darkened as if she didn't believe him. "You never say my surname."

He narrowed his gaze. "What?"

"Petrulengo. You never introduce me as Martine Petrulengo. Only as Martine."

Thinking back to the times he'd introduced her, Declan realized what she said was true. "I don't know why. Maybe I was worried there may be animosity against your clan."

She tipped her head at him. "I can understand, but even if there is, I am still a Petrulengo."

"Why didn't you tell me this before?" He lifted her up and pulled her onto his lap. She shifted closer to him, tucked into his lap. Warm, soft—and all his. "I am in awe of your strength. You have endured so much and yet here you are in London, away from those you love."

She tangled her fingers in his chest hair, tickling along his skin. "'Tis nothing compared to what you have endured." She nibbled his ear.

He kissed her brow, fierce love prompting him to say, "I am proud of you. Proud to call you my betrothed. And I will be doubly proud to call you my wife."

A knock resounded on the door.

"Enter," he called without moving an inch. Damn anyone who dare criticize how he and his betrothed conducted themselves.

Little cleared his throat. "M'lord, 'tis a guest."

Martine scrambled from his lap, fluffed her skirt, and sent a quelling look in his direction. God, he couldn't get enough of her. Her gown smoothed over her curves, allowing him a view of her beautiful breasts. Her tsk made him chuckle.

"Aye, Little, send them in."

He cleared his throat again. "M'lord, I believe you would be more comfortable in the parlor."

He mentally rolled his eyes. Honestly, he'd be more comfortable in bed with Martine. In fact, all he could think of was heading upstairs and delving into her. He wanted her flesh against his. He wanted to feel her love as she wrapped her legs around him.

Martine nodded toward Little. "Aye, please escort the guest to the front parlor."

"Hmmm. Aren't you the queen of the castle," he teased his betrothed.

She swatted at him, but he could tell she was pleased. "'Tis child's play."

He offered her his arm and they headed toward the parlor and the unexpected guest. Just being this close to her had him itching to run past Little, up the stairs, and into their bed. "Shall we make a run for it?"

"Poor Little would be scandalized," she countered with a sensual smile. "No matter how much I'd love to."

"Perhaps later."

"Aye," she said with a wiggle of her brow.

They laughed as the entered the grand room. He stopped in his tracks.

The mantel clock ticked.

A carriage rambled by.

His breath caught in his throat.

On the overstuffed settee near the fireplace sat his mother.

She stood. Tears glistened in her eyes. "My son," she cried as she walked toward him, her hands outstretched as if he'd clasp them and all would be well.

"Mother," he rasped, uncertain what to say or do. He glanced at Martine and then Little, but neither offered any help at the moment.

She let her hands fall, pain etched tightly on her features. She'd aged, he noticed, but then who wouldn't after so many years.

After a moment of regard, she turned toward Martine. "I'm Lady Lillian Wright."

"My betrothed, Martine Petrulengo."

Martine squeezed his hand as his mother gasped in surprise.

"You're betrothed?" She smiled and looked at him adoringly.

"Aye."

He felt Martine looking at him, imploring him to be kind. But, *bollocks*, he felt anything but kind.

He had suffered. He had the physical and emotional scars to prove it.

"Sit," Martine said. "We'll have tea."

His mother's gaze shifted between them and she nodded.

Little brought tea and quickly left the parlor, closing the doors as he did so.

"My son," Lillian Wright said. "How many years have I waited to say that? There is nothing . . . nothing I can do to make amends for the past."

Fist clenched, he looked directly at her. "Aye, you are correct." Ice ran through his veins as he looked at her. As far as he was concerned, she was a woman who'd come to visit him, not his mother.

The light shining through the windows highlighted the tight lines pinched around his mother's eyes. Tears raced down her wrinkled cheeks. "Not a day has gone by that I have not thought of you."

He smirked.

"I speak the truth," she said as she walked toward him. Her fingers grazed his cheek as she looked at him greedily. "You have changed so much."

He shrugged. "Aye, that can happen after twenty years."

She sobbed, making him feel wretched no matter how detached he tried to be. "Your father. He was crazed. I had to leave. He had—"

"Tea?" Martine asked as she handed his mother a cup. "Certainly we won't settle all of this over afternoon tea. But let's try to be civil."

His mother granted Martine a smile. How he wanted to yell at her, force her to leave. "Thank you, my dear."

He cocked a brow and asked, "If father was such a horrid man, why did you leave me with him?"

The teacup clattered. She set it down. "You wouldn't leave."

"Nay," he shouted as he stood. "You left, but he told me you died."

She gasped as she brought her hand to her mouth. "He didn't give you the letters?"

He fisted his hands at his waist. She spoke nonsense. "What are you talking about woman?"

"Declan," Martine chastised as she gripped his arm. A quick squeeze and a patient look forced him to nod.

Regardless, he glared angrily at both of them. "I received no letters."

His mother stood, worrying her napkin as she gripped and twisted the linen. "I wrote to you, begging you to come with me. But you always refused to leave your father. Each time I wrote to you, I hoped I'd see you at my doorstep."

Dear God. He pinched the bridge of his nose. "I never received your letters."

Lilian Wright crumbled into a heap. Declan and Martine raced to her side.

"Mother," he called as he lifted her onto the settee. "Water, get her water."

Martine dipped a handkerchief into a pitcher of water. Declan patted her brow, an unfamiliar sentimentality overcoming him. "Mother?" he asked when her eyelids fluttered.

"Mother?"

She opened her eyes, and confusion filled her features. She touched the side of his face as if to determine if he was real or not. "What happened?"

"You fainted."

She scoffed. "Nonsense. I have never fainted."

He grinned despite the desire not to. "Regardless, you fainted."

His mother ignored him. "My dear, when is the wedding?"

"The wedding?" Martine darted her gaze. "I'm not certain."

"Not certain?" His mother sat up and patted his hand. "We will need to begin planning at once." She pinned him with a glare. "Do tell me there is a chaperone in the house."

"No," Martine answered as she looked furtively between them.

She fanned herself. "No, she says." She stood as if she hadn't been on the floor a few moments before. "I will arrange one immediately."

"We do not need a chaperone."

Lillian Wright glared down her nose at him. "I will not have scandal swatted around the *ton* about my son and his bride to be."

He scoffed. "I care not what society thinks."

She gasped. "You know not what you say."

He cocked a brow. Truly he could care less. "The letters," he reminded her with a stern tone. "You said I wrote you back."

A haunted look passed over her face. "Yes. I received responses to nearly every letter until four years ago. Then," she confided, "they stopped, no matter how many times I wrote."

He rubbed the back of his neck. His heart pounded at the news of the letters. Of the news that she'd cared. Thought upon him. *Bollocks*. Declan was at a loss. 'Twas obvious his father had answered the letters. And upon his death they stopped.

Did he forgive her? Or did he continue to loathe her?

A man strode into the room, concern obvious on his face. He was tall with a regal, elegant quality that came with inherited money. The man protectively pulled his mother to him.

His mother gave a watery smile. "Robert, I'd like to introduce you to someone."

No matter how hard he tried not to, Declan basked in the prideful look she gave him.

"Anything, darling."

"This is my son, *Lord* Declan Forrester."

Wright stepped forward. "I know who he is. I knew you would come one day." He held out his hand and despite Declan's desire to remain aloof, he shook it. "You know all?" His cool exterior chilled the room.

"Aye, I know all." Did this distant man deserve the adoration his mother was bestowing upon him?

Lord Robert Wright stared at him with such scrutiny that he felt as if the man were boring into his soul. Wright nodded, then said, "I will not allow my wife to be hurt further."

Aghast, Declan just stared at the man.

With a beseeching glance, his mother grasped her husband's arm and tried to guide him to the door. "Robert, dear, perhaps you could allow my son and I time alone."

Lord Wright stood rigid, unyielding.

"Please."

He looked at his wife, then cast a disparaging glare in Declan's direction. "I will see you at dinner?"

"Yes, my dear."

He left, but not before he turned back and hesitated. His mother waved and he turned to leave.

There was more to this, Declan guessed. More than what Broderick told him, and mayhap Broderick didn't know the details he was certain Wright had kept close.

"Until the wedding, I shall move in."

"Nay, Mother."

She waved at him. "I insist. Now, Martine, tell me how you met my son."

It wasn't his life. This was not the life he'd lived for as long as he could remember. In his life, there wasn't a mother and fiancée discussing wedding plans.

Nay, his life was filled with pain and uncertainty. He tried to shake off the feeling that his life was still in a precarious position. No matter that his mother was here, that she'd written to him all along. No matter that Martine was his and would soon be his wife.

"I must be on my way," his mother announced unexpectedly. "I will ready my luggage and be ready to move in by the week's end."

With a flutter of her fingers and a quick peck on his cheek, she left.

He turned toward Martine. "What the hell just happened?"

Chapter 26

Declan nuzzled the apex of her neck as she tried to dress for the second time in an hour. "Please, let me see to our meal."

"I could feast on you."

"Pah, you'd likely starve."

He caressed her round bottom, loving the soft flesh and her whimper of pleasure. "I think not."

She swatted his hand away and moved out of his reach. "'Tis lazy you are. All you want to do is lie abed all day."

He smiled, feeling contentment at how they resolved their problem. "I could get used to it." Especially if she were in bed, naked—ready for him.

Martine slipped on a pair of slippers, sat before the vanity and brushed her luxuriant hair. He rose and stood behind her, lifting the brush from her hand, and gently ran it over her hair as he inhaled the fresh, musky scent of roses and lovemaking. He lifted the silky waterfall of her locks and nibbled on the back of her neck. She shivered and her reflection in the mirror flushed and her eyes darkened. Passionate. She reached her hand back and held onto his head as he trailed kisses along the length of her neck and onto her shoulders.

"Shall we return to bed?"

A throaty, sexy chuckle trickled from her lips. "You're insatiable, Declan."

He smiled against her skin. "Aye, 'tis the truth of it."

A knock on the door interrupted their foreplay.

"My lord?" Little called through the oak. "Your mother has arrived."

She chuckled at Little's obvious distress at an early house guest and Declan's look of surprise and uncertainty.

Declan quickly dressed in a pair of breeches and his comfortable leather waistcoat. "Are you ready, my love?"

Martine cocked her brow then rushed from the room before he could capture her and lead her back to bed.

He gave chase and captured her before she descended the stairs. The tinge of pink on her cheeks, the laughter in her eyes, made him smile. He leaned in and suckled on her plump lower lip.

"We've a guest," she weakly protested between kisses.

Declan fingered her loose hair, the silky strands curling around his finger and slipping through his hand. "Aye, 'tis lovely hair." He whistled. "You cut a fine strap in that dress." Another look at her décolletage prompted him to say, "You should have grabbed a shawl."

She grinned, a sly look narrowing her eyes. "'Tis the fashion."

"The hell with fashion," he groused as he tried to pull the dress up.

She slapped his hand away, tightened her grip on his arm, and led him to the parlor.

"Ah, here he is, Gwyneth." His mother strolled forward and grasped his hands. Her smile filled her face and the hint of tears shimmered in her gaze. "Didn't I tell you he was handsome?"

Declan tried to pull away, but her grip surprised him with its strength.

Her gaze lit as she took in Martine. "And this is his fiancée."

Martine flitted her gaze back and forth between Declan and his mother. How was one supposed to act with the mother of the man she was sleeping with?

His mother pulled Martine to her side and slipped her arm around her shoulders. "Tell me, how long have you been engaged to my son?"

Despite her unease, she found Declan's mother welcoming. "Just before we left Ireland."

"Excellent," she said with glee. "We'll begin introducing you through London, and we must have a ball to celebrate."

Martine looked over her shoulder at him, hoping her pleading look would stop all discussion about a ball. He shrugged, looking as uncertain as she felt. Hmmm, mayhap the man had spent too much time in Ireland and wasn't privy to the ways of the *ton*.

She focused on the other woman in the room. She was sitting quietly near the hearth with her hands folded in her lap. She cocked her brow at Declan when he continued to stare at her. Tension filled the room and clearly vibrated around the woman.

"Oh, I have been remiss," Declan's mother said. "Please let me introduce you to Gwyneth."

Declan bowed slightly as Gwyneth remained silent.

"Gwyneth," his mother said sharply. "Greet your brother properly."

Oh, dear.

"I am pleased to meet you, Lord Forrester." Her voice was clipped, English, and she was obviously vexed. She rose and executed a mocking curtsy.

Lady Wright, her grace—Martine was uncertain of the proper title—strode to Declan and gripped his hands in hers. "I know this is a great shock to you. But I never had the chance to tell your father and . . . so many years have passed."

He sat and stared at his sister. "She isn't my half-sister?"

"You heard her," Gwyneth said. "Please direct your questions to me, if you please."

Martine sat between Declan and his sister. She touched Gwyneth on the arm, ignoring her flinch. "I'm so pleased to meet you."

Gwyneth raked her gazed over Martine and remained silent as she stood to leave.

"You promised," his mother said with tension and tears thick in her voice. Her heart broke at the pain on Lady Wright's face.

His sister bobbed her head and sat once again, still unyielding and horribly rude.

"We were just about to break our fast, would you care to join us?"

"No," his sister nearly shouted.

"Excellent," his mother said as she cast a fierce scowl at Gwyneth. "We'd love to. Robert is at his club."

"Mother," Declan said as he offered his arm. "This way."

'Twas obvious he was uncomfortable, uncertain. First his mother was alive and now he had a sister. Her heart went out to him as he led his mother toward the dining room. She glanced at Gwyneth and received an icy glare. She held her hand out toward the chamber's entrance and they followed Declan and his mother.

His mother waved at them. "Please excuse your sister's behavior. Such a shame she chooses to pout on a grand occasion such as this."

Gwyneth rolled her eyes and scoffed. "I am certain my brother does not care for my problems." Though her tone sound bored, as if she were merely tolerating their presence, there was a sadness hidden in her cautious gaze.

Martine gave a sympathetic smile and said, "But of course we care. Don't we, Declan?"

Again Gwyneth's hawk like gaze narrowed in on her. "Where are you from?"

"'Tis enough," Declan said with authority. "My betrothed is English."

His sister ignored him and narrowed her gaze. "Your accent is rather queer. In fact, there is something strange about this entire situation."

"Gwyneth," Lillian hissed. "Mind your manners."

"I hardly think that I should be chastised for asking a question." Anger straightened her shoulders as she challenged them with a hard look. "You are not English. Certainly Martine is not an English name."

All blood left her face. How did she answer?

His mother went to speak, yet Declan stopped her with a raised hand. He regarded his sister coolly, feeling the rising wave of his anger that she should so disgrace his wife. 'Twas more to the matter than he knew, 'twas obvious. However, her cold exterior was cracking and he witnessed the flash of fury that tinged her cheeks red. Despite her fair skin, she had the look of him. Dark as pitch hair, neatly coiffed in what he assumed was the latest fashion, and her eyes were blue. Not the dark blue of his, more like a clear day when the sun illuminated the sky and it reflected back on the earth.

No one, not even his new-found sibling would be allowed to speak rudely to his wife to be.

Declan leaned his elbows on the table, earning a furrowed grimace from Little. He steepled his fingers and rested his chin upon them. "Never," he said while gazing ahead, "speak to Martine in such a manner again." He left no room for discussion in his steel-edged tone and he intended for her to obey. Why was he not surprised that she didn't?

Gwyneth threw her napkin onto the table and rose, shoving the chair to the ground as she brushed by with her full skirt. She raced out the room in a most unladylike pace, knocking past a surprised Finn Randolph as she did so.

"I apologize, Lady—Martine." Lillian wiped a tear from the corner of her eye. "She has not been the same since her betrothed was killed in a carriage accident."

Martine clutched her chest. "How horrid for her."

"Yes. I am afraid she blames herself. God knows why, yet she will not speak to me about it."

As Declan's sister left, Finn walked into the dining room.

Barely paying attention to the conversation between Martine and his mother, Declan watched Randolph rakishly gaze at his sister as she rushed past him in the corridor. When Finn turned his attention back to his mother and wife, worry etched across his features. Curious, Declan called to him. "Join us, Finn."

He held out his hands and looked down at his clothing. "I'm not dressed, to be sure."

Indeed, his friend had the look of a man who'd just enjoyed the many pleasures of a pub.

"Pah. You're always welcome," Martine said with a smile.

Finn executed a bow. "Thank you, my fair Martine."

She blushed beneath Finn's attention. Vexed, Declan cleared his throat. "Did you have something to tell me?"

Chuckling, Finn reached for a napkin and deliberately draped it on his lap. "I met with your friend Captain Brooks."

This should prove interesting. "Aye?"

Finn shrugged. "I'll be sailing with him when he leaves port."

He was surprised speechless. He stood, then raked his fingers through his hair. With his hand resting at his waist, he looked down the long table at his lifelong friend. He'd be sailing with the Captain Brooks. Aye, there were times when he didn't see Finn for several weeks, but he always knew he was covering his back.

Randolph bit into a biscuit. "I'll keep an eye on the old bird and maybe even create an adventure for myself."

Declan forced a smile. *Bollocks*, he was being selfish. "'Tis a sound plan." He hated the hollow sound of his voice. "Brooks can be a tricky ticket."

He felt Martine's scrutiny. If he looked at her, he knew the hard veneer he masked his emotions with would shatter. His wife knew his attachment to Finn. And now he was leaving. "When do you go?"

"On the morrow."

"Time for a brandy, my friend." He nodded to his mother, then kissed Martine on the cheek. "Please excuse us."

"A bit early for a brandy, my son."

He glanced at her and tipped his head. "'Tis a salute to a dear friend. I pray you excuse us."

"I'll meet you in your study." Finn bowed and left the room.

"You have remained friends for a very long time," his mother observed.

"Aye." Declan had relied on Finn for more than friendship. He was like a brother to him. Family when he had none. It would be as if he were losing a limb.

Sympathy welled in Martine's eyes. Those clear, windows he couldn't get lost in or else he may shatter. Too much had happened. While it was necessary to come to London, Declan wondered if he'd have been better off remaining in Ireland with Martine and his past be damned. "I must see to Finn."

He left the women in his life and headed toward the study—one of them he couldn't live without, the other was a part of his past he thought gone. Now his mother had miraculously re-appeared. He needed steady; he needed predictable. Having the rug pulled out from beneath him every day was getting tiresome.

And now Finn would be leaving. He raked his fingers through his hair, then pushed open the study door.

Another change. Another upheaval.

"Ah, the lord himself." Finn handed him a brandy and held his up in toast. "Here's to women, money, and sailing on the high seas."

"Who is the woman?"

Declan pointed to the doors that led to the gardens. "She's my mother."

Finn rolled his eyes. "Not her, ye *eejit*, the lovely one. Not that yer mother isn't lovely," he said quickly. "I just meant the younger one."

Laughing, Declan slapped Finn on the back. "She's my sister."

Finn stopped in his tracks. "I didn't know ye had a sister."

"Neither did I." The stern countenance of his friend's face was clear in the early morning light. "Quite a nasty girl from the looks of it." He cocked a brow at his friend. "Why do you ask?"

They continued to the rear of the property, the ewe trees shielding them from intrusive eyes and the busy London streets.

"She was the one," Finn said with a puzzled look on his face. He shook his head and his rakish demeanor returned.

Declan's cocked his brow.

"The lass being snatched into the carriage."

Declan stopped and faced him. "The Wright carriage?"

Finn looked into his brandy and scowled. He set the drink on the base of a statue. "There was fear, Declan. I'd bet my life on it."

More to worry about. He shook his head, then pinched the bridge of his nose. "Why would she be running?"

His friend shrugged. "She's yer sister, not mine. Ask her yourself."

Declan thought for a moment. He'd have to ask his mother questions, questions he didn't think he wanted the answers to. Would she share the Wright family secrets with him? He clapped his hand on his friend's back. "Are you certain you wish to sail with Brooks?"

"As certain as I can be." Finn set his hands at his waist and looked up at the sky.

"You'll send word if you need me?"

"'Tis I who looks out for you, lad," Finn said as he lightly punched his friend. He opened his mouth, then shut it.

Aye, he felt the same. "Ha. You're older, to be sure, and quite a bit uglier."

Finn pulled a face. "That's not what the ladies in Dublin say. Remember that buxom redhead who—"

"Not so loud. My mother's in the house."

Laughing, they moved toward the house. Before they entered, Finn stopped. "I'm leaving now, Declan. Nate will be talking to you about the other men."

He sighed and shook his hand. His stomach clenched as if in warning. It would be a long time before he saw his friend again—if ever. "Aye."

Finn pulled him into a hug and roughly patted his back. "Marry her soon. She's a treasure."

"Aye, to be sure."

They awkwardly parted, many words left unsaid, but known regardless. Declan went inside as Finn went to the stables.

Now to join Martine and his mother. They were most likely discussing wedding details that he wanted no part of.

He just wanted to wed her, not partake in the lengthy rituals of the *ton*.

A smile quirked his mouth. He was certain his bride to be would feel the same.

Chapter 27

Martine woke to shouting. Angry voices with fierce tones emanated into her chamber. She stumbled out of bed and into the hallway.

"Stop," she yelled. "Leave him alone."

Two strangers wrestled with Declan as another man stood aside. He cast a look her way, then resumed watching the fight before him.

Lillian's husband?

"Cease, Forrester. You have no choice but to return."

Martine struggled down the stairs. "Return?"

"Go back to your room, Martine. I'll handle this," Declan yelled. He forced one man from him, but the other held tight.

Lord Wright stood at the bottom of the stairs. His demeanor was terse and frightening. He removed his gloves and slapped them against his palm. "Do as he said and leave."

"Little," Declan growled. "Bring her to her room."

Martine shoved Little aside. Panic ruled her actions as she tried to reach Declan. "Why aren't you helping him?"

The old man paled as he looked about the room. She hoped he was looking for a weapon. "I've tried, but I'm no match for their brawn."

"I'll go." Declan shook off the men and straightened. "Leave her alone. I'll go with you."

A satisfied smirk tilted Wright's mouth.

Martine rushed over to Declan. Her body shook with fear. "What is happening?"

He held her and whispered into her hair. "'Tis nothing but a misunderstanding."

"He is to go back to prison," Lord Wright decreed.

Martine turned to Wright and went to push him. "*No. He's done nothing.*"

He nodded to one of his men who pulled her away.

"Hurt her and you're a dead man," Declan said with lethal calm.

Wright merely smirked, smoothed his jacket, and adjusted his cravat. "There seems to be some discussion as to the legality of Forrester's earlier release."

'Twasn't possible. "You vile man. Let Declan go."

Declan pulled Martine back into his arms. "I'll be fine." He kissed her and said in a low voice, "Send Little to my mother."

She nodded. Aye, his mother would be able to help. She may be able to find his men as well, but she had no idea where they were.

"Time to go, Forrester," Wright said with too much enthusiasm. "You have people to answer to."

"I have proof," he yelled. "I have proof of my innocence."

Wright gave a humorless laugh as he stared down his patrician nose. "From Broderick? The man is a twit and has lost all hold on reality. Come with us and she remains unharmed."

Declan let go of Martine and followed Wright out the door. He looked over his shoulder and offered a small smile. She moved toward him, straining as Little tried to hold her back. Terror struck her with a force that buckled her knees. His face a mix of anger and sharp angles. A thunderstorm roiled in his gaze. Och, her heart ached for him. How could this happen? Again?

She tried to follow, yet blast the man, Little supported her. She collapsed against the old man as she wept unabashedly.

Her heart tore from her chest as they led the man she loved away.

"You must hurry," she told Little as he held out a handkerchief to wipe her eyes. "Make sure she knows it is of the utmost importance."

"I'll not let you down," the butler vowed. He gave her a compassionate look and said, "I'll do my duty."

"Aye," she assured him. "Please take care."

"Aye, m'lady."

He left quickly and all she had to do was wait. Each minute turned into another as time passed with torturous slowness. She walked into Declan's study and ran her hand along the hard wood surface of the desk. She sat in his chair, easing into the soft cushion of the leather. He spent so much time here, she could still feel him.

The overwhelming events of the day took their toll. Martine tried to fight it. She rose in order to revive herself and paced to the double doors that led to the gardens. She didn't walk out into the glaring sunshine of the day.

Pah, when would Declan's mother arrive? Her thoughts spun and swirled in her mind. How could it come to this? She crossed her arms before her chest and watched Betsy play in the distance. The staff, save Little, had kept their distance when Lord Wright was here. She felt terrible she hadn't made a better effort to get to know them, yet so much had happened that she hadn't the time.

Betsy skipped down the mulch-covered path and playacted with some imaginary friend. Watching the sweet girl helped her stay calm and not watch the timepiece incessantly.

"I came right away."

She turned at the voice. Hope flared when she saw Lady Wright bustle into the room. "I'm so glad you did." She moved toward her and grasped her hands.

"Of course I came. My dear, you look wretched." Lillian led her to the chair and bade her to sit.

"Pah. I'm not worried about me. 'Tis Declan." She accepted the glass of water handed to her by Little. "You must help Declan."

Lady Wright sat in the chair across from the desk. She

appeared elegant with her high-fashion gown and regal posture. "Of course I will help my son."

Martine summoned the courage to look directly into the woman's eyes. "Your husband came and took him away."

Lillian blanched as she fanned herself with her hand. "I cannot believe Robert would do such a dreadful thing."

"He took him away and will send him to prison unless you stop him."

She stood and wiped tears from her face. "How could this happen? He raged after I said I was moving in as chaperone." She wrung her hands. "He's not a bad man. Robert fears . . . fears I will leave him." A fretful look took over her features. "I do not know why he'd think such. I've been nothing but loyal to him since we wed."

After she took a sip of her tea, Lady Wright set the cup down. "Right. Well it appears as if I must go to Robert." She stood up. "I will force him to release my son. I will *not* lose him again."

Martine prayed Declan would be found and that his mother wouldn't be too late. "Please bring him back to me."

Lillian swept over toward the desk and gathered Martine's hands. "My dear, I promise I will save Declan." Tears filled her blue eyes and flowed over her lashes. "I missed the chance to save him once before and, because of my cowardice, I failed him miserably."

"I'm certain you did the best you could." Martine squeezed her hands. "I'm so glad you came."

"I'll never be far away again." Lillian masked her features from sympathetic to a hardened veneer. The transformation helped Martine accept the fact that Declan's mother could actually accomplish the tremendous feat.

Lillian nodded her head and straightened her shoulders. A formidable expression hardened her features. "I must be on my way."

"You'll send word?"

"Absolutely, my dear." The woman appeared to be on a mission as she slipped her hands into kid gloves and bustled out of the room in a hurry.

"You, Little," Martine heard her say. "Come with me, man. We have business to attend to."

Martine couldn't help but smile and felt better than she had all day.

Still, she wondered whether they were fated to endure continuous problems? Or would this be the last interruption to their happiness?

Time would tell, she supposed, and prayed no more would infringe on their path to marriage.

Declan thrashed against the locked door that imprisoned him. He gasped for air as the walls closed in, and he stumbled away. He raked his fingers through his hair, then wiped the sweat from the back of his neck.

Vicious memories along with Martine's face, pale and sad, cluttered his mind. *Bollocks.* Declan pushed himself up from the floor and resumed pounding on the hard wood door. Still no one answered.

'Twas no different than Newgate, even though there were no other prisoners groaning and screaming for release. And it wasn't release from prison they had wanted, it was release from life. Declan closed his eyes and tried to envision Martine in the garden with the sunlight streaming down on her dark tresses and kissing her skin. Flowers surrounded her in their springtime buds and vibrant colors. She smiled, a smile made of promise and love—devotion. He clung to the vision.

God, he missed her. The sight of her, touch of her, the mere scent of her.

A noise sounded in the distance. Declan opened his eyes and was greeted with the bleak darkness of the room and no comfort save his musings.

Keys rattled and the knob turned. He watched the door as a cat watches its prey, ready to leap in a flash to devour its next meal.

The door opened a creak as a thin stream of light breached the darkness. Declan crouched down on his haunches.

The door opened further and a silver tray clanked on the floor. Declan leapt toward the door and wrenched it open and grabbed the servant who'd delivered the tray.

Slamming the door closed, he tossed the young boy in the corner. Even in the darkness he could see the lad quiver. Declan leaned against the door and contemplated what to do. This was an opportunity, he knew, but Wright would always be there, just over his shoulder.

"What's your name, lad?"

The boy's eyes widened then he scowled. "'Wot's it to ya, gov?"

Declan paced forward and stood before the boy. He was young, to be sure, with a mop of dark hair and the gangly limbs of a boy on the verge of manhood. "I asked your name."

He thrust his chin forward. "Glendale. Jon Glendale."

"Well, Jon, 'tis time for you to tell me what's happening beyond this door."

The scrappy lad stood and brushed his pants free from dirt. "There's talk of ye. About yer breaking out o' Newgate."

Declan smirked. So that was how they were playing it. As if anyone had survived escaping from Newgate. The lad moved toward the door, but Declan stopped him with his hand. "Stay here if you wish to remain safe."

Jon mutely nodded and tucked back into the wall. Declan reopened the door and looked out to ensure no one was guarding the hallway. Quietly he left the room and headed in the direction of raised voices. He stilled outside a room closed off by two large oaken doors. Angry voices permeated the wood and greeted him with a surprise.

If he was not mistaken, one of the voices was his mother's. He waited until the shouting ceased and placed his hand on the cool brass doorknob. After a moment's hesitation, he turned the knob and entered the room. All discussion stopped as Wright, his mother, and Broderick turned to face him.

"A lovely afternoon, to be sure."

"Declan," his mother exclaimed as she rushed towards him. She framed his face with her hands and stared at his face. "They have hurt you."

"It was his own doing." Wright shrugged his shoulders. "He fought to escape."

Declan glared at the arrogant man, yet remained silent. He gripped his mother's wrists and removed them from his face. Emotions raged within him. He was pleased that she came and irritated he had to seek her help. "I appreciate your help, but you must leave."

She shook her head vehemently. "No . . . no, I will stay with you, my son."

"Once again you chose your son, thus your blasted first husband, over me." Wright swiped all the papers from his desk. "This bastard of a son who killed in prison. He killed a man, Lillian."

Declan moved his mother behind him. "Aye, I killed a man. It was kill or be killed in Newgate. I make no apologies."

"Listen to him, Robert. You sent him there." Tears flooded her eyes and trickled down her face. Her skin was ashen as she gripped a nearby chair. "You sent him there," she whispered.

"I had to. We had to," he said as he pointed at Broderick. "Or else the king would have targeted us as well."

Broderick blustered. "I've no account for this . . . this new attempt at revenge. We arranged for him to go to prison the first time to save our own necks."

"And you wanted Lillian as your own," Wright spat.

"We all wanted Lillian," Broderick countered. "She was how we lived with ourselves. Saving her from the crazed husband."

His mother straightened her spine and glared at her husband. "Gwyneth will come with me. I will no longer reside under this roof." She clutched Declan's arm. "You will never attempt to hurt my son or his betrothed in any way. I know too much, Robert. Too much of the past and your part in it."

Declan watched the man and took perverse pleasure in the range of hues that surged up his neck and over his face.

"Come, my son. We must return to your home. Your betrothed is plagued with worry." She patted his hand and gave a stunning smile. "I will tell Grimes to inform Gwyneth of our new address."

He just nodded and escorted her from the estate. She'd left her husband, home, the comfortable place in society to support him. Something akin to joy surged through his heart. Although she had abandoned him so many years ago, her current loyalty had helped to heal the festering wound. He owed his strength to her, and for that he'd be forever grateful.

"Excellent," she said. "I have not felt so alive in many years." She nodded to the footboy and entered the carriage. "It is settled then. And your sister will be pleased to stay with you as well."

Declan frowned, but decided not to comment on Gwyneth. If she lived up to previous behavior, he knew she'd prefer to sleep on the docks than stay under his roof.

Maybe he should allow Finn to take her away.

Chapter 28

Martine tossed and turned as her thoughts tumbled about in her mind. She woke, not able to coax her mind to a better, happier path. Pah, she was worried about Declan. No word had been sent and she fretted all the more because of it.

Instinct led her to the broad windows. She searched the garden, looking for what pulled her there. At the rear gate, there he stood. "Declan," she whispered.

She raced from the room and down the front stairs, shoved past Gertie, and threw the doors that led to the garden open.

She ran right into Declan's open arms and kissed him all over his face.

"Easy, my love," he said between laughter. "I'm here to stay."

"I missed you so," she said between tears.

He hugged her close to his body. "'Twill never happen again."

Martine pulled back and allowed her gaze to absorb every detail of his handsome face. Bruises marred the perfection of his jaw line and a deep gash intersected his brow. She lifted her hand to gently touch his wounds, her heart fretting all over again. "How could they hurt you so?"

He shook his head and rested his forehead against hers. "'Tis nothing. Let's go inside." He linked his arm through hers and led her back through the open doors.

As they entered the back of the house, Lady Lillian Wright bustled through the front. A hint of anger quivered her lip and flashed in her eye. She methodically removed her gloves and slapped them on the table. Lillian came before them and stood.

"Thank you for saving him," Martine said as she leaned down and gave the woman a kiss. "Thank you."

Declan's mother gripped her shoulders and a proud smile flashed on her mouth. "I would never allow him to return to prison."

She nodded and glanced at Declan with a hint of pleading in her gaze. Tight lines surrounded her eyes, eyes that were just as blue as her son's. He remained aloof, a stern scowl on his face and the rigid line of his back only indicating his ire more.

"No matter what the bastard tried to do?"

His mother scoffed. "Really, son. Your language."

"*Mother*."

"Right. I do not know about you, but I need a bracing cup of tea." She walked to the parlor, her kidskin shoes clicking in rhythm to her brisk steps. "Come along, we have much to discuss."

Declan followed his mother, needing the answers and the right to ask more questions. She sat like a queen in the chair nearest the fire. The crisp spring air had obviously warranted one to be lit. He bypassed the tea and headed straight to the decanter of brandy. He poured a healthy dose and turned back to his mother.

Tragedy had visited his life too many times to count. But what mattered most were these two beautiful women before him. One he'd lost long ago and had the luck to find, and the other was such an obvious match to his soul, the other beat of his heart. He enjoyed them a moment longer before he strode to the couch opposite his mother and sat. It took the cock of his brow for her to begin her rushed explanation.

"He will never bother you again. I have knowledge that would ruin him as a peer, not to mention his political dealings. Your imprisonment notwithstanding." She sipped her tea and patted her lips with a small napkin, behaving as if this were any other day, except he saw the slight tremor of her hand. "I will never lay eyes on him again. Excellent," she exclaimed when Little brought in a tray of tea cakes and buns. "A row always leaves me famished."

Martine chuckled as she served his mother.

"I cannot believe how vicious my husband was being. I do not understand," she said as she sniffed into a napkin. "He never treated *me* in such a way. Why would he treat my children that way?"

"Has he treated Gwyneth badly?" Martine glanced at Declan, then back to his mother. "Is that why she's so unhappy?"

"No, no." Lillian shook her head as she continued to wipe her nose. "My daughter is in turmoil over the death of her fiancée. Tragic, tragic accident. Although her relationship with Robert has never been congenial, now it is downright frigid." She tapped her chin. "I wonder why I never noticed it before?"

"Finn said he saw her running from Wright's carriage," Declan offered. If his sister were here, he'd question her until she revealed all.

Something shifted in his mother's eyes. He witnessed it. Martine obviously sensed it and quickly looked to him. He was tired of secrets, those of his family, his own. They only ruined lives and bore distrust.

"I'll leave you to talk," Martine said as she exited the room.

"She is lovely, my son." His mother watched him, waiting perhaps, but there was also relief in her expression.

Declan sat across from his mother. God, it was strange sitting with his mother as if he did so every day. They both drank—him brandy, her tea in contemplative silence. "Aye, she is the love of my life."

"Ah, 'tis the lord himself."

Declan turned, then groaned. "Grand. Just what I need to make my day pleasant—a visit from the *Kapo*."

Rafe Petrulengo entered the room with a catlike grace and poured himself a drink. "Fine brandy you have."

The man had the nerve to sit at his desk, kick up his feet, and rest them upon the wood surface.

"We don't have to pretend to tolerate each other," he said with a quick glance at his mother. God only knew what she was thinking. A gleam of curiosity brightened her eyes. "What do you want?"

The Gypsy smirked and mocked a salute at Declan and his mother. "As you wish." He refilled his brandy and swirled it as he looked at Declan. "My grandmother missed Martine."

Declan chuckled. His mother was paying rapt attention to their exchange. He knew he'd have to explain at one time or another, but now was not the time. "If you think I believe that, you've underestimated me."

Rafe gave an arrogant shrug. "Believe what you want, Irish. I brought Anya here. And she plans to stay, no matter how I try to convince her otherwise."

Actually, he had no problem with Anya residing with them. Martine would be ecstatic to have her grandmother in their home. In fact, why hadn't he thought of it before? Martine would love the idea of having her family close by.

"Declan?" his mother question.

He dragged his fingers through his hair and sighed. "Mother, meet Martine's brother, Rafe."

The Gypsy had the impudence to grin, roguishly accepted her hand, and kissed its surface. "A pleasure, my lady."

"It is a pleasure to meet one of Martine's relatives." She shot a look at Declan and quirked her brow. "I am certain there is more to this story than I know."

Declan nodded. "I will tell all over luncheon." He looked at Rafe, who had refilled his glass once again. "Does Martine know Anya wishes to stay?"

Rafe shook his head. "I was waiting to see if you'd permit her to stay."

He narrowed his eyes and looked at the man before him. His clothing marked him as a Gypsy, as did his dark eyes and skin. Yet he felt somewhat of a kinship with the nomad. Declan rubbed his eyes, entirely too weary to argue. "I will always welcome Anya in my home."

"A Gypsy in a lord's home?" Rafe said with a sardonic edge.

He watched his mother cast her glance up and down Rafe as if weighing who this man was. Most women would have run screaming, but nay, his mother stood straight and observed the interaction as if it was a normal occurrence.

Declan scowled. "Pour me one."

Again that arrogant smirk. "Where's my sister?"

"We both know she's not. Let go of the pretense."

Rafe shook his head and waved his fingers at Declan. His rings glinted in the sun streaming through the window. "You'll never understand, but she brought a certain peace to my family."

"How can that be? The Rom are notorious for not accepting outsiders."

Rafe took a sip and held it. After he swallowed, he spoke, "The children refuse to believe she's never coming back. Even the elders speak of her absence with dismay."

Declan nodded to the chair for the *Kapo* to sit. "She refuses to see her family."

The Gypsy's gaze did not waver as Declan attempted to pin him with a withering look. "They aren't her family, the family of her heart."

Aye, he'd agree to that.

"You'll remain for our wedding?"

Rafe gave a careless shrug. "If it is written in the stars."

Damn if Declan didn't chuckled at the arrogant man. "Aye, *Kapo*, then I have a plan."

Declan assisted Martine from the carriage. The church was quiet save for their small group. Rich stained glass, archways, and stone flooring greeted them as they entered. The gleaming pews were set in rows and lit candles graced a large altar—all of the elegant niceties the wealthy and those of the *ton* expected.

"Ah, m'lord, 'tis good to see ye again, lad."

Declan turned toward the priest. He was garbed in the traditional collar and black hassock, although it pulled tight over his rotund stomach. The jovial man bowed to Martine, yet couldn't hide the curious twinkle in his eyes. "How can I be serving you today?"

Declan clasped Martine's trembling hand in his own. "We wish to wed."

The priest's eyes widened in shock as he rocked back and forth on the heels of his shoes. "Ahhh, the banns need to be considered, to be sure." He tugged on his double chin. "You'll have to wait a fortnight."

Martine gasped and looked at him expectantly. "Father, we need to wed now."

Father Anthony gathered her hands in his. "It is the tradition and church law, my child."

Declan scoffed. "You know there are ways around the banns. Many a marriage was performed after a large donation."

The man looked over their shoulders to see if anyone else was in the church. "Yes," he allowed with a grin.

Declan laughed. The tension eased out of the situation as Martine and Father Anthony chuckled as well.

He reached for his money pouch. "I've enough to placate the delicate rules of the church."

"A lovely donation does well to soothe the church," the priest said as he patted Declan enthusiastically on the back. "Let's be done with it then."

Declan went to the carriage to gather their witnesses. They stood near the altar with Father Anthony before them. Declan's mother, Little, and a disgruntled Gwyneth were their only witnesses. Candlelight flickered around in a hazy, golden sheen. Martine nervously gripped her skirt, then rubbed the blue silk between her fingers. Declan had given her a bouquet of flowers and the sweat from her palms made holding them uncomfortable. Yet she felt a blessed peace. She belonged with Declan. Of that she was certain. Och, how she loved him. She watched him, proud and confident in a deep gray suit and a white shirt that offset his tanned skin and blue eyes. His dark hair was slicked back and lay over the collar of his shirt.

He was so handsome. Strong and generous. Honorable and loving. Martine let go of her gown and slipped her hand into his. Father Anthony cocked his brow at the gesture, yet he continued directing the wedding vows.

"One moment, Father." Declan nodded, then called to the rear of the church. "'Tis time."

One by one Matthew, Lange, Nate, Rufus, and Pierce made their way down the aisle and into the empty pews. Each man had groomed in one way or another, making them presentable for such an occasion. The priest chuckled as the men awkwardly pulled at their starched collars.

"Are we ready, then?"

"Aye, father." He cast a warm smile at her and then said, "We've another witness."

The door of the church opened. Rafe led an older woman with a tuft of white hair who came into the building with her head ducked.

"Grandmother?"

Declan grinned. "We thought you would like her to be here."

Martine wrapped her arms around his neck and kissed him soundly. "Thank you," she whispered as tears threatened. "Thank you."

She released him and went to welcome her grandmother. "I'm so glad you're here."

Anya laughed. "Pash. I would never miss this day."

She turned toward her brother. "Thank you."

He embraced her and kissed her on the forehead. "For you I'd bring the moon."

Anya patted her arm as Martine led her to the first pew. Declan's men moved aside so Anya and Rafe could be the closest to the couple.

"Grand," the priest said. "Are we ready, then?"

"Aye, father."

"Heard that before, Lord Forrester." The priest reopened his Bible and began reading a marriage blessing.

Happiness infused her. The moment was perfect. She kept stealing glances at her groom and nearly pinched herself to make sure this was real, not some fairytale.

"Lord Declan Forrester," Father Anthony announced. "You may kiss your bride."

A rousing cheer filled the church as his mother, men, Anya, and Rafe offered their congratulations.

She was now a married woman.

"Right," Father Anthony said. "Never boring around you, my lord."

Declan hugged her. He leaned back and gently cupped her face. She would take pleasure in looking into his face for the rest of her life. He kissed her lips softly, and then they turned to accept the congratulations from the well-wishers.

They enjoyed a luncheon and after most had left or gone to bed, Martine had one last goodnight to say.

Her brother gave a curt nod. "May we speak?"

With an apologetic smile toward Declan, Martine left the room with her brother.

"What can be so important you can't wait until morning?" Although she knew the answer, sadness filled her as she watched Rafe. No matter if their relationship had experienced ups and downs, he was her brother.

"Anya will be staying with you?"

She chewed on her lip. "Pah. Is that what this is about?"

He paced the foyer with quick strides. Her brother was flustered, not a trait she knew he possessed. "Am I to be the only one remaining? The last of the true Petrulengos?"

Ah, that was it. He was lonely. Men were a hard sort. "I would like you to stay as well."

He glared at her. "And be stuck in this city with its noise and the English?"

She stilled his pacing by resting her hand on his forearm. "Anya would be pleased, as would I." His muscle tensed beneath her hand.

"Don't you understand? I will never belong here." He pounded his chest as he said, "I am *Rom*."

She crossed her arms before her chest and pinned him with a glare. "Yet you expected me to marry Magor, Rafe. And I am not Rom."

His jaw flexed and the hard expression in his eyes softened. "I always wished you were. Tell me, you are *Guaja* and Rom. How will you live with these people?"

"I will, have no worry." Martine tipped up on her toes and kissed him on the cheek. With Declan's love, all was possible. "Please stay."

He shook his head and sighed. "I cannot."

He embraced her, one that reminded her of when they were younger and without his vast responsibilities. She held tight, knowing 'twould be a long time before she saw him again.

"Please," she whispered. "Visit us again. Anya and I will need to see if you are well, and I want my children to know their uncle."

His smile was indulgent, tender. He brushed the side of her face with his hand. "Tell them their uncle is the *Kapo* and their mother was his *siskkaar*."

He walked across the marble foyer, his leather shoes clicking in rhythm to his lengthy strides. She watched him, held back threatening tears, and wished he'd turn around and decide to stay. Yet she knew his pride would never allow it and fleetingly wondered if he was right. He was Rom and would never be able to remain in one place too long.

Declan had watched from afar. She was visibly shaken. He walked forward and embraced her from behind. "All will be well," he whispered. She nodded and turned toward him. He gathered her in his arms and carried her up the stairs.

Just being near her had his body ready, longing to be within her. She tipped his face toward hers and reached up for a kiss. Their mouths clashed as he devoured her lips and slipped his tongue into her mouth, loving the taste of her. He pulled back, his breath heaving.

"Have I told you how much I love you, lass?"

She feigned innocence as she tangled her fingers in his dark hair. "Nay, I don't think you have."

"Let me show you," he said with a husky voice as he unbuttoned the bodice of her gown. "Let me show you."

"I love you, Rom, Irish, or English. Never doubt that." He pulled her into him. Her body fit against his, perfect, absolutely perfect.

They kissed, a probing kiss filled with desire and sealed with their devotion. Ah, Declan mused as he slipped deeper into Martine's embrace, his life had changed. For the better, to be sure.

And all for the love of a Gypsy.

About The Author

Madelyn Hill has always loved the written word. From the time she could read and all through her school years, she'd sneak books into her textbooks during school in order to devoured books daily. At the age of 10 she proclaimed she wanted to be a writer. After being a "closet" writer for several years, she sent her manuscripts out there and is now published with Soul Mate Publishing. And she couldn't be happier! A resident of Western New York, she moved from one Rochester to another Rochester to be with the love of her life. They now have 3 children and keep busy cooking, watching their children's sporting events, and of course reading.

Authors love to hear from readers!

Please connect with Madelyn
Facebook: https://www.facebook.com/madelyn.hill.94
Twitter: https://twitter.com/AuthorMaddyHill
Website: www.madelynhill.com

Other books by Madelyn Hill
Wolf's Castle – released July 10th, 2015

Also from **Soul Mate Publishing** and **Madelyn Hill**:

WOLF'S CASTLE

Can he forget the past and embrace the future?

He's the beast of Lomarcan Castle. Tortured, angry, and bound and determined not to allow Vivian Stuart to invade his lair. Lord Galen Maclean refuses to be endeared to the lovely woman who has landed on his island looking to study alchemy. The island possesses secrets, secrets too horrid to share with the gentle woman. However, her beguiling nature brings light to the darkness of the castle and the few quirky inhabitants and edges into his heart.

Can she tame the beast within him to gain his love?

She was stranded on a remote island, her father dead and dishonored by her betrothed. Still, the lovely Vivian Stuart wears her heart on her sleeve and strives to redeem Lord Maclean. She knows his heart is good and the castle can be filled with love. Through science she learns more about the troubled lord and slowly but surely, the torture lord's icy heart begins to thaw as Vivian shares the magical healing power of love.

Available now on Amazon: **http://tinyurl.com/q7fm7pg**